BUTCHERS HILL

By Laura Lippman

Baltimore Blues

Charm City

Butchers Hill

In Big Trouble

The Sugar House

In a Strange City

The Last Place

Every Secret Thing

By a Spider's Thread

To the Power of Three

No Good Deeds

What the Dead Know

Another Thing to Fall

Hardly Knew Her

BUTCHERS HILL

LAURA LIPPMAN

wm

WILLIAM MORROW

An Imprint of HarperCollins*Publishers*

Originally published in 1998 as an Avon Books paperback.

BUTCHERS HILL. Copyright © 1998 by Laura Lippman. All rights reserved. Printed in the United States of America. No part of this book may be used or reproduced in any manner whatsoever without written permission except in the case of brief quotations embodied in critical articles and reviews. For information address HarperCollins Publishers, 10 East 53rd Street, New York, NY 10022.

HarperCollins books may be purchased for educational, business, or sales promotional use. For information please write: Special Markets Department, HarperCollins Publishers, 10 East 53rd Street, New York, NY 10022.

First William Morrow hardcover edition published 2008.

Library of Congress Cataloging-in-Publication Data has been applied for.

ISBN 978-0-06-125571-7

08 09 10 11 12 OV/RRD 10 9 8 7 6 5 4 3 2 1

For Susan Seegar,
who taught me how to read,
encouraged me to write,
and convinced me to cut
all the hair off my Barbie.
I'm glad I was never an only child.

ACKNOWLEDGMENTS

I am indebted to the usual suspects: John Roll and Joan Jacobson, my first readers; Mike James, Peter Hermann, Kate Shatzkin, and many more colleagues at the Baltimore *Sun* shared their advice or support along the way; Holly Selby andd Connie Knox deserved to be thanked long ago, but they know me well enough to tolerate my tardiness.

I am grateful to Lee Anderson, the most resourceful searcher I know, and Patti White, who introduced us.

I also want to thank every worker and volunteer who ever fielded a question from me about homelessness, poverty, child care, foster care, adoption, or welfare. You make Baltimore—and the world—a better place.

When years without number
like days of another summer
had turned into air there
once more was a street that had never
forgotten the eyes of its child

W. S. Merwin, "Another Place"

PROLOGUE

Five years ago . . .

HE WAS DEEP IN HIS FAVORITE DREAM, THE ONE ABOUT ANNIE, WHEN HE thought he heard the scratchy sound of pebbles on his window-pane. *Snick, snick, snick.* No, he had been the one who had thrown the pebbles against Annie's window, so many years ago, back on Castle Street. Then he would sing, when he saw her pull back the curtain: "Buffalo girl, won't you come out tonight, come out to-night, come out tonight." And she did.

What a skinny, long-legged girl she had been, creeping down the fire escape in her bare feet, high-heeled shoes stuck in the pock-ets of her dress, bright red birds sticking out their long necks. "Patch pockets," she had said when he had marveled at them. He marveled at everything about her—the white rickrack she sewed along the hem and neckline of her dress to give it what she called pizzazz, her heart-shaped face, the hollow at the base of her throat, where he hung a heart-shaped locket.

No matter how many times she crawled down that fire escape to meet him, she always hesitated on that final step, about a half-story above the ground, as if she were scared of falling. But he knew she was a little scared of him, of loving him, of what it meant for a young, high-spirited girl to love a man so serious and solemn. She would hang, the toes of her bare feet curling in fear as she swung above the street, and he would laugh, he couldn't help himself, at that skinny long-legged girl swinging above Castle Street. His Annie. "The prince is supposed to take a girl to a castle, but you already live on one," he used to tell her. "Where am I going to take you, Princess?" He promised to take her to Europe, to Jamaica, to New York City. In the end he had taken her the five blocks to Fairmount Avenue, with a week at Virginia Beach every August.

Snick, snick, snick.

But that was forty years ago and Annie was dead, almost ten years now, and he was alone in their bed. The little burst of noise at his window must be a tree branch, or sleet on the pane. But there were precious few trees on Fairmount Avenue and it was early June, June third. Even half-asleep he knew the calendar to the day, knew which numbers had come in, because he always wrote them on that day's date. 467 on the Pick Three, 4526 on the Pick Four, which he had straight for $350. His lucky day. But that was yesterday. He had already collected on the ticket down at the Korean's. He would have to check his dream book in the morning, see what the number was for a lost love, for a heart, for the color red.

Snick, snick, snick. Then a thicker sound, one he recognized immediately, the now all too familiar sound of breaking glass. Window glass, straight below him—no, a windshield this time. The sound shattered what was left of his sleep, his dream, his Annie.

Those damn kids, the ones from over on Fayette. Well, *no more*, he resolved, then said it out loud. "No more."

He kept his gun in his bottom bureau drawer, in a nest of single socks he held on to, because their mates might show up one day. They made for good cleaning rags, too, slip one over your hand and dust the woodwork. The bullets were with his never-worn cufflinks, in the tiny drawers on either side of the old-fashioned chifforobe. He loaded the gun with care, not rushing. After all, they weren't rushing. When those kids got started, they took their sweet time, knowing no one would call the police, and it wouldn't matter if they did. Everyone in the neighborhood, so scared of those little kids, and the cops so indifferent it could make you cry. "It's just property," they said, every time he called. Not *their* property, though. Just his car, his radio, his windows, his front door. His, his, his.

He moved slowly down the staircase in the dark, huffing a little. Lord, he was getting fat, he'd have to start putting skim milk on his cereal. Nasty stuff, skim milk, not much more than white water. But a man had to do what a man had to do. John Wayne had said that, he was pretty sure. Saw that movie with Annie in the old Hippodrome theater, or maybe the Mayfair. One of those. It was hard to hold on to your memories with any exactitude the way the city kept tearing things down. And the things the city didn't tear down just fell down all by themselves. He and Annie had gone dancing afterward, he was sure of that, over on Pennsylvania Avenue.

When he came out on the stoop, the children were too engrossed in their nightly game of destruction to pay him any heed. They dragged sticks along the sides of the parked cars, methodically kicked in the headlamps and banged the fenders with rocks. Eventually, he knew, they would break all the windows, then steal the radios, if the radios were worth stealing. Those who didn't have a good sound system in their cars were rewarded with ripped upholstery, garbage on the floor, dog shit on the seats.

The marble steps were cool and slick beneath his bare feet. He missed the bottom one, falling to the sidewalk with an embarrassing dull, heavy sound, a too-ripe apple dropping to the ground. Startled, the children looked up from their work. When they saw it was him, they laughed.

"You go inside, old man," said the skinny one, the one who always did all the talking. "You need your sleep so you'll be ready for all that napping you have to do tomorrow."

The short, chubby one laughed at this great wit, and the others joined in. There were five of them, all foster kids living with that young Christian couple. Nice as could be, well intentioned but they couldn't do a damn thing with these kids. Couldn't even keep them in nice clothes. Just kept taking kids in and watching helplessly as they ran wild. The skinny one, the chubby one, the boy-and-girl twins, and the new one, the scrawny one who always needed someone to tell him to wipe his nose. Yeah, that was the one thing these anticrime streetlights were good for, letting you get a good look at the criminals as they went about their work.

"This is gonna stop," he said. "It's gonna stop right now."

They laughed even harder at this, at this pitiful old man sitting on the ground, telling them what to do. Then they unloaded everything they had in their hands, pitching rocks, sticks, and soda cans at him. He didn't try to cover his face or head, just sat there and let their trash shower down on him. When all the rocks and sticks had been flung, when they had shouted the last crude thing they could think of—it was then, only then, that he showed them the gun.

"Shit, old man, you ain't gonna use that," the skinny one said, but he didn't seem as cocky as before.

"That what you think?" He fired straight up, into the sky.

"He's gonna kill us. He's gonna kill us all," the girl screamed and began running. She was fast, that girl, faster than the rest, although her twin was almost as fast. The two of them were at the end of the block and turning north before he knew what was happening. The chubby one took off then, while the tall, skinny one tugged at the littlest one, the snot-nose one, who seemed frozen not so much in fear as in open-mouthed stupidity.

"C'mon, Donnie," the skinny one pleaded, yanking at his arm. "The old man's got a gun. He ain't messing with us this time."

Snot-nose hesitated for a moment, then began heading toward the corner in a clumsy, loping stride, more or less keeping even with Skinny's long-legged sprint. He could have caught them, if he wanted. Instead, he fired again, then again, the gun a living thing in his hand, separate and apart from him. A car was turning onto Fairmount as they ran, someone raised a window and shouted to stop all the noise down there, and there was a backfire, a young boy's voice screaming, another backfire, and the gun just kept shooting. The noises all jumbled together, he couldn't tell which had come first. The littlest one stumbled and fell, and now the skinny one was screaming, high and thin like a girl.

And then the street was empty, except for a crumpled little pile of clothes near the corner.

He looked at the gun, still held out at shoulder height in his strangely steady right hand, but quiet now. He was waiting for something to happen, then realized it already had.

He went inside and put the gun beneath a pile of quilts on the floor in Annie's closet, a door he seldom opened. He grabbed his broom and his dustpan, put on some shoes to protect his feet. By the time the police and the paramedics arrived, he was almost done sweeping up the broken glass from in front of his house. Wouldn't you know, this would be the one time they would get here so fast, when he had so much to do.

"Give me a minute," he said, and the police officers, speechless for once, waited as his broom hunted down the last few bits of glass and trash on his little patch of Fairmount.

"Okay," he said, leaning the broom and dustpan against the stoop, knowing he would never see them again. "I guess I'm ready."

ONE

TESS MONAGHAN'S BLOTTER-SIZE APPOINTMENT CALENDAR WAS THE LARGEST, whitest space she had ever contemplated. Thirty boxes of June days, vast as the Siberian steppes, stretching across her desk until it seemed as if there were room for nothing else. She thought she might go blind staring at it, yet she couldn't tear her gaze away. Thirty perfect squares, all awaiting things to do and places to go, and only today's, the fourth, had a single mark on it:

> *9:30: Beale*
> *10:30: Browne*
> *(SuperFresh: Dog food)*

There was also a doodle in the lower left-hand corner, which she thought a pretty good likeness of a man in a wheelchair taking a long roll off a short pier. In terrible taste, of course, unless one recognized the man as her erstwhile employer, Tyner Gray, in which case the drawing took on a droll charm.

She had told Tyner that June wasn't the right time to open her own office, but he had pushed and nagged as usual, promising enough work from his law office to carry her through those early dry months. At her darker moments—this one would qualify—she believed all he had really wanted was to free up a desk for his summer clerk.

Well, she had only opened for business last week. One expected things to be a little slow just after Memorial Day weekend. Then again, July and August would be quieter still, as most of Baltimore escaped to Ocean City and the Delaware beaches.

"But not us, Esskay. We're working girls," she told her greyhound, who was doing a fair imitation of a Matisse odalisque from her post on the lumpy mauve sofa. "The Pink Nude." No, "The Black, Hairy Nude with the Pinkish Belly." A one-time racer, Esskay was now a world-champion napper, putting in about eighteen hours a day between the sofa here and the bed at home. Esskay could afford to sleep. She didn't have overhead.

Overhead—now there was a wonderfully apt word. Tess was over her head all right, deep in debt and sinking a little more each day. So far, her Quicken accounting program showed only outgo at Tess Monaghan, Inc., technically Keyes Investigations, Inc. The business took its name from a retired city cop whose credential was essential if Tess wanted to operate as a licensed private detective in the state of Maryland. She had never actually met Edward Keyes, who put in the incorporation papers in return for a small percentage of her profits. She hoped he was a patient man.

But now her first prospective client, a Mr. Beale, was due in ten minutes. She suspected he would be pathologically punctual, given that he had literally tried to be here yesterday. He had called just after eight the night before, as if his need for a private detective were a craving that required instant gratification. Tess, who had stayed late in a futile attempt to make her new office look more officelike, wasn't in a position to turn down any client, but she thought it wiser to let this one stew in his own juices overnight. Or unstew, as the case may be. Beale had sounded the slightest bit drunk over the phone, his words pronounced with the elaborate care of the inebriated. Tess had given him a nine-thirty appointment, after much ostentatious fretting about the havoc it would wreak in her busy,

busy day. Yes indeed, she had cut her morning workout by almost thirty minutes, rowing her Alden racing shell only as far as Fort McHenry.

Last night, in the almost-summer twilight, the office had looked clean and professional, a few easy touches away from being a first-class operation. Today, with bright sun slanting through the plate glass window, it looked like what it was—the bottom floor of a too-often-renovated rowhouse in one of the iffier blocks on Butchers Hill. Almost 100 years old, the building had long ago buckled with fatigue, its linoleum floors rippling like tide pools, the doors and the jambs barely on speaking terms. Eggshell paint, even three coats, could only do so much.

If Tess had more money, she might have done better by the old storefront, bringing in real furniture instead of family castoffs. Of course, if she had more money she would have taken a better place in a better neighborhood, a bonafide office with wooden floors, exposed brick walls, maybe a harbor view. In nicer surroundings, her junk could have achieved funk status. Here, it was just junk.

Her Aunt Kitty's office-warming gift of framed family photographs, seemingly so whimsical and inspired, only made things worse. What type of businesswoman had a tinted photograph of herself smeared with chocolate, holding fast to the neck of a coin-operated flying rabbit while her grandmother tried to pry her off? Impulsively, Tess yanked this off the wall, only to be reminded that the enlarged photo hid the small wall safe, where her gun rested in solitary confinement. Petty cash would be housed there, too, as soon as she had some.

A hand rapped at the door, with such force it sounded as if it might crash through the glass pane at its center. Eager-beaver Beale, ten minutes early by the neon "It's Time for a Haircut" barbershop clock that hung on the wall, another contribution from her aunt. "Come in," Tess shouted over her shoulder, looking around quickly to see if there was anything else she could hang over the safe. The doorknob rattled impatiently, reminding her that she kept it locked, a sad but necessary precaution in Butchers Hill.

"Right there," she said, placing the picture back on the wall. She could find something more appropriate later. Poker-playing dogs were always nice.

"Miss Monaghan?"

The man she let into her office was barrel-chested with skinny legs that seemed ridiculously spindly beneath such a large bulk. He stepped around Tess, as if encased in an invisible force field that required him to keep great distances between himself and others, then settled slowly into the chair opposite her desk. His joints creaked audibly, the Tin Man after a long, hard rain. No, it was another Oz character he reminded her of, the lesser-known Gnome King from the later books in the series. He had the same rotund girth atop skinny legs. What else? The Gnome King had been deathly afraid of eggs.

"So this is Keyes, Inc.," her visitor said. "Would you be Keyes?"

"I'm his partner, Tess Monaghan. Mr. Keyes is, uh, semi-retired."

"I'm retired myself," the man said, eyes fixed on his own lap. For all Tess's last-minute worrying, nothing in the surroundings seemed to register with him—not the furnishings, not the photograph, not even Esskay, who had opened her eyes and was doing her adorable bit, just in case the visitor wanted to toss her one of the biscuits that Tess kept in a cookie jar on her desk.

"I guess you know who I am." His voice was meek, but his chest, already so large, seem to swell with self-importance.

She didn't. Should she? He was an elderly black man, which in his case meant he had skin the color of a stale Hershey bar—dark brown, with a chalky undercast. He wore a brown suit two shades lighter than his face, and although it was clean and neat, it wasn't quite right. Too tight in the shoulders, slightly baggy in the legs and paired with a rose-pink shirt and magenta tie. He held a once-white Panama hat, now yellow as a tortilla chip. No woman had watched him dress this morning, Tess decided.

"I'm afraid I don't," she admitted.

"Luther Beale," he said, as if his full name would be enough. It wasn't. She did hear in his voice the same ponderous, overenunciated quality that had led her to think he was drunk on the phone.

"Luther Beale?"

"Luther Beale," he repeated solemnly.

"I'm afraid I don't . . ."

"You might know me as the Butcher of Butchers Hill," he said stiffly, and Tess was embarrassed at the little noise she made, halfway between a squeal and a gasp. The nickname had done the trick. In fact, her former employer, the defunct *Baltimore Star*, had bestowed it on him. The *Star* had been good at bestowing nicknames, while the surviving paper, the stodgy *Beacon-Light*, was good only at attracting them. The *Blight*, most called it, although *Blite* was beginning to gain currency, thanks to a new media column in the city's alternative weekly.

Luther "the Butcher" Beale. The Butcher of Butchers Hill. For a few weeks, he had been famous, the leading man in a national morality play. Luther Beale, evil vigilante or besieged old man, depending on one's point of view. Luther Beale. His name had been invoked more often on talk radio than Hillary Clinton's. Hadn't "60 Minutes" done a piece on him? No, that had been Roman Welzant, the Snowball Killer, acquitted almost two decades ago in the shooting death of a teenager tossing snowballs at his home outside the city limits a decade earlier. Beale had killed a much younger boy for breaking one of his windows. Or was it a windshield? No matter. The main thing was that a county jury let Welzant walk, while a city jury sent Beale away.

"Yes, Mr. Beale. I remember your . . . incident."

"Do you remember how it ended?"

"You were convicted—manslaughter, I guess, or some lesser charge, not murder, if you're sitting here today—and you went to prison."

Beale leaned forward in his chair and wagged a finger in Tess's face, an old man used to teaching lessons to insolent young folks. "No, no, no. I got *probation* for the manslaughter charge. It was the gun charge I had to do time for. I killed a boy, a terrible, terrible thing, but they would have let me stay on the streets for that, because I had no intent. They put me away for using a gun in the city limits. Mandatory sentencing. Isn't that something?"

Tess was inclined to agree. It was indeed something, something twisted and warped. But she recognized the question as a rhetorical one and sat back, waiting. She had met people like Beale before. They were like one of those minitrain rides at the zoo or a shopping mall, just going around and around on the same track all day long.

"So what can I do for you, Mr. Beale?"

"You know, I was sixty-one when I went to prison. I'm sixty-six now, out for three months. This neighborhood is worse than it was when I went in. I guess even hell can get hotter. Which is why I took notice when I saw a nice girl like you opening up a business here. I hope you have some protection, Miss, something besides that skinny dog. You should have a gun. Because you can bet the little boys 'round here have them. Yet I can't have a gun any more. I'm a convicted felon. Isn't that something?"

This time, he seemed to expect an answer. Tess tried to think of a noncommittal, noninflammatory reply. "It's the law."

"The law! The law is foolish. The Bible says thou shalt not kill, not thou shalt not use a firearm in the city limits. You know I'd never done a thing in my life before they arrested me for shooting that boy? They looked, believe me they looked. They wanted me so bad. I never understood that, why did those police officers and those prosecutors want me so bad? It was as if locking me up would make everything right in the city. But I had no record. I didn't even have an unpaid parking ticket. You know what they found on me, after all that looking and looking?"

Tess shook her head, if only to indicate she was listening.

"Sometimes I did contracting work on the weekends, but I didn't have a state license for home improvements. Oh yeah, they had themselves Public Enemy Number One, right then and there, that they were sure of. Man goes out and paints rooms and cleans gutters, doesn't have a state license. Lock him up and throw away the key."

"I hear they've got a warrant out for Bob Vila, too," Tess offered.

Beale swatted the air, as if Tess's joke were a pesky gnat. "So now I have a record. It's all I have. It's all anyone knows about me. Used to be, people saw me on the street, they might say, 'Oh there's Luther Beale, he lost his wife Annie to the cancer.' Or, 'Luther Beale, he works over at the Procter and Gamble in Locust Point, he could afford a nicer house in a nicer place, but he likes Fairmount Avenue, lived here all his life.' You know what they say about me now?"

She waited a beat. "No, I guess I don't."

Tess thought she saw tears in the corners of Beale's eyes. "They say, 'That's Luther Beale. He'd kill you as soon as look at you. He killed a little boy one time, just for throwing rocks at some cars.' "

Well, you did. But there was no percentage in antagonizing a prospective client with the truth. Tess couldn't see any percentage in this conversation at all. Had Beale confused her with a street-corner psychiatrist? Or did he assume, as so many men did, that a woman's primary function on earth was to listen to a man? Maybe she could make some extra money that way, just listening to men speak of their troubles. Forget phone sex. How about 1-900-UBOREME, or a web page, www.tellyourtroubles.com.

"Mr. Beale, is there anything I can help you with today?"

"Retribution."

The word, pronounced with great care in Luther Beale's deep, growly voice, seemed to hang and shimmer in the air. Tess envisioned it in black plastic letters on the marquee outside one of those hellfire churches on the Eastern Shore, the little cinderblock buildings that stood in the middle of vast cornfields. *Today's sermon: Retribution. Don't forget Guild Ladies annual scrapple breakfast.*

"Retribution," he repeated. "A beautiful word, don't you think?"

She thought not. "Vengeance is an ugly business. You may have a legitimate grudge against the system, but if that's what you're after, Mr. Beale, you better find someone else to help you with it."

"You're an educated woman, Miss Monaghan? A college graduate?"

"Yes, Washington College, over in Chestertown."

"I would hope such a fine school might have taught you the meaning of such a common word. I read a lot in prison—the Bible, history. But I also read the dictionary, which is one of the best books we have. No lies in the dictionary, just words, beautiful words, waiting for you to make something of them. The heart of retribution is tribute. From the Latin, to pay back. It can mean to reward as well as to punish."

Beale was enjoying his little vocabulary lesson. Tess wasn't. Several replies of varying degrees of heat and wit occurred to her. But her aunt and her former employer had repeatedly impressed upon her that running one's own business meant eating several healthy doses of crap every day.

"Okay, so to whom do you wish to make tribute?"

Beale twisted his hat, kneading the brim with fingers as plump and long as the Esskay Ballpark Franks that had given the greyhound her name. *Hot dog fingers and ham hands*, Tess thought, then wondered why she had pork products on the brain. Apparently her usual morning bagels weren't going to hold her until lunch today.

"As I told you, I worked at the Procter and Gamble on Locust Point. It was a good place to work—decent pay, good benefits. The company shut it down while I was . . . gone."

Prison, you were in prison. For killing a little boy.

"That was hard on folks, but the stock went up, up, up. That was my retirement fund and I couldn't touch it for almost five years, so it went up even more. I'm a rich man by my standards, richer for not working than I ever would have been working. I couldn't spend all this money if I tried. And I've got no wife, no kids, no family at all, no one to leave it to."

Tess nodded, although she still wasn't sure what he was getting at.

"Now there was a television show, before your time, 'The Millionaire.' A guy named Michael Anthony used to show up, tell folks they were going to get some money. My wife and I always liked that show. I got to thinking—maybe I could have my own Michael Anthony, someone who could find the children, then help them out. Not with millions—I'm not doing that well—but with a thousand here or there."

"The children?" He had lost her completely.

"The ones who were there that night. The ones who saw what . . . happened."

Tess tried to remember the news stories about the Butcher of Butchers Hill. There had been much about his victim—Donnie Moore, it was coming back to her in bits and pieces. The media had worked hard to find something of interest to say about an eleven-year-old who wasn't particularly nice or bright, yet didn't deserve to be shot in the back for an act of vandalism. The best they could come up with was that Donnie was a work in progress. The other children, the witnesses, had been virtually anonymous figures by law and custom. As foster children, their names were confidential and the local media kept them that way during the trial. The court artists hadn't even sketched the children on the stand, if memory served.

"Why would you do this? Those kids taunted and tormented you."

"And one of them was killed. That's not God's justice. I may be right with the courts now, but I'm not right with myself, and I'm not right with God. I can't do anything for the boy who died, except pray for both of us, but I might be able to help the others. Scholarships, if they want to go to college. A car to get to a part-time job. Help at home. I don't know. Doesn't everybody need money?"

He had her there. Boy, did he have her there.

"So who are these kids? Where are they?"

"Well, there was the chubby one. And the twins, I remember their names. Truman, that was the boy, and the girl was Destiny, I think. Then another boy, a skinny one who did most of the talking."

"You don't have full names?" She tried not to sigh audibly.

"No'm. They were foster kids, lived with the Nelsons, a nice young couple that took in lots of kids. They meant well, but they couldn't handle those kids, couldn't even keep 'em in clean clothes. The Nelsons moved away after the shooting, and the kids all went to new homes. But they'd be eighteen now, out on their own anyway, right?"

"If they were at least thirteen at the time, they would be. But if they're still minors and in foster care, they're going to be hard to find, even *with* names. Donnie was only eleven, there's no guarantee the others were much older. We can't even expect them to have drivers' licenses. City kids—" She had started to say "poor black kids," but caught herself. "City kids often don't, you know."

"Oh." Beale thought for a moment. "I think the chubby one was named Earl. Or Errol."

"Errol?"

"Maybe Elmer. An E name with an L in it somewhere, I'm pretty sure of that. Does that help?"

Tess forced another would-be sigh back into her throat. "Look, Mr. Beale, I have to tell you the odds I can find these kids are pretty slim and, while it won't be expensive, it will cost money, probably more than you ever dreamed. You'll pay not only my hourly rate, but any expenses I have. Mileage. Fees for computer searches."

"I can pay," he insisted.

"Before I can begin working on your case officially, you have to visit an attorney named Tyner Gray and ask for a referral to a private detective." She opened her desk and pulled out one of Tyner's cards. "He'll draw up a contract for my services. That guarantees our relationship is privileged, which may not seem important to you, but it's extremely important to me."

"It means you don't have to talk to people about me, right?"

"Yes." *Maybe.* Even Tyner couldn't guarantee that the cops wouldn't challenge her on this some day. The trick was to stay away from the kind of matters that interested cops, which she had every intention of doing. "Tyner will charge you his hourly fee for your visit. It may seem like a lot for not much work, but there's no getting around it if you want me to take your case."

"I told you, money isn't a problem."

"In my experience, money is always a problem eventually. You have to understand, this isn't a fee-based result. I look, you pay. Finding people is easier today than it's ever been. But not when you don't have their names. You'd be surprised how many kids are named Destiny in Baltimore alone."

"Destiny doesn't matter so much. She's a girl."

Healthy doses of crap, healthy doses of crap, Tess chanted to herself. "And why don't girls matter?"

Beale wasn't so self-absorbed that he couldn't sense her irritation. "I didn't mean—it's just that I'm a man, and I'm worried about the young black men I see. The girls sometimes find a way out on their own. It's harder for the boys. It's hard to be a black man, but it's even harder to get to be a black man, if you know what I mean."

Tess knew, much in the same way she knew certain facts about Bosnia, Singapore, and the Gaza strip. Parts of Baltimore were foreign countries to her, places she couldn't reach even with a passport. That was just the way it was, the way it had always been, the way it was always going to be.

"Okay, I'll try to find the boys *and* the girl, once I figure out who they are. Let's say a miracle happens and I locate them all. Then what? Do you want me to arrange a meeting?"

"I wouldn't mind meeting them, but I guess they're not much interested in seeing me again. No, you just find 'em and figure out what they need, and what it might cost. I'll write you a check, then you'll write them a check. I have to be anonymous in this. I don't want to risk them turning down the money, out of some strange sort of pride."

Tess jotted these instructions on her desk calendar, although she doubted there was much chance Beale's philanthropy would be rejected. That kind of virtuous pride was the stuff children's stories were made of, not real life.

"If you give any one of them more than ten thousand dollars, you can't be anonymous with the IRS. There's a gift tax, you know. You might want to consider setting up a foundation or nonprofit of some sort. Tyner can walk you through the process. It might be advantageous, tax-wise."

"I'm not interested in saving on my taxes. I am interested in—"

"Retribution, I know. From the Latin. To pay back. A reward as well as a punishment."

Beale stood and looked at her. From the look of his furrowed brow, he was trying to decide if she was mocking him or simply demonstrating what careful attention she had paid.

"You're a smart girl, Miss Monaghan, aren't you?"

She decided to let the "girl" pass. This time. "I'd like to think I'm reasonably intelligent, yes."

"But you're not yet wise. Do you know your Bible? 'Wisdom is the principal thing; therefore get wisdom: and with all thy getting get understanding.' Proverbs, Chapter 4, Verse 7."

The broad, sunny smile on Tess's face could only be described as a *non*-shit-eating grin.

"Before you leave, you should know the getting of wisdom in this case requires a sizable retainer."

TWO

BY THE TIME BEALE LEFT, TYNER'S CARD CLUTCHED IN HAND, TESS HAD thirty minutes before her next appointment. She decided to take Esskay for a quick walk, find a snack to tide her over to lunch, explore a little more of her new neighborhood. She grabbed the leash from its peg by the front door and Esskay was instantly alert, rolling off the sofa in one fluid movement and tapping her toenails on the linoleum, happier than Gene Kelly on a rainy day.

But this was a perfect day. Spring had started out cool and wet in Baltimore this year, then settled into a pattern of eerily exquisite days. Sunny, dry, not too hot, the tiniest city gardens riotous with azaleas and then lilies that never seemed to wilt or lose their blossoms. To top it off, the Orioles were playing .600 ball. Naturally, all this Edenic perfection made the natives nervous. The local wisdom was that good things always had a hidden price, like those rent-to-own deals where you ended up paying a thousand dollars for a three-hundred-dollar television set. Sooner or later, the bill would come due.

Esskay stopped abruptly and Tess banged her knee against the dog's pointy tailbone, hard enough to bruise it. "What the—" She should have known. The dog had stopped here every day for the past week, since the unparalleled thrill of seeing a cat sunning itself on the windowsill of this particular rowhouse. Esskay had already forgotten what she had seen, but she hadn't forgotten the sensation. *Happy, happy, joy, joy*, her quivering muscles seemed to sing. Tess allowed the dog the moment, then flicked the leash.

"Walking means moving forward from time to time, Esskay. Let's keep going."

They crossed the street into Patterson Park, entering through ornate stone portals. "The city's emerald jewel," an overwrought *Beacon-Light* editorial writer had once christened the park. Sure, a gem that had fallen out of its setting and now rattled around in someone's drawer, too expensive to insure or wear. Baltimore was full of such inconvenient treasures. The city's standard solution was to auction them off, or let them go to ruin, but there was always a Save-the-Something group that interceded at the last minute, like the mountie in an old-fashioned melodrama. Talk about hollow victories. What was the point of citizens rallying to save, for example, the beautiful old pagoda that rose here in Patterson Park's northwest corner when the city crews wouldn't even cut the grass on a regular basis. Just a week ago, a jogger had found a woman's body in the overgrown weeds at the pagoda's feet, her throat slashed, her face literally beaten off. The *Blight* had given it a paragraph on page three. *City woman killed.* Tess knew how to translate this particular bit of newspaperspeak, how to decode the clues offered up by the story's very placement and brevity. *Drugs, prostitution claim another deserving victim.* The piece had caused an uproar in the neighborhood, but only because the paper had placed her body in Butchers Hill instead of Patterson Park proper. So bad for property values, those carelessly strewn corpses.

Butchers Hill. The name had made a conveniently macabre and alliterative nickname for Luther Beale, but its origins couldn't be more stupefyingly literal. At the turn of the century, the city's prosperous butchers had lived in the precincts west of Patterson Park, building fine houses on the proceeds from their tenderloin empires. And it was on a hill, providing a view of the harbor below. Butchers. Hill. End of story, with one ironic postscript. Beale's house technically wasn't even in the neighborhood. But the Butcher of Fair-mount Avenue just didn't have the same ring to it.

However you drew the boundaries, the butchers had fled the area long ago. Now the neighborhood was an uneasy mix of old-timers, poor folks, and gentrifiers. Nearby Johns Hopkins Hospital had proved to be a sturdy Lorelei, luring fresh supplies of urban homesteaders to dash themselves on the bricked-in fireplaces and leaded windows. Tess could tell the neighborhood was sizing her up, trying to figure out where she fit in. White+young+whimsically named dog usually equaled yuppie around here. But then, how to explain the twelve-year-old Toyota, with the muffler held on with duct tape?

She checked her Swiss army watch, a parting gift from Tyner. "Parting gift," she had mused. "Isn't that what you get on a game show when you've lost?" "Good up to 330 feet," he had replied, as if she ever planned to be even ankle-deep in the Patapsco again, much less the ocean. Almost ten-fifteen. She tugged on Esskay's leash. The dog had literally stopped to smell the roses, relics of some for-gotten garden that continued to thrive in this corner of Patterson Park.

"We have to move if we're going to have time to grab some coffee and be on time for our next appointment. If you behave, there might even be a Berger cookie in it for you. Did you hear me? If you want a *treat*, get moving."

Esskay, spoiled by having Tess to herself for so much of this spring, paid no attention. The hot sun elicited new, exciting smells from the earth every day, while the harbor-borne breezes made the grass move intriguingly, as if field mice and rabbits were running there. And although the dog had no idea what a Berger cookie was, she knew what "treat" meant, and she knew she always got one after a walk, no matter what. Happy, happy, joy, joy.

* * *

THE TEN-THIRTY APPOINTMENT WAS WAITING OUTSIDE THE OFFICE, A bright yellow flame among the faded bricks. Tess could tell the woman was impatient and put out from the moment she rounded the corner, coffee and an open package of Berger cookies in hand, a half-eaten one clenched in her teeth.

"I don't like to be kept waiting," Mary Browne said as Tess fumbled with her keys.

A blushing Tess choked down her mouthful of chocolate-iced cookie, unlocked the door, and ushered the woman into her office. "I'm normally very punctual, but I went out to walk my dog and—"

"Fine. You're here now, may we begin?" She took the seat opposite Tess's desk, crossing her legs at the knee, then tugging her skirt down as if Tess might be inclined to look up it.

Tess threw the greyhound the promised piece of cookie, stealing a longing look at the others, nestled in their open box. The one she had gulped on her way back to the office had only whetted her appetite. Perhaps she should put them on a plate, offer them to this unsmiling Mary Browne in the guise of courtesy. Then she could have a few more herself.

"Would you like a cookie, perhaps a glass of water?" Esskay chose this moment to wander into the bathroom at the rear of the office and begin lapping noisily from the toilet bowl. A very classy operation, this Keyes Investigations. "I also have some orange juice in the refrigerator. And a six-pack of Cokes—"

"I prefer to discuss business," she said, pulling a small brown envelope out of her purse.

Unlike Luther Beale, who had been oblivious, Mary Browne took in her surroundings with one quick, impassive glance. The fresh eggshell paint seemed to peel beneath her eyes, revealing every decade of the building's inglorious history: the recent incarnation as a cheap studio apartment, when a makeshift kitchen had been shoehorned into the back; its brief fling as a bar; the years as a dry cleaner, which had left a vague chemical smell scored into the walls.

As her prospective client studied the room, Tess studied her. Mary Browne could be Exhibit A for any Afrocentric curriculum that wanted to claim ancient Egypt as its own. Her features were as fine as Nefertiti's, her skin a velvety dark brown, which looked even darker against the yellow suit and matching straw hat. Her hair appeared to be cut very close to the scalp, but not so close that it still didn't curl. With her long neck rising like a stem from the deep V of the suit, and her dark, smooth face framed by the broad brim of a hat with a yellow band, she resembled nothing so much as the black-eyed Susans that would bloom in late summer.

"Miss Monaghan?" Mary Browne's tone was as cold and treacherous as thin ice.

"Please, call me Tess. I'm probably younger than you, after all."

"I'm only thirty-two—"

"I'm twenty-nine." It occurred to Tess that telling a prospective client that she looked older than she was might not be one of Dale Carnegie's tips. "But it's not that you look over thirty, it's that you look so much more . . . polished. More sophisticated, I guess I'm trying to say."

"I didn't come here to talk about my age or my clothes." Mary Browne's speech was almost comically precise, her diction clipped and hard. "I wish to find my sister, who has been estranged from the family since she was a teenager."

"Estranged? Did she run away? Or was she kidnapped by a non-custodial parent?"

The question seemed to throw Mary Browne. "She left of her own free will when she was eighteen. It was quite legal, given her age, but not exactly intentional. I mean . . ."

"I've found it helps," Tess said, "if people just tell the truth from the get-go. I'm not here to judge you, and what you tell me is confidential."

"Fine. My sister became pregnant when she was eighteen and my mother threw her out when she announced she was going to put the baby up for adoption. That's not done among our people. Is that enough 'truth' for you?"

"Your people?" She was only parroting Mary Browne's words, yet the words sounded a little ugly in her mouth.

"Black families take care of their own, even if they need a welfare check to do it. In the neighborhood where I grew up, it was unheard of for a girl to give her baby away. To give it to her mother or grandmother—that was acceptable. My mother wanted to raise her grandchild, but Susan had different plans. So my mother threw her out and I watched, knowing Susan was doing the right thing, but too intimidated by my mother to object. She was a formidable woman, my mother. Our mother. One didn't cross her, unless one was willing to lose. Susan was. I wasn't."

"And you've had no contact with Susan—in how many years exactly?" Tess found a steno pad in her desk drawer and took some notes. Mary Browne's officious manner made her want to seem more businesslike.

"Thirteen. Thirteen years ago this month."

"No contact at all? What about your mother?"

"My mother died last year. I suppose that's why I want to find her. She's all the family I have now."

"Okay, let's get formal." Tess turned on her Macintosh, which sat on a computer table next to her desk. "I explained rates and expenses when you called. You've already been to see Tyner, so all I need to do is put you in my files. I have a form here with your name, address, and phone number, but there are a few other things I need to get started. May I ask what you do for a living?"

"I'm self-employed. I raise money for nonprofits on a contract basis."

Self-employed. That set off a mental alarm. Tess might want to check Mary Browne's credit rating, make sure she had the money to hire her.

"How did you hear about this office, Ms. Browne?" Aunt Kitty, always the entrepreneur, had recommended she ask this in order to identify her marketing needs.

"I wanted to hire an independent businesswoman like myself, and I remembered seeing the item in the *Daily Record*, announcing you were joining Mr. Keyes's firm as an associate. Your name rang a bell. You were in the news this winter, weren't you? I can't recall all the details—someone tried to kill you, or you almost killed someone when you were attacked in Leakin Park?"

"Something like that," Tess said unhappily and her ribs, although fully healed, winced a little at the memory of what a well-placed foot could do. "Sister's full name?"

"Susan Evelyn King."

"King?"

"Different fathers," Mary Browne said shortly, her eyes daring Tess to make something of it.

"Have a Social Security number?"

"Why—no, I'm afraid not. Is that necessary?"

"Nope, just makes it a little easier. How about a birthdate?"

"She was thirty-two on January seventeenth."

Tess turned back to face Mary Browne. "I thought you said *you* were thirty-two. How can your sister be the same age?"

Given the rich, deep color of her skin, it was impossible to say Mary Browne actually blushed, but something in her manner suggested she was embarrassed.

"I meant I'll be thirty-two, in December," Mary Browne said stiffly. "We were born in the same year, almost exactly eleven months apart."

Vanity, thy name is woman. But what was it to Tess if Mary Browne wanted to shave a few years off her age? She was probably thirty-four or thirty-five and already lying about her age. Once Tess was on the other side of thirty, she might feel the same way.

"I've got two sets of first cousins like that on my father's side," she said, typing in Susan King's date of birth. "He calls them Irish twins. When my Aunt Vivian had her second boy in the same calendar year, the doctors at Mercy threw in the second circumcision for free."

Mary Browne allowed herself a small, lips-together smile, then handed Tess the brown envelope she had taken out of her leather briefcase at the beginning of the interview. Inside was a photograph and a check for the retainer.

"Is this her?" Tess asked. The girl in the photo was big-boned and plump. Her oversize glasses had caught the camera's flash, so her face was little more than a dark smudge beneath two exploding stars. She wore an apron and held something by its handle, a broom or a mop. It could be Jimmy Hoffa, for all Tess knew, or Madalyn Murray O'Hair, another missing Baltimorean. Totally useless, this photo, but the check—well, it was bad form to stare too hungrily at the check.

"That's her at seventeen."

"Not much of a resemblance, is there? But you did say you're only half-sisters."

"She was actually a pretty girl, just not particularly photogenic."

"Sure," Tess said dubiously.

"It's all I have." Mary Browne managed to sound apologetic and defensive at the same time. "But I guess it is about as helpful as someone trying to find you with that photo on the wall."

Great, Mary Browne's miss-nothing eyes had landed on the flying rabbit photo. Tess definitely had to find something else to hang over the safe.

"That was taken outside the old Weinstein's Drugs on Edmondson Avenue. Remember, it was in the same shopping center as the old Hess shoe store with the barber shop and the squirrel monkeys in the window?"

"We didn't buy our shoes at Hess, but, yes, I know the place of which you speak." *The place of which you speak*—close your eyes, and it could be the latest BBC production of Jane Austen. "My mother would take me to see the monkeys."

"Just you?" Tess assumed Mary Browne hadn't told her everything. People seldom did. Maybe there was more to the story of why Susan King had bolted, the ugly, unfavored duckling growing up in the shadow of this swan.

"Susan, too, of course."

"Well, that photo marks the day I learned a tough life lesson. My grandfather owned Weinstein's, so I thought I was entitled to endless rides on the flying rabbit. But when my quarter was done, it was done, same as anyone else's. Poppa was a soft touch, he would have let me ride forever, but Gramma had rules about such things. 'You'll pay like the other kids!' No free rides and no free treats at the soda fountain, although Poppa sometimes slipped me something chocolate."

"This may sound strange, but you look like that little girl who was on television years ago, the one who jumped on the sofa with the plastic slipcovers."

"You mean"—Tess slipped into the Baltimore accent her mother had made sure she would never acquire—

" 'Hey, you kids, stop jumping on that furniture! You'll *rune* it!' "

"Yes, that one. I remember wanting my mother to buy those covers, because I thought it meant you could then jump on the sofa with impunity."

With impunity, yet. Jane Austen, meet Joe Friday.

"Actually, that was my cousin Deborah on the commercial, Deborah Weinstein. Funny you'd pick up on the resemblance. We don't look anything alike now. She's still fair, while I got dark."

"You think you're dark?"

It was Tess's turn to blush and stammer. "Well, I mean my hair got darker."

"I'm just giving you a hard time. Actually you haven't changed as much as you think."

"Really?" Tess believed she had changed extraordinarily, that it was almost impossible to find the more-or-less hard-bodied, more-

or-less grown-up Theresa Esther Monaghan in those plump limbs and that face round with baby fat.

"Yes. You still wear your hair in a braid and you still have a smudge of chocolate on your face." Mary Browne didn't say good-bye, just allowed herself another no-teeth-showing smile and left even as Tess dabbed at the errant bit of frosting from her Berger's cookie. She must have had that dimple of chocolate on her face for the entire interview.

"Wait a minute!" she called after Mary Browne, her computerized form not even close to complete. But when she reached the door, Mary Browne was pulling away in a baby-blue, late-model Taurus with Virginia tags. Virginia tags often meant a rental car in these parts, but Tess took down the license plate, just in case. Homicide detective Martin Tull had recommended such mnemonic tricks to sharpen her powers of observation.

Back at her desk, she allowed herself the venal pleasure of staring at the two checks she had collected that morning, filling out a deposit slip with great ceremony. Mary Browne might be a little mysterious, but finding Susan King was going to be a slam-dunk. This was the kind of case she needed—easy, lots of cash up front. The check was even a money order, so she didn't have to worry about it bouncing.

A money order? Why would someone pay with a money order? Did Mary Browne have a husband at home who might ask questions about a checkbook entry to Tess Monaghan, private investigator? Or, appearances aside, was she scraping so low she didn't even have a checking account? Tess looked at the application form still open on her computer. A P.O. box for an address. That hadn't seemed so strange when she had called, but now Tess's heart jumped up and out, beating against her ribcage as if it wanted to escape.

Her fingers clumsy with nervousness, she punched in the phone number Mary had left, only to hear the precise, silky voice that had so recently filled her office: "You have reached the pager-voice mail for Mary Browne. Please leave a message at the beep, or punch in your number and I will return your call as quickly as possible."

Tess smothered her relieved laugh. "I just wanted to tell you to plan on seeing your sister by the fourth of July, Mary Browne," she told the pager. "I almost guarantee I can find her by then."

Actually, Tess couldn't find anyone who wasn't in the phone book. But she knew someone who could, and she wasn't too proud to delegate.

THREE

THE THIRD-FLOOR LADIES ROOM AT THE ENOCH PRATT FREE LIBRARY was empty. It usually was, which was why Tess had chosen it for a meeting place. She didn't know why the library's top floor, home to the humanities department and the Mencken Room, should be so relentlessly male, but it was, and always had been. There was probably a class-action suit in this, but it would have to find another plaintiff. Tess had long cherished this island of privacy in downtown Baltimore, with its view of the verdigris-domed Basilica of the Assumption.

"Hello, Wee Willie Keeler," she said, waving to the blank windows across Cathedral Street. That was Kitty's pet name for the cardinal, Kitty being about as lapsed as anyone named Monaghan could be.

Tess had her own lapses. Once, as a college senior home for winter break, she had taken an over-the-counter pregnancy test in one of the stalls here. She didn't dare try it at home, and yet she couldn't stand the suspense of waiting until she returned to school. The test had been negative and she had celebrated by meeting Whitney Talbot at the bar at the top of the old Peabody Hotel. Wearing slinky little dresses, they had lied about their ages, names, and just about everything else to the men who insisted on buying them drinks. "Auditioning new sperm donors," Whitney had called it.

The Peabody was gone, demoted to a chain hotel with polyester bedspreads and no rooftop bar. And her best friend Whitney was gone—at least temporarily to Japan. Ah, the local litany of loss. Now that was the real Baltimore Catechism, the ecumenical prayer known to every native. Tess curled up in the window well, deep and low enough to be a proper window seat, and skimmed a copy of Mary McCarthy's first volume of memoirs while she waited. Soon enough, she heard the heavy tread of hiking boots on the tile floors. A plump woman, as soft and disarrayed as an unmade bed, entered the room.

"About time—" Tess began, but Dorie Starnes held a finger to her mouth, in imitation of the librarian stereotype.

"Did you check the stalls?"

"The doors are all open, Dorie. See?"

Unsatisfied, Dorie pushed each of the stall doors, then glanced up at the ceiling, in case someone might be clinging to one of the light fixtures.

"You can't be too careful, you know," she said, closing and locking the heavy wooden door to the outside corridor.

"Actually, you can. There's a point where precaution has a diminishing return. For example, let's say you're so afraid to fly that you drive everywhere. That's not only more risky, statistically, it also costs you money through lost time."

"I *don't* fly."

"Right, because you're afraid."

"Because I've never wanted to go anywhere that was more than three hours from Baltimore by car."

"Oh." Tess tried to think of a nonflying analogy about the benefits of risk-taking, but nothing came to mind. "I take it back. Maybe *you* can't be too careful."

"You better believe it. If my titular bosses ever find out I've opened my own shop while still working for them, that would be the end of little Dorie. This may seem like cloak-and-dagger bullshit to you, but it keeps my health insurance and 401-K safe for another day."

"Nice use of titular. Still doing those vocabulary builders?"

"Yeah. It's a twelve-cassette program, for kids taking the SATs. I already know what most of the words mean, this way I get to hear how they should sound." Dorie glared at Tess, in case she was mocking her. But Tess had learned early in their relationship never to aggravate the *Beacon-Light*'s systems manager. From her cubicle at the newspaper, Dorie ran a vigorous trade in black-market information, tapping into the newspaper's on-line resources and, more valuable still, the business side's computers, something even the reporters couldn't do. Forget the hand that rocks the cradle. It's the fingers that can access your credit rating that truly rule the world.

"It's not only your vocabulary. Your voice sounds different, too. Fuller."

"I've been listening to Derek Jacobi read the *Iliad* on tape. It's like, I don't know, twenty hours altogether, and if I keep my headphones on too long, I start sounding as if I'm from a whole different kind of Essex."

"Indeed," Tess said. Dorie had mispronounced the English actor's name, but she'd never hear about it from Tess. "Well, duchess, let me tell you what I need."

Dorie listened intently, taking it all in. Tess would have gladly given her copies of her files, but Dorie was paper-averse. She maintained that her "organic hard disk" was the safest way to store information. No power surges, no system crashes, and not even the world's best hackers could get to it.

"Jeez, Tess," she said after hearing the details of the two cases, shaking her head. "I mean, normally, no problem, but it happens I've got a few people with rush jobs. People who pay me considerably more money than you do."

"Hey, I qualified for my lifetime discount by suggesting you set up this little sideline, remember?"

"Sure, and I'll take you for a ride in my new Ford Explorer someday to show you how grateful I am. In the meantime, the *Beacon-Light*, my employer of record, has a few things they expect of me as well. Tyrannical despots. Can the Susan King search wait a couple days?"

"Sure." In fact, it was probably better that way. A too-swift result might prompt the demanding Mary Browne to wonder if she had been charged too much. "What about the Beale case? Can you help me on that at all?"

Dorie ran her fingers through her shortish hair, whose tendency toward cowlicks gave her the look of an exotic bird, the faintly cross-eyed ones with the comical little crests. "You gotta be kidding. First names only, and the geezer isn't even sure of those? Minors, no less, probably in state custody at some level, whether it's foster care or the juvenile justice system."

"The state has computers," Tess wheedled. "Department of Juvenile Services, Department of Human Resources—all their stuff must be on a mainframe somewhere."

"Look, I'm not saying I can't hack my way into the state system, but once you get there, it's a mess. None of the agencies' files are compatible, and there's no cross-referencing. And even within the state bureaucracy, Tess, you gotta have more than a first name. I could get you the clips on Beale's trial pretty fast, though. Maybe the kids are named in there."

"I already thought of that. But as minors in foster care, their identities wouldn't have been publicly disclosed."

"Then try the old-fashioned shoe leather approach in the neighborhood. Maybe someone knows where they all went, or can hook you up with the foster parents. Use those long legs for something besides rowing that stupid little boat of yours."

"Okay." It was the answer Tess had expected, although she had half-heartedly hoped Dorie might know some secret, omnipotent database.

Dorie started to leave. Tess knew the drill, knew she would have to wait five minutes before she departed. She may have chosen the site, but everything else about their meeting had been dictated by Dorie.

"So what are you doing later?" Dorie asked as she unlocked the door and checked the corridor. "Want to grab a beer somewhere?"

"Sure. Oh—no, I can't. I'm having coffee with Martin Tull when he gets off."

"That *shrimp?* What, is he the next big romance? He's too small for you. Throw him back."

"Just a friend. I need friends more than big romances right now."

Dorie laughed knowingly. "Sure you do, Tess. Keep telling yourself that."

"He's a buddy, nothing more. I like him. Besides, it can't hurt to have a friend who happens to be a homicide detective."

"Hey, maybe he can help you with this Beale thing."

"No shit, Sherlock." It wasn't often that Tess got the last word with Dorie, but when she did, it was sweet. Fleeting, but sweet. Tomorrow, there would be a sarcastic e-mail on her computer, a subtle reminder of just who needed whom in this relationship.

AT HER APARTMENT THAT EVENING, TESS OPENED UP TWO CANS FOR dinner—ravioli for her, Pedigree for Esskay. Having read somewhere that single people shouldn't stint on the niceties, she took the time to put the ravioli on a plate and made a salad with a mustard vinaigrette from the pages of Nora Ephron's *Heartburn*, one of the two "cookbooks" she owned. She even added a drizzle of olive oil to Esskay's food, then carried both dishes out to the "terrace," a sooty expanse of roof reached by the French doors off her bedroom. During the warm-weather months, it was her dining room of choice, as long as Esskay kept the dive-bombing seagulls at bay.

A few weeks back, she had gotten overly optimistic about where the decimal point belonged in her checking account and ended up purchasing a cafe table and matching chairs from the Smith and Hawken store. She had intended to buy only one chair, but the saleswoman had made her feel so odd that she had ended up taking home four, overcompensating as always. She tried to remember to sit in a different one each night, just in case the green-painted metal was susceptible to wear patterns. She felt like Goldilocks, going from place to place, only these were all the same and never quite right.

Was she lonely? That wasn't the word she would put to what she felt—the quick, rapid pulse in her throat, the dryness in her mouth, the constant sensation that somewhere, somehow, she had left an important task undone. No, loneliness was melancholy and still, a feeling experienced when one was far from family and friends. Sure, Whitney had moved to Japan and she was—thankfully, really—on a hiatus from romance, but she had other friends and an embarrassment of relatives rattling around Baltimore. What she was feeling must be anxiety over the new business, pure and simple.

"But things are looking up," she told Esskay and herself, picking at her food with uncharacteristic delicacy. "We put money in the bank today. We've got a cushion now."

The greyhound gazed soulfully at Tess's plate, as if to say, *Well, then, let me help you celebrate by finishing your dinner.* Tess used the leftover ravioli to lure Esskay back into the apartment, then went downstairs to the bookstore on the first floor, hoping a visit with the proprietor, her Aunt Kitty, might take the edge off her strange mood.

Kitty was in the front, shelving a new shipment of books. Women and Children First had started as a family deal struck at a crab feast several years back, when a suddenly flush Kitty Monaghan literally collided with a not-so-suddenly bankrupt Poppa Weinstein. Of course he had been taken with the petite redhead—almost all men were—but he had also admired her idea for a specialty bookstore in what had once been his flagship drugstore. "I always served women and children," he told Kitty, as they swung their crab mallets, "so why not books for women and children? Make me an offer."

But the *Titanic*-inspired name was a misnomer within a year. "Women and Children First, but not *exclusively*," Kitty had decreed, gradually adding male authors to the women's side of the store. Her only requirement was that the men's books must have strong female characters, a stipulation that excluded many famous writers.

"I mean, you can sequester yourself, but what does it accomplish?" she asked Tess this evening, unpacking books by yet another round of interlopers. Amis, Ellroy, Updike, the two Roths, Henry and Philip, and the latest from the local guys, Madison Smartt Bell and Stephen Dixon. "You can shut yourself off for a while, but eventually you've got to face them."

"That's why I fought against going to Western High School," Tess said, sitting on the old U-shaped soda fountain that still sat in the center of the store. "A public all-girl high school is a nice concept, but I never wanted to be safe in some little namby-pamby girl world."

"Bullshit," Kitty said, breaking down and flattening the now empty boxes. "You didn't want to go to Western, my dear niece, because you came out of the womb with a taste for testosterone. You hated Western because you resented being in a flirting-free zone."

"You've got it backward. We could flirt all we wanted—out in the quad at lunch time, with the boys from Polytechnic. I wanted to argue with them, compete with them for the highest grades and see if they would still ask me out."

"Tess, you were a C-cup at age twelve. Einstein could have gotten a date with a Poly boy if he had breasts. In fact, Einstein with breasts is probably the Poly ideal to this day."

Kitty's latest boyfriend, who appeared to be twenty-five to her forty-whatever, picked this moment to enter the store, clutching an armful of irises whose ragged stems indicated they had been pilfered from someone else's garden. Will Elam. Will He Last, to Tess. A graduate student, he was a little scrawny and a lot too brainy for Kitty. The smart ones never went quietly at the end of the two, three weeks she allotted her boyfriends. They always wanted to know *why*, when there was no why, other than Kitty's low threshold for boredom.

"Now that you mention it, I think I know which side of the family that boy-crazy gene came down on," Tess said.

Kitty, cooing over her flowers, ignored her. Will was lost in Kitty-land, that tiny country where the flag was the color of strawberry-blond curls, the official scent was Garden Botanika freesia, and the only sound one heard was a contralto whisper.

"I'm going out," Tess announced, on the off chance someone might be paying attention to her. "Don't wait up."

FOUR

AT THE DAILY GRIND, TESS INSISTED ON PAYING FOR MARTIN TULL'S latte and chocolate biscotti.

"I take it you want a favor," he said dryly.

"How crass. Did it ever occur to you that maybe I want to treat for once, instead of having you grab the check as if I were a charity case?"

"And maybe you want a favor."

"Maybe," she said, stirring a little sugar into her cappuccino. No reason to rush. Tull's curiosity would eventually get the better of him. He had an avid interest in her little business, in part because he had played matchmaker between her and his retired colleague, Edward Keyes. Tess suspected the switch to private detective was a change he might make himself one day, if the commissioner ever made good on his threat to rotate him to other departments. Homicide was Tull's calling. As long as he was allowed to practice his vocation, he wouldn't leave.

But he was distracted just now, his eyes sliding over to the recreation pier across the street from the coffeehouse.

"They're not there," Tess said.

"Who?" His voice was all innocence, as if he hadn't glanced at the pier several times already.

"Your alter egos. They're on hiatus. I always forget, which one is based on you? The blond one whose eyes are too close together or the bald, smoldering one?"

"He's not bald anymore and he's leaving the show, even if it gets picked up for another season."

"Thought you didn't watch."

"It's in the papers, sometimes. I read the articles to make sure the show isn't going to be a shoot in my neighborhood. They close streets and everything, it's a real hassle. They like Hamilton, I guess. There's a lot of variety in the houses up in Northeast District. Looks good on TV."

Tess smiled. Leave it to Baltimore, usually so finicky about its national image, to embrace a television program that spotlighted its murder rate. The network television show about Baltimore homicide cops was such a part of the city now that a robber had once surrendered to the actors by mistake. True, production could be something of a pain, especially here in Fells Point, where the recreation pier stood in for police headquarters. But the show got the city right, and after all those years of being force-fed Los Angeles and New York locations, it was thrilling just to hear some pretty boy say "Wilkens Avenue" and "Fort McHenry Tunnel" on national television, as if they were real places.

"But it's why we always meet here, isn't it? Because you like to sneak peeks at the actors."

"I like coffee, and I don't like bars," Tull said. "You live in Fells Point. Where else are we going to meet?"

"Another coffeehouse?"

A blonde at the next table was trying to catch Tull's eye, with no luck. He never noticed women. Well, almost never—an ex-wife lurked somewhere in his past. Then again, maybe that's why she was an ex, because he hadn't paid any attention to her. Tull was maddeningly reticent on the subject. Meanwhile, women were always heaving and sighing in his presence, practically falling at his feet, but this ace detective just couldn't crack the case of his own intriguing looks. Inside, he was forever a short, skinny kid with bad skin, not to mention those comically small hands and feet.

Tess didn't have any romantic yearnings toward him. She would remain under her self-imposed dating ban until she figured out why her judgment in these matters had been so historically wretched. Of the last three men in her life, one was dead, one was in jail, and one was in Texas. She wouldn't wish any of those fates on Tull the tee-totaler.

"Do you have a drinking problem?" she asked suddenly.

"Now that would be a cliché, wouldn't it?" replied Tull. "The alcoholic cop."

"A cliché is merely a truth that's become banal through repetition."

"What if I told you I think *you* drink too much, so I make you meet me here, where you can't abuse anything but caffeine?"

Tess considered this. Such personal observations fascinated her, even unflattering ones. Did she drink too much, or was Tull simply trying to deflect her question? She followed H. L. Mencken's tips for responsible alcohol consumption: Never drink before sundown and never drink three days in a row. Well, she more or less followed those rules. Obviously, you weren't supposed to wait for evening once daylight savings time kicked in. And an occasional glass of wine at lunch was merely civilized.

"I'd say you were trying to change the subject on me," she said. "Besides, talk about clichés. Everyone thinks I do everything to excess. I can go cold turkey on anything, any time. Just try me."

"Like men. Which means I can't try you." He was teasing her. Tull would have run for the exits if he thought she had a romantic interest in him. Tess was suddenly aware of Nancy LaMott's voice on the sound system, rubbing against them like an affectionate cat. It was one of those uncanny moments when background music suddenly became a suitable soundtrack. "Moon River" in this case. Two drifters. Huckleberry friends, whatever the hell that meant.

"*Breakfast at Tiffany's,*" Tull said.

"Great story, crappy movie." Tess sobbed every time she saw it.

"Did I ever tell you how George Peppard got me through insomnia? Some station was showing 'Banacek' reruns every night. Cleared up my problem in no time."

"When was this? After your divorce?"

"I don't remember." So near, so far away. She had run smack into another one of Martin Tull's internal firewalls. He could remember the details of every homicide he had worked in the city, but he always claimed virtual amnesia when asked a personal question.

"So, I actually had clients today," she said, knowing this was a subject he would welcome.

"Yeah?"

"*Two* clients in one day. One very direct, slam-dunk missing persons thing. God bless Autotrack."

Tull snapped his biscotti in two with his small, very even white teeth. "A lot of that computer stuff is illegal, or should be. I don't want to know too much about how you do what you do. Puts me in a difficult position."

"I don't do it personally, if that's any comfort. But it's the other case I want to ask you about. It involves finding minors, possibly in foster care. The computer is useless, or so I'm told."

"In Baltimore?" Tull drummed his fingers against the table, instantly engaged.

"Maryland. I think. I hope. I don't even have their full names."

"Who wants to find them? Why?"

She sidestepped the first question. It was none of Tull's business who came to her door, but the why, if finessed, might be enough to get the help she needed. "They testified in this court case several years back. My client feels indebted to them, and he wants to make good on it."

"Car accident?"

"An accident of sorts. These kids were the only witnesses. He doesn't remember their last names, though, and isn't sure of their first names."

"Tess, that's a no-brainer. I mean, it's so easy, you should be ashamed of yourself for not knowing how to do it."

She pretended to pout. "Okay, I'm ashamed of myself. I'm totally lost. What do I do? Where do I start?"

"These kids were witnesses in a court case, right? So all you have to do is put the case name in the court computer, and the witness list will pop right up. Even minors have their full names on file if they're called as witnesses. Even in a civil case."

Tess sipped her cappuccino, feeling smug. "Of course, I didn't say it was civil. That was your supposition."

"Civil or criminal, same difference, but you said—" Tull looked at her. "You yanking my chain, Tess? Who is your client, anyway? Someone on my side of the street?"

"The names of my clients are confidential, Detective Tull, as you know."

"Criminal, criminal, criminal," he muttered to himself. "Homicide?"

"None of your business."

"Homicide it is. A homicide with kids as witnesses." Tess could almost see Tull riffling the mental files of his mind, processing each of the two thousand-plus cases the city homicide squad had handled in the past seven years. "Kids, kids, kids. The one who was shot by the guy in Cedonia, for bringing his daughter home too late from the movies?"

"If I told you the name of my client, Tyner could be disbarred. Besides, you couldn't be further off."

"The one where the guy shot the fourteen-year-old for jostling his car when he walked by, setting off the car alarm?"

That caught her off-guard. "How did I miss that one?"

"No, that can't be it. The *kid* was killed, the witness was an old woman sitting on her porch." Tull snapped his fingers. "Dead kid. Kid witnesses. Beale. Luther Beale. That crazy motherfucker."

"I don't know about crazy. A little odd, but then who wouldn't be, given the circumstances?"

"Then it *is* Beale." In his delight, Tull actually slapped himself five, high and low. "Man, I can't believe you're gullible enough to believe anything that old bastard has to say."

Tess stood up abruptly, angry at how easily he had tricked her into confirming his hunch. Tull took one look at her face and said, "Why don't we pour our coffee in to-go cups and take a walk?"

Fells Point was crowded and rowdy on a Friday night, but Tess and Tull knew how to leave the drunken throngs behind. They walked down Fell Street, a narrow block of newer townhouses and condominiums jutting into the harbor on a long spit of land. There wasn't enough parking for cars to be prowling for a space here, and the only bar was a relatively sedate place. They made their way to the dock and sat on its edge, staring out across the water to Locust Point. Tess could see the remains of the Procter and Gamble plant where Beale had once worked, alongside the Domino's plant. The "Sugar House" to the locals, with a blazing neon sign that had written itself across a thousand Baltimore memories.

"Luther Beale is trying to make amends for what he's done," she said. "Is that so hard to believe? Do you have to be *gullible* to think someone might want to do the right thing?"

"I'm sorry," he said. "I shouldn't have used that word. But Luther Beale—Jesus, Tess, he's the devil. His name should be Lucifer Beale."

"The devil? That old man, in his brown suit? Oh, Martin, I know he killed a little boy, and it sickens me, but he's not evil. He's an old man who made a terrible mistake. He wouldn't be the first guy with a gun to do that. At least he wants to make amends, or try."

"*That's* the problem. He's still a vigilante at heart, making up his own justice system as he goes along. First he was the judge and executioner, now he wants to be the jury, allocating the punitive damages."

"He made a mistake. One horrible, terrible, tragic mistake. I'm not saying it's defensible, but it's not what you're making it out to be."

"One mistake? *One* mistake?" Tull's voice rose almost to a shout. He stopped himself, fighting for control. "I bet he told you he didn't have a record, right?"

"He said there was a rap on him for doing home improvements without a license—"

"Run his name, Tess. You'll find an agg assault arrest from fifteen years ago. If the other guy hadn't been 250 pounds and six-foot-six, that probably would have been Beale's first murder charge. He got PBJ—probation before judgment."

"I know what PBJ is," Tess snapped. "I also know it's the legal equivalent to having a clean record, so Beale told me the truth. If I ran it, I wouldn't find anything."

"Yeah, Beale learned something important from that encounter," Tull continued, ignoring her. "Pick on someone your own size. No. Someone smaller, a kid. An eleven-year-old kid, Tess, who weighed maybe seventy-five pounds. He had some rocks. Luther Beale had a .357 Magnum. It wasn't exactly a fair fight on Fairmount."

"I met him," Tess objected. "I talked to him. He's genuinely contrite. If anything, he feels he hasn't paid enough for what he's done. That's all this is about. He was quoting the Bible. He wouldn't be the first criminal who found God in prison."

"Yeah, and he wouldn't be the first one to lose him again once he got out." Tull looked up at the moon, a full one rising over the harbor, fat and sickly green-yellow. "Tell me, Tess, didn't you feel anything weird, anything off about this guy? I've got a lot of faith in your instincts. I met you over a dead body, and I trusted your feelings about *that*."

"Not at first," she reminded him. "Not until I almost died, too."

Good, her little barb had hurt him, although it really hadn't been his fault. He had hurt her, too, questioning her judgment.

"Yeah, okay, point taken. But didn't Beale give you the creeps?"

"No, not really," she said. "Kind of annoying, in that attention-must-be-paid, listen-to-your-elders kind of way. Abrupt to the point of rudeness. Truth be told, talking to him wasn't much different from talking to my grandmother."

"Rude doesn't begin to describe it. Word around the courthouse was that he wanted to take the stand, claim self-defense or some other crazy-ass scenario. His lawyer talked him out of it, which didn't improve Beale's disposition any. Donnie Moore's mother came to that courthouse every day, sat through every minute of that trial. All she wanted was for Beale to say, 'I'm sorry.' You know what he said to her, when they finally met in the hallway?"

"No," Tess said, even as her memory began retrieving all those soundbites from five years ago. "I don't need to know."

"I'll tell you, anyway." Tull leaned closer, lowering his voice the way an old woman might if forced to repeat a vulgar epithet. "He said to this woman, grieving for her only child, 'If you had been a good mother in the first place, Donnie wouldn't have been living in my neighborhood, and he wouldn't be dead now.' Nice guy, huh? Real sweetheart."

Tess said nothing, just stared at the man in the moon. All her life, she had looked to the moon when it was full, hoping to see the smiling face you were supposed to see. But she always saw a sad one, the mouth formed in a tiny rueful O, as if he were whistling a sad tune.

Tull put his hand over hers, a strange gesture for him. A strange gesture for *them*, newly minted friends that they were, and neither one a touchy-feely type. "I'm going to tell you one more time, Tess, and you can ignore me one more time if you like, but it's true: Luther Beale is bad news. Drop him."

"Did you work the case?"

"No, but I knew the guys who did—"

"So this is hearsay on your part."

Tull nodded reluctantly. "I guess you could say that."

"You really hate vigilantes, don't you? Is it a cop thing? Is it because you honestly fear for what will happen if people start taking the law into their own hands? Or is it because every Luther Beale is evidence of the police department's failings? If the cops had stopped those kids, he wouldn't have been driven to do what he did."

"That's not fair, Tess."

No, it wasn't. But friends got to disagree, piss one another off, forgive and forget. Even in her anger, Tess realized she and Tull had passed a little milestone in their relationship. They had fought, and now they were making up.

"What is it that bothers you so much about Luther Beale? I really want to know."

Tull took his time answering. "I don't like vigilantes because their sense of justice lacks proportion. They take lives for property. They value themselves more than they value anyone or anything. We're close enough to anarchy as it is. We don't need any more Luther Beales to rush us there."

"But he was right, wasn't he? As cruel as he was, he was right."

"Right to kill Donnie Moore?"

"He was right that Donnie Moore wouldn't have been on Fairmount Avenue in the middle of the night if his mother had done her job in the first place."

"You're harsh, Tess."

This time, she didn't bother to defend herself.

FIVE

SOMEWHAT TO HER CHAGRIN, TESS FOUND HERSELF HUMMING A GARTH
Brooks song as she finished up her row along the Patapsco early the
next morning. One of her beloved routines, and how she had missed
it when injuries kept her off the water earlier this year. Her mind
was a screen on a rain gutter, she couldn't help what got caught
there—but *Garth Brooks*, for God's sake, the synthetic poseur with
the big hat. Still, her parody fit nicely with the movements propel-
ling her Alden through the murky water. *I have low friends*, took her
from the start to the top of the stroke, while *in high places* brought
her to the finish. Four verses, each a little faster than the last, were
enough to power her from the Hanover Street Bridge to the boat-
house.

She did, in fact, have a handy supply of friends and relatives in
the city's key institutions. Uncle Donald had worked in virtually
every state agency over the years, while her dad's job as a liquor
board inspector had earned him an interesting assortment of indebted types across Baltimore. She also knew a reporter who, unlike
Dorie, didn't charge for his services. A reporter who was running a
real favor deficit on Tess's ledgers. Magnanimous Tess decided she
would give him a chance to settle his account simply by pulling the
file from Luther Beale's court case and finding the list of witness
names. She'd leave a message on his voice mail as soon as she got

home and by the time she finished her shower, her work would be done.

THE CLARENCE MITCHELL COURTHOUSE HAD A HEAD START ON THE summer doldrums. No satellite trucks outside, which meant no hot trials inside. The air trapped inside its dim hallways was cold and stale, like your refrigerator after two weeks at Ocean City.

"Who's that tap-tap-tapping at my door?" a voice growled when Tess knocked at the press room.

"It's the littlest Billygoat Gruff, you troll. May I cross your bridge?"

"Not by the hair on your mother's chinny-chin-chin."

"You're mixing up your fairy tales. That's what the three little pigs said to the big bad wolf."

"Eat me. Oh, I'm so sorry, that's what Hansel and Gretel said to the witch."

The door swung open. As usual, Kevin Feeney hadn't even bothered to get up to open it, just rolled across the floor in his office chair, phone cradled to his ear, then rolled back to his desk, berating someone all the while.

"You useless sack of shit. I've known that for weeks." A source, Tess decided. If it had been a boss, Feeney would have been much harsher. "Yeah, well, tell me something I don't know. Really? Well, I hear there's breaking news out of Spain the world is round."

As he spoke, he pawed through a pile of papers on his desk, then handed Tess the printout she had asked him to pull from the court computers. Yes! Easy as that, there were the names. Destiny Teeter. Treasure Teeter. Salamon Hawkings. Eldon Kane.

"Amazing. Beale was one for four." One name right out of four, and it was the one who mattered least to him, the girl, Destiny. He had been right about the "El" name, too—that must be the little chubby one he had spoken of.

"Yeah, yeah, yeah," Feeney muttered into the phone, motioning to Tess to stay put. "Why don't you call someone who gives a shit? I am so tired of this crap. You know I don't write the fucking editorials or the goddamn headlines. You want to jaw at me about delivery, too? Are we getting the paper right on your porch, or do you have to walk all the way out to the sidewalk?"

A pause, while his caller murmured something. "Lunch? Sure. Next Wednesday is good for me. Let's go to the noodle place in Towson. Noon? Make it twelve-thirty."

"Your latest girlfriend?" Tess asked when he hung up the phone.

"Your *mama*. Only she likes to go to those cheap motels over on Pulaski Highway for nooners."

"I *wish*. I might respect my mother more if I thought she ever lost control. Or learned to just say no to my grandmother. Gramma's throwing my mother a fiftieth birthday party tonight, which really means she's making my mother put on her own birthday dinner at Gramma's apartment."

"Not that I'm not absolutely fascinated by the ins and outs of your wacked-out family, but I've got some more stuff for you. I ran all the kids' names through the newspaper's electronic library in case one of them grew up to be a National Merit Scholar or a cabinet member. I even tried Nexis, although it was a long shot, but I like spending the paper's money on frivolous shit. Two came up. I'm pleased to be the first to tell you—Eldon Kane, just eighteen, has graduated to the adult justice system. Don Pardo, why don't you tell the folks at home what Eldon has won."

Feeney switched to the smooth tones of a television announcer. "Well, Bob, Eldon has qualified for a bench warrant on car theft charges, because he didn't show up for his arraignment. He's now a wanted man and is probably no longer in the state."

Tess, who was beginning to hope Feeney had done more of her work than she even dreamed, slumped. "Great. If the cops can't find him, how will I?"

"You've got another shot, though. Another name came up in the *Beacon-Light*'s files. The Hawkings kid won some statewide forensic contest three years ago, while he was an eighth-grader at Gwynn's Falls Middle School, just over the city line. Only a list, in agate type yet, but there he was."

"That's something," Tess said, making a note on the printout. "Maybe the middle school can tell me where he went on to high school."

"You got parents' names? Sure would help."

"Hey, I didn't even have their names until you handed me this. What about the foster parents, though? Anything on them?"

"Yeah, George and Martha Nelson. They're in D.C. now. Privatization and the current political climate has been very, very good to them. During the last spasm of back-to-the-orphanage chatter, they picked up a big grant to run a combination home-boarding school for 'at risk' young black men. The Benjamin Banneker Academy. Got glowing write-ups just two months ago in both the *Washington Post* and the *Washington Times*, probably the only thing those two papers have ever agreed on. But neither article mentioned what happened in Baltimore five years ago. Chances are the reporters didn't make the connection and the Nelsons didn't volunteer it."

"Maybe they figured they might not get such big grants if they admitted a kid got killed in their care."

"Look, they didn't exactly give him permission to go out at two a.m., breaking windshields." Feeney flipped through the pages of his reporter's notebook. "I dug up an address on Donnie Moore's mom—she tried to file a civil action against Beale while he was in prison, figuring she could attach his pension and Social Security. Here it is—she's in those projects they're about to blow up, over on the west side."

Tess made another note on her legal pad, copying the address scrawled on the inside cover of Feeney's reporter's notebook.

"What happened to her lawsuit?"

"She settled. It was sealed, but word around the courthouse was she ended up with less than five figures after her lawyer took his cut. It's a little ugly, how they do the math in these cases. Donnie Moore's worth was calculated on his future earning potential."

"Damn, I wonder what I'd be worth according to that formula."

"Hell, Tess, they'd get more for you if they sold you for parts." Feeney cackled at his own joke.

"Thanks. You want to get together for dinner sometime soon?"

"Maybe later this summer. I'm taking four weeks off. I've got so much vacation banked they're ordering me to take some of it."

"Where you headed?"

Feeney looked embarrassed. "California. My sister lives in Long Beach and I haven't seen her daughters for three years. We're going to do some family junk together. Go to the zoo down in San Diego, stuff like that, then I'm going to head into Baja by myself, sit on the beach and drink. You ever been there? Beautiful, beautiful place."

Tess wasn't distracted by his babbling about Baja. "Feeney, are you going to Disneyland with your nieces?"

He nodded, mortified. The phone rang and he grabbed it, shouting into the phone in glad relief: "Yeah? Well, fuck you too, Bunky. You know, if I wanted shit from you, I'd squeeze your head."

Tess waved good-bye, still grinning at the idea of Feeney and his nieces bobbing through the Pirates of the Caribbean, Feeney with the animatronic Lincoln, Feeney being accosted by various Disney characters, who would be drawn like a magnet to his surly countenance. If only she could obtain photographic evidence, the extortion potential alone would allow her to retire.

THE MAIN OFFICE AT GWYNN'S FALLS MIDDLE SCHOOL WAS IN A FIGURA-tive and almost literal meltdown—sweaty miscreants lined up outside the vice principal's office, all the phone lines lit up, and the air conditioner on the fritz. Tess, who had been called in by the vice principal a time or two during her own middle school days, felt guilty and paranoid just standing in the midst of this bedlam, as if the unpunished sins of her youth might suddenly come to light.

"Can I help you?" The harried secretary at the front desk didn't bother to make eye contact with Tess and her clipped words made it clear that she hoped she couldn't help.

"I'm trying to get some information about one of your former students."

Tess was nonchalant, as if it were perfectly routine for some stranger to request a student's record, but the secretary was having none of it. A black woman with dyed blond hair, grass-green eyes, and a crumpled linen dress of a tropical pattern with glints of both colors, she stared at Tess as if trying to match her to some of the faces she had seen on the wall during her last trip to the post office.

"I take it you're not a parent."

Tess considered lying, but decided she wouldn't get away with it. She hadn't seen a single white student in the office, nor in the school's gloomy corridors. "No, I'm a private investigator who's been hired to find this student."

"By a custodial parent?" The secretary drew out the legal term, cu-sto-di-aaaaaaal, as if to warn Tess she knew what was what.

"Um, no, but my client does have a legitimate interest in finding this child."

"Really? How can anyone—someone who's not a parent, probably not even a relative—have a *legitimate* need to find one of our students? If it were the law, you'd have a badge. If you were from Child Protective Services, you'd have a state ID. If it's not the law, and it's not the state, then you're not legitimate and I don't want you in my school."

Tess decided to pull rank. "Look, maybe you should just get the principal. This is a sensitive matter, it requires someone who has authority, and the discretion to use it."

"I *am* the principal, Missy, and you're the sensitive matter. Strangers who walk in off the street are something we take real seriously around here. Now clear these premises, and don't come back. If I see you again, I'll have you arrested for trespassing."

Tess left the way she had always left the principal's office—head down, cheeks hot, certain everyone she passed knew of her mis-deeds.

DONNIE MOORE'S MOTHER WASN'T AT THE ADDRESS FEENEY HAD PRO-vided. The apartment had been taken over by her sister, a spaced-out woman probably ten years younger than Tess. She might have looked younger, too, if not for crack cocaine, which had cooked her body down until it was nothing more than a little skin stretched over some long, knobby bones. Or perhaps her habit was heroin; she seemed in mid-nod when Tess knocked. Head swaying dreamily, like one of those plastic dogs you still saw sometimes in the back of souped-up Chevies, she leaned against the door frame and directed Tess to a rowhouse on Washington Street.

"Near the hospital?"

"No, farther south." In her drug-soft mouth, the phrase came out: "Farver sauf."

"But that's practically back in Butchers Hill." Tess felt as if she had been driving all morning, only to find that what she wanted was a few blocks from her own office.

"Yeah, that's where Keisha's new house is. Her baby's fahver helped find it for her." The sister faded out for a second, closing her eyes. Then her eyes popped open again. "He treats her *good*."

"Her boyfriend?"

"Her baby's fahver," she corrected. An important distinction, ap-parently. "Say hey to her for me, will you? Tell her Tonya says hey."

"Donna?" Her words were virtually without consonants, almost impossible to understand.

"Uh-uh. Tone-ya. Like Toni Braxton, you know, 'cept different. Hey, you know my cousin know a girl who know one of her sisters, down in Severna Park, where she's from?"

"A girl knows your sister?"

"No, she know Toni Braxton. She says she's really nice, not at all stuck-up. She say she comes home and sings in the backyard, and they have chicken. They gonna call me next time she visits." Tonya closed her eyes and hugged herself, thinking of her private back-yard barbecue with Toni Braxton.

A RAT WADDLED DOWN THE SIDEWALK IN FRONT OF KEISHA MOORE'S rowhouse. The house looked neat, but dark, its windows shut and curtains drawn against the bright sunlight. It had the feel of a place where everyone was fast asleep, although it was now almost noon. Tess knocked several times and was about to leave when she heard footsteps on the stairs.

"What you want?" The woman who flung open the door wore nothing but a bra and a pair of baggy athletic shorts. At least, the shorts had been designed to hang loosely. Her substantial frame filled every fold. She wasn't fat, really, but big and solid in a way Tess imagined was probably appealing to most men. Certainly, this wasn't the wasted frame of an addict.

"Are you Keisha Moore?"

"You from Social Services?"

"No—" Tess fumbled with her knapsack, trying to find her wallet and her wallet and her P.I.'s license.

"Because I *told* you, there's no man living here."

"No, really, I'm a detective."

Poor word choice. "I ain't done nothing. What the cops want with me? I ain' done nothing and Lavon ain't done nothing. Why you got to be hassling us all the time?"

"I'm a *private investigator*, not a cop." Tess found the license at last and thrust it at Keisha. "All I want is to ask you a few questions about your son, Donnie Moore."

The woman's face seemed to go dead at the mention of Donnie's name. She sucked on her lower lip, looking at Tess's license.

"That was a long time ago," she said softly. "Why you coming around now?"

"Can we talk inside? It's awfully warm out here in the sun."

But the rowhouse was far hotter, stifling and close. In the small front room, two small children slept on two old sofas, which had been set up like church pews, facing the altar of a brass wall unit with a television set and VCR. The children looked tired in their sleep, if such a thing was possible.

"My nephews," Keisha said, stopping for a second to look at them. "They was up late last night."

"They belong to your sister, the one I met in your apartment?"

"Tonya told you how to find me? She never did have good sense. No, these are my brother's children. I'm watching them for my sister-in-law while she's at DSS, trying to straighten out her food stamps. They's trying to cut her off because of one of those new rules, but she don't even know which one she broke."

"Where's your brother?"

"Gone," Keisha said, and something in her voice kept Tess from asking for more details.

Somewhere above them, a baby began to cry. Keisha ran upstairs, her cloth bedroom slippers slapping on the uncarpeted stairs, and returned a few minutes later with a fat, copper-colored baby in a diaper. She had taken the time to throw a plaid cotton shirt over her bra, although she hadn't bothered to button it.

"She needs a change," she said, leading Tess into the middle room. This would have been the formal dining room when the house was built, but now it was empty, except for an old-fashioned deep freezer against one wall. Keisha used this as a changing table and while her movements were lovingly efficient and competent, it made Tess nervous to see the baby lolling on the slick, hard surface.

"She's pretty," she said tentatively, not sure if that was the appropriate word. More puckish, really, making a fish mouth that reminded Tess of Harpo Marx, but what mother wanted to hear that?

"You got any?"

"Uh-uh," Tess said politely, trying to project the kind of longing she knew mothers expected of nonmothers. She didn't have much of a baby jones. Still, there was something appealing about this chubby girl, a life-of-the-party light in her eyes, a way of churning her arms and legs as if ready to dance.

"This is Laylah," Keisha said, making the baby wave a tiny hand at Tess.

"Lay-lay-lay-lah," Tess sang a little riff to the baby, then felt embarrassed. "I guess people do that all the time."

Keisha looked puzzled. "There's a song with my baby's name? Isn't that something? I'd sure like to hear that sometime."

"Yeah, Derek and the Dominoes." Keisha looked blank. "You know, Eric Clapton."

"Oh yeah, that guitar player. The one whose little boy fell out the window. The one who did the song with Babyface."

Funny, the different contexts people brought to the world. Then again, Tess hadn't known Toni Braxton was from Severna Park. "How old are you, if I may ask?"

"Just turned thirty-one this past April."

"So when you had Donnie you were"—Tess stopped, in part to do the math, in part because the math made her feel rude.

"Fifteen. Yes'm. But what do you want to know about Donnie for? Sure was a long time ago."

"I'm trying to find the other children who were with him at the Nelsons', and I thought you might know where they were."

"Why? I mean, why do you want to find them?"

"Because someone asked me to." That sounded a little sinister, so she added, "There may be some money coming to them, because of what happened."

"Money for them, but not for Donnie?"

"No, I'm afraid not." She didn't owe Keisha any further explanation, but decided to make one up, in case Keisha was distracted by her own grievances. "Because of your lawsuit, I guess. Double jeopardy and all that."

"Oh," Keisha said. The baby's diaper was the kind with tape, and Laylah wasn't a squirmer, but it still took Keisha quite a bit of time to fasten the sides. "Well, I don't know where they are. I never even met 'em."

"What about the trial? Weren't you at the trial?"

"Uh-huh."

"They were there, too, weren't they? I know they were called as witnesses."

"Oh I s'pose we might have spoke, once or twice. But we didn't meet in any real way."

Keisha reminded Tess of the weight you had to pick up from the bottom of the pool to pass Junior Lifesaving. Sometimes, if you didn't come at it just right, you had to surface, take a breath, and make another pass. "Why was Donnie in foster care?"

"I don't s'pose that's anyone's business now, is it? It wasn't right, I'll tell you that much. It was all a stupid mix-up. They took my boy from me for no reason and they got him killed, and they didn't have to pay."

"They put him in foster care just like that, with no hearing?"

Keisha hugged Laylah to her, dropping her head so she could sniff the back of her daughter's neck. She smiled, as if the baby's scent was a kind of aromatherapy. Tess wondered if you had to be a mother to smell it, or if babies' necks smelled good to everyone.

"Look, that was all a long time ago, and I don't remember much about it. I don't want to remember much. I got Laylah and I'm a good mother now, a real good mother, and my baby's father is good to me. What's it to me, you do something for those other chil'ren?"

In the front room, one of the sleeping nephews whimpered like a puppy. Keisha Moore didn't move, just stood in the shadowy dining room, rocking Laylah in her arms.

Tess put her card on the freezer/changing table. "Just in case," she said. "For what it's worth, Laylah really is a cutie."

When she passed through the front room, the two little boys slept on, their cheeks patterned by the rough weave of the old sofas, their clothes twisted and wrinkled on their skinny, compact bodies. She hadn't noticed before that they were wearing their shoes, high-top athletic shoes with Velcro fasteners at the ankles, shoes that had cost someone dearly. They had probably been too tired to take their sneakers off when they went to sleep. But why hadn't Keisha or her sister-in-law followed behind, undoing the straps and sliding the shoes gently down their ankles so as not to wake them?

Tess remembered running barefoot through her summer days, careless and free, a stubbed toe or a dropped jar of fireflies her biggest fears. On Washington Street, the children couldn't even afford the luxury of running barefoot through their own dreams.

SIX

ALMOST A DECADE HAD PASSED SINCE GRAMMA WEINSTEIN HAD GIVEN
up her big old house in Windsor Hills and moved into a cramped
apartment in the suburbs northwest of Baltimore. "So urban," she
had said, and the family had been pleased at this uncharacteristic
rhetorical restraint on Gramma's part. But in the end, the changing
neighborhood was less important to her than the cost of maintain-
ing the house, a rambling wreck of a place with rotting wooden
shingles and a weed-choked yard. "I am a woman of reduced circumstances," she liked to tell her children and grandchildren. "You
know, Poppa didn't leave me that well fixed." They knew, they
knew.

Yet Gramma still wanted to entertain on the scale to which she
had become accustomed when Poppa was alive. For Judith's birthday dinner, she had invited all five of her children, their spouses,
the grandchildren and the great-grandchildren. It added up to
twenty people, which would have made her apartment feel like an
overcrowded elevator, an elevator filled with tsotchkes and china
springer spaniels, each one with its own name and history.

Her children had handled the situation as they always did, by
going behind her back. Tess's mother, Judith, called her four brothers and they agreed to draw straws for the dinner. The losers at-
tended, while the others made up credible excuses for why they

could not attend. Even Tess's own father ended up wiggling off the hook, claiming a work conflict. The Monaghans and the Weinsteins still didn't get along that well. So the guest list was limited to Gramma, Uncle Jules and Aunt Sylvia, their daughter Deborah and son-in-law Aaron, Uncle Donald, Uncle Spike, Tess and, of course, the guest of honor, Judith, who had organized it all.

"Where is everybody?" Gramma asked, as Judith sliced her birthday cake and passed pieces around the table.

"Commitments," Judith said. "People's lives are so hectic now."

"Well, Isaac and Nathan were always so driven. That's why they're successful. But I'd think your husband might have been here, at least. Don't the Monaghans celebrate birthdays? God knows, they celebrate everything else."

"Patrick's taking me to the Inn at Perry Cabin this weekend." Judith broke off a piece of cake with her fingers and crammed it into her mouth. *She'd kill me if I did that*, Tess thought.

"A cabin? He takes you to a cabin for your fiftieth birthday?"

"It's a five-star restaurant and hotel, Gramma," Tess said, as her mother's mouth was still full of cake.

"Very fancy, I'm sure. I just can't understand why things can't be like they used to be."

Tess could. It wasn't just the loss of the house, although it had been a wonderful place for parties, that overgrown Victorian perched on a hill above the Gwynn's Falls, full of secret places, like an old dumbwaiter and the remains of a wine cellar. No, it was the loss of Poppa that had changed the nature of their family gatherings. Overworked and overextended, he had still managed to throw his love at them with both hands, like a little kid pushing up waves of water in a swimming pool. Gramma, in defiance of every known stereotype about grandmothers Jewish or otherwise, had served inedible food and begrudged them every mouthful. Unless one ate too sparingly, in which case she was offended.

"Tessie, you're not eating your cake," Gramma said now, watching Tess halve her slice, then divide it again and again. It was hard to find a cake that Tess didn't love, but Gramma always managed, serving a soggy pineapple store brand with the consistency of frozen concentrate straight from the can.

Judith gave her a warning look. As if Tess needed to be reminded of the ground rules for this evening: No candor, no simple truths, nothing that can be construed as an insult. Unless, of course, you were Gramma.

"I'm so full after that wonderful meal."

"Well, Judith can't open her gifts until you finish your cake. Would anyone like another cup of coffee? I'll make some."

"No!" Judith almost shouted in her panic to keep her mother from committing yet another culinary felony. "I mean, I'll make it, Mama. I know where everything is."

"Does it look like Judith is putting on weight?" Gramma asked after she had disappeared behind the kitchen's swinging door. "Or is it that dress?"

You should talk, Tess thought sourly, still breaking her cake into crumbs. Grandma Weinstein was one of those older women who appeared to be all bosom from shoulder to waist. Tess often wondered if this was the fate that awaited her own body, no matter how much she lifted, ran, and rowed. Every day, it seemed, the papers brought more proof that biology was destiny, that genetics would get you in the end.

"You're certainly looking *healthy* yourself these days, Theresa Esther," Grandma said slyly. Tess flinched. Her grandmother's euphemisms had a way of cutting deeper than anyone else's insults. Needle, needle, needle. It was like going to a bad acupuncturist.

"She's a beautiful girl," said Uncle Donald, missing the subtext as usual. Funny, in his days as a political fixer, he understood the meaning of the tiniest gestures in Annapolis, could predict a bill's fate by the way the speaker scratched his head. But he seemed to miss all the nuances in his own family's interactions. "When I walk down the street with Tess, I see the men stealing looks at her, wondering how an old man like me got such a gorgeous companion."

"Feh," said Gramma, unimpressed. "A woman who puts stock in that kind of attention is like a soup bone who thinks the dog has honorable intentions. Nothing counts until you've got a ring on your finger. Don't forget that, Tess."

Which was the only cue Aunt Sylvie needed: "And when am I going to dance at your wedding, Tesser?"

"When the Maryland General Assembly outlaws the Electric Slide."

Deborah smiled at Tess over her son's head, two-year-old Samuel, named for Poppa. Now thirty-seven, Deborah had spent five years and an estimated fifty thousand dollars to produce Samuel, insistent that her child have the same DNA as his parents. As the Chinese say, be careful what you wish for. Samuel was a miniature Aaron and Aaron, in Tess's estimation, wasn't worth anywhere close to fifty thousand dollars. Deborah might have done better shopping around for some sperm that didn't come with that pale, beady-eye, no-lips gene.

"Oh, Mama, Tess is a career woman," Deborah said. "I heard you opened your own office down on Butchers Hill. How's business?"

"Great." The afternoon couldn't have been worse. Tess and Esskay had canvassed Beale's neighborhood, to see if anyone knew the whereabouts of Destiny, Treasure, Salamon, and Eldon. It turned out almost everyone knew who her client was and those who didn't assumed she was a cop. Neither camp was inclined to help her beyond "Hello," "Nope," and "Good-bye." Oh, they had been polite enough; they just wouldn't talk to her. She had never felt so *white* before. Until today, she had thought she was pretty good at inspiring confidence in people, but her open countenance and ready smile hadn't beguiled these folks. Not even Esskay, with her ingratiating little snorts, had been able to break the ice.

"Aren't you nervous in that neighborhood?"

"It's not so bad."

"Really? Didn't I read in the paper last week that a prostitute was found near the Patterson Park pagoda, stabbed and beaten?"

Good old Deborah. She probably couldn't name the current president of the United States, but she had managed to find that one-paragraph item in the *Beacon-Light*.

"Was she black?" Gramma asked.

"The paper didn't say."

"It's not supposed to," Tess said. "They don't put race in unless it's relevant—"

"Black," Gramma decreed. "Well, let them murder one another. She probably left behind five children we'll all have to pay for." Everyone looked at the ceiling, and Uncle Donald cleared his throat nervously, but no one said anything.

Judith poked her head around the kitchen door. "The coffee's ready. Raise your hand if you want a cup."

"Theresa Esther, you lazy girl, get in there and help your mother," Gramma said. "It's her birthday, after all."

As with everything at Gramma's house, there was a strict hierarchy to the gift ritual. Uncle Spike always went first, as his actual relationship to the family remained somewhat dubious. The Weinsteins suspected he was a Monaghan, the Monaghans were sure he must be a Weinstein. He kept everyone guessing by attending all events, even ones like this, where he wasn't actually invited.

This year, he and Uncle Donald had gone in together on Judith's present and when Tess passed the large, heavy box to her mother, she had a sinking feeling. It felt like a piece of electronic equipment. Uncle Spike, a bartender and a bookie, tended to buy such things off the backs of trucks, while Uncle Donald had been known to use his state government job to write awfully creative procurement orders.

"One of those radio–CD players," Judith said happily. "How did you know I wanted one for the kitchen?"

"I've got my spies," Uncle Donald said, winking at Tess. "Is it okay? We can always . . . exchange it if it's not what you want."

Uncle Spike looked up anxiously from his second slice of pineapple cake. So he had been responsible for finding this year's gift.

"No, no, it's exactly right. Thank you, thank you both."

Uncle Jules came forward next, with a box wrapped with the trademark yellow ribbon and green-and-yellow-striped paper of his jewelry store. Every Weinstein woman received one of these boxes on her birthday. Always lovely, but not necessarily quite right for the recipient. Tess had long suspected the pieces were estate items Jules picked up on the cheap, or merchandise he couldn't move. This small box held a pair of sterling silver combs set with turquoise stones, the kind of thing Judith would never wear, although Tess might. Trust Gramma to point that out.

"Jules, those are much too young for Judith. What were you thinking? She's fifty now, after all, getting up in years. Maybe Tessie could wear them, they'd be nice with her eyes. Oh, I forgot. It's Deborah who has the green eyes, yours are more grayish-blue, aren't they, Tessie? Very nice in their own way, though."

One more gift for Mom to open and I am outta here. Tess had presented her gift in private, back at her parents' house. A set of hand-hammered pewter measuring cups, with matching spoons. Judith had seemed to like them, but it occurred to Tess now that her mother, although quite accomplished, found no joy in cooking. As the only daughter of a woman who seemed to revel in destroying food, she had been forced into the kitchen at a young age and remained there by default.

Gramma handed Judith an envelope. It was always an envelope, always with a check for fifty dollars. That is, her four sons and one daughter received fifty dollars, the grandchildren were allotted twenty-five dollars at birthdays and Hanukah. Tess assumed Judith and her brothers received larger checks because the system was structured like war reparations. Those who had suffered the longest received the most.

But instead of the familiar green check with Gramma's spiky handwriting, Judith pulled out a photocopy folded into quarters.

"What's this? It looks like a land deed."

"My big surprise," Gramma said triumphantly. "I'm giving all my children and grandchildren equal shares in that acreage that Samuel left me in north county. It just happens to be part of the parcel where they want to build a new shopping center. The deal should go through later this summer. Poppa finally made a good investment, even if it did take ten years after his death to pay off."

"I'm surprised he didn't have to sell this when he filed for bankruptcy," said Uncle Jules, putting on his reading glasses to inspect the deed. After all, he would share in this windfall, too, as would his Deborah.

"It was a personal investment, held outside the corporation. Samuel wanted to build a house in the country for when he retired. Who knew it would ever be worth anything, so far out? But what was considered far doesn't seem so far anymore, the way people are fleeing the city every day. I paid the taxes and held onto it, and now our ship has come in. My lawyer says we might get as much as two hundred thousand dollars for the land if we play our cards right."

The deed moved around the table, from hand to hand, until it was Tess's turn to study it. Five kids, four grandkids, two hundred thousand dollars—so this was a chit, worth more than twenty-two thousand dollars. If they played their cards right.

The Weinsteins had finally caught a break. Lord knows they were due. *She* had caught a break. If the sale went through, she'd have a nest egg, more than enough to float her through the lean times.

Good old Poppa. It was as if he had reached out from beyond the grave and slipped a quarter in the slot, giving her one more ride on the flying rabbit.

SEVEN

IT WAS COMMONLY BELIEVED THAT THE MAYOR OF BALTIMORE AWOKE every morning and turned southward, a huge smile on his face. No matter how poorly his city was run, he could count on Washington, the nation's capital, to be in even worse shape. Higher homicide rate, dumber schools, bigger potholes and a convicted drug user at the helm, until the city finally despaired and turned the whole mess over to a control board. Yes, things could always be worse, the streets of Washington seemed to sing, as Tess's car bumped and jolted its way to the Nelsons' school on Capitol Hill.

The Benjamin Banneker Academy was a former bank, a sandstone building with fortress-thick walls on a not-too-bad block east of the Capitol. Although she knew the area fairly well, Tess could never accustom herself to its checkerboard quality, where a block of restored townhouses suddenly gave way to rowhouse slums. In Baltimore, neighborhoods were good or bad, and it was easy to avoid the trouble spots. On Capitol Hill, you could buy a three-dollar cup of coffee and a dime bag of heroin within five minutes of each other. One wrong turn, and you were suddenly starring in your own private version of *Bonfire of the Vanities*.

Tess tried the oversize door of the Benjamin Banneker Academy. Locked—unusual for a school, but plain common sense here. The Nelsons were probably hypersensitive about safety, given the circumstances in the death of Donnie Moore. She pressed the buzzer and waited on the stone steps. A round-faced young man poked his head out and said, "No visitors during lessons, ma'am."

"Mr. and Mrs. Nelson are expecting me."

He looked her over, closed the door without comment, then returned several seconds later, opening the door to her. Tess saw now that he wore a dark blue uniform in a military style. His black shoes were mirror shiny, his trousers had a knife-sharp crease. Although his full cheeks gave his face a babyish cast, the rest of him was hard and slender, with the big, defined muscles of a weight-lifter pressing at the seams of his uniform. "I'm sorry, ma'am. But as the monitor, I have strict instructions not to admit anyone, especially reporters."

"I'm not a reporter."

The young man looked puzzled, as if he knew of no other occupation for white women who came to the door of the Banneker Academy. A slight woman in a floral shirtdress came out into the hall, pulling a white cardigan over her narrow shoulders. The woman's posture was even more formidable than the monitor's, so straight and proper that it made Tess's spine ache just to look at her.

"Miss Monaghan?"

"Yes, I'm the one who called to talk about Donnie—"

"Of course." The woman touched the young monitor's elbow. "Drew, you may go back to your post. Mr. Nelson and I will be in the study if you need us."

She led Tess into a small, shadowy room lined with bookshelves, but no books. Apparently the Banneker Academy's endowment was not a lavish one—everything looked used and threadbare. She glanced at the globe standing in the corner. It was enormous, a beautiful world of dark, lush colors, and bright blue oceans. That kind of globe usually cost a fortune new, but this one was at least ten years old, with Europe, Russia, and Africa all hopelessly out of date.

Mr. Nelson, a compact man with a moustache and close-cropped hair, rose from a faded wing chair by a casement window and offered his hand.

"Welcome to Benjamin Banneker Academy," he said, but his voice didn't sound particularly welcoming, and his hand slid quickly through hers, as if he found the contact distasteful.

"Thank you. I'll admit I'm a little confused. Is this a school or an orphanage?"

"Both," Mrs. Nelson said, "although we don't like the term 'orphanage.' The Banneker Academy is a charter school, a private school that receives monies from the district under a program designed to make the public schools more competitive. At the same time, it's a group home. The boys admitted here as students are placed through the city's foster care program."

"So you're double dipping."

Mr. Nelson frowned. "We're not doing anything illegal if that's what you're suggesting. These are two separate programs under the same roof."

"I didn't mean to imply—"

"I'm sure you didn't," he said stiffly. Great, she had managed to offend him in what was supposed to be the innocuous, buttering-up portion of the conversation. Step aside, Dale Carnegie, let Tess Monaghan show you how it's done.

Mrs. Nelson interceded, trying to smooth things over. "We convinced the district to allow us to open a private school for the boys who have become our wards. We are the faculty, we are the parents. If George and I have learned anything from our . . . missteps over the years, it's that it's no use rearing children right, only to send them into schools where our teaching is undone."

So now it was the Baltimore school system's fault that the Nelsons' wards had been running wild in the streets. Was anyone to blame for what happened on Fairmount Avenue five years ago?

"Our boys have consistency now, and they flourish," Mrs. Nelson continued, her voice quiet but impassioned. "I grant you, we can't teach them advanced calculus, or physics, but if we have a boy who wishes to study those subjects, we can obtain the services of a tutor from the district. One day, we'll have our own gifted-and-talented program, and teachers will be fighting to work here."

"One day," said Mr. Nelson, who seemed less starry-eyed than his wife. "We have a ways to go."

"You said you learned from your missteps. I assume you mean Donnie Moore."

The Nelsons looked at each other. Tess saw him nod, ever so slightly, as if giving her permission to speak of what had been so long forbidden.

"Donald," Mrs. Nelson said. "Yes, I was referring to Donald."

"I'm trying to find the other children who lived with you when *Donald* was killed." Tess had never heard anyone employ this more formal version of his name—not his mother, not Detective Tull, not even the newspaper accounts of the time—but she was willing to appropriate the usage if it helped her gain some small rapport with the Nelsons.

"Why?"

Tess was ready for this question, more ready than she had been with Keisha Moore.

"A local victims' rights group is interested in helping the children."

"Now? Doesn't it seem a bit late? They've probably just begun to heal, and you—your victims' group—wants to remind them of the horror they saw." Mrs. Nelson pulled her sweater over her shoulders, as if just thinking about Butchers Hill gave her a chill. "I don't see much love in that kind of philanthropy, Miss Monaghan."

"No one's asking that they relive what they've been through. I thought if you ever heard from them, if you knew where they are—"

"No," Mr. Nelson said sharply. "We never hear from them. They don't even know where we are, and we don't know where they are. That's how foster care works, you know. We took them, we cared for them, we loved them, but we had no rights. They were our children, as surely as if they had been born to us. But when Donald died, they took them from us that very night. That evil old man might as well have killed all of them, so thoroughly did he destroy our home and the work we were doing."

Mrs. Nelson was crying now, silent tears running down her face. Mr. Nelson took Tess by the shoulders and turned her to the casement window behind the wing chair. "Look there," he said, gripping Tess's shoulders, as if she might try to wrest away from him. She saw ten young men in formation, running drills in the courtyard, marching and turning to a leader's shouted commands. It was a hot morning and sweat ran from their faces, but they worked in grim determination, their movements crisp and sharp.

"These young men love discipline," he said. "They *yearn* for it. They've waited their entire lives for someone to say, you are good enough to meet the highest standards. Donald and the others lived in a world where people said, *You're nothing, you'll never do anything, just show up, go through the motions, that's all you can do.* And then, just in case those poor children didn't get the point, didn't know how little their lives were worth, a judge gave a man less time for killing Donald than some people get for killing a dog."

The young men marched in place now, shouting in cadence. Although Tess couldn't hear the words they were chanting, she could sense the joy in their movements as they answered their drill instructor's calls.

"Leave our children alone, Miss Monaghan," Mr. Nelson urged her. "Let them forget. Forgetting is their only salvation now."

"Those who cannot remember the past are condemned to repeat it."

"Do you really believe that?"

Tess shrugged. The Santayana chestnut had been worth a try. "Sometimes."

Her candor seemed to thaw Mrs. Nelson by a few degrees at least. "If it's any consolation, I couldn't help you even if I wanted to.

Those children are lost to us, too. I suppose that's our punishment, for not taking better care of them."

"But you'll save these bo—young men." It was more of a question, a hope, than a statement of fact.

Mr. Nelson shook his head. "I wish I could promise them that. I can only promise them safety here, on this little patch of land, for as long as they're with us. Eventually, they'll go forth in the world, and then there's only so much we can do. But no, there will never be another Donald Moore, not on our watch."

What was left to say after such a speech? Luther Beale's compensation plan, his desire for retribution, seemed trite and puny in the face of the Nelsons' commitment to their wards.

"Go in peace, Miss Monaghan," Mrs. Nelson called after her, her voice still a little shaky from her quiet tears.

The same monitor showed Tess out. Impressed by his perfect posture, Tess found herself standing a little straighter, throwing her shoulders back and sucking her stomach in.

"Do you like it here?" she asked him as he unlocked the front door.

"Oh yes, ma'am."

"What do they—in the curriculum—I mean, what do they teach you here?"

"Survival."

"What do you mean?"

The young man gave her a smile at once sweet and superior. "They're teaching us how to live in our world—and how to live in *yours*. Now be careful going to your car, ma'am. We've got some real bad people in these parts."

TESS WAS HEADING NORTH ON THE BALTIMORE-WASHINGTON PARKWAY when her knapsack started ringing. Startled, she almost swerved out of her lane, then remembered the cell phone she kept in the litter of pens and crumpled ATM slips at the bottom of her old leather book bag. Past experiences had convinced her that she couldn't afford to be without a portable phone, but the balances on all those ATM slips indicated she couldn't afford to use it, either.

"It's Dorie. God, I hate cell phones."

"Not as much as I hate this always-under-construction road. I'm crawling along down here."

"You going slowly enough to take some notes? Or you want to pull off at the next exit and call me back? I've got the Susan King info you wanted."

"I'm pulling into a rest stop even as we speak. I'll call you on the *Blight*'s 800 number."

Tess pulled her Toyota into a lane banked by a row of public telephones. It must have seemed so cutting edge once, a highway rest stop built so you could make a call without leaving your car. How quaint, how adorably low-tech. But it was a cheaper, better connection than the cell phone provided.

"Okay, I've got my notebook out. Shoot me what you have on Susan King."

"First of all, she's not Susan King anymore—she's Jacqueline Weir. Changed her name legally when she was eighteen. Probably thought that was good enough to keep her relatives from finding her."

"It would have been, if her relatives didn't now have access to Dorie's magic fingers." A little stroking was all part of the package with Dorie. "Why do you assume she changed her name in order to hide? The way her sister explained it, they just lost touch after she had a falling-out with their mother."

"Jacqueline Weir has the best reason of all to hide from her relatives—money. For someone who's only thirty-two, she's done pretty well for herself. She has her own business. A consulting firm, according to the file, but that could be anything. She must be doing well, because she has a huge line of credit. She also has a mortgage of sixty-five thousand dollars on a Columbia condo."

"That's not such a big deal," Tess objected, even as she wrote down the address Dorie rattled off.

"No, but the loan is secured by her own stocks, and not many thirty-two-year-olds have a portfolio like that. Approximately two hundred thousand dollars at market close yesterday. How much do *you* have in savings?"

"Don't tell me you pulled her credit report, Dorie. I thought we agreed you weren't going to do that unless it was absolutely necessary."

"Okay, I didn't pull her credit report. Let's just say my sixth sense tells me it's excellent. What else? Oh yeah, she leases a brand-new Lexus, only through her company, so it's a tax thing. Very crafty, this Susan King-Jacqueline Weir. I did find some sort of legal action filed on a Susan King when I ran the Chicago Title search, but it's after she changed her name, so I'm thinking it's not the same Susan King, or else it's no big deal. If someone had been really serious about collecting, they would have gone to the trouble of finding her. Probably parking tickets, some penny-ante shit like that."

"If she's so wealthy, wouldn't she pay her parking tickets?"

"Look, I'm not saying she's rich, but she's obviously got enough money on hand so relatives who aren't so well off would feel comfortable yelling for hand-outs."

Tess thought of Mary Browne in her expensive yellow suit, which matched the shoes, which matched the ribbon on her straw hat. Tess's mother dressed that way and it didn't come cheap, that matchy-matchy look. The shoe bills alone were staggering. "Her sister didn't look as if she was hurting."

"Yeah, well that's part of the trick of getting money, isn't it? Not looking like you need it. By the way, I ran Mary Browne with the birth date you gave me."

"And?"

"Even limiting the search to Maryland, I found about a hundred. With e's, without e's, but at least a hundred who could be her. Yet not a single one with that particular DOB."

"I *knew* she was lying about her age."

"Maybe." Dorie didn't sound convinced. "Or maybe she's not

using her right name, either. Or maybe she's not from where she says she's from. Maybe she's not this woman's sister, and maybe you don't really know why she's looking for Susan King, who's trying to make a new life for herself as Jacqueline Weir."

Tess looked at her watch. "Look, I'm not far from the turn-off to Columbia. Tell you what—I'll buzz by her place and if Jacqueline Weir is home, I'll try to figure out her story without letting on who hired me. Will that make you happy?"

"Not as happy as the check you owe me for this."

Tess hung up the phone and, not without some effort, wedged her way back into traffic. Idling along, she couldn't help thinking about what Dorie might find on Theresa Esther Monaghan in her electronic data bases. A twelve-year-old Toyota. No mortgage, although she had a loan for the business, co-signed by Kitty and Tyner. No other record of the business—after all, it was in the name of Edgar Keyes, although Tess's name showed up on the incorporation papers as vice president. It made her feel safe and smug, knowing how few electronic tracks she had left. It also made her feel like something of a failure. Surely important people couldn't move so anonymously through life.

She was so busy thinking about her electronic profile that she almost missed the turn-off for Columbia. She caught Highway 175 at the last possible moment and headed west, into the heart of Maryland's last fling with Utopia.

The planned community of Columbia, brought forth during the giddy optimism of the sixties, was to have revolutionized the suburbs with its "villages" and mandated proportions of green space. A new town, as it had been called, a different way to live. But Columbia's only real legacy was its strangely named cul de sacs—Proud Foot Place, Open Window Way, Sea Change. Utopia was just another suburb, a bedroom community for Baltimore and D.C. The late developer James Rouse was better known for his much imitated "festival marketplaces," from Boston's Faneuil Hall to Baltimore's Harborplace, than he was for his new city. He had wanted to change the way people lived and ended up changing the way tourists shopped. *So much for life as a visionary*, Tess thought. At least he had walked the walk, living in his own creation, and using his retirement years to build housing for the inner-city poor.

Jacqueline Weir's condo was in a development known as the Cove, which at thirty-years-plus was Columbia's equivalent of Colonial Williamsburg. Tess wandered through the cluster of stucco and brick buildings for almost fifteen minutes before she found the address. It was a two-story apartment that backed up to a small canal along the man-made Wilde Lake, stagnant and bright green with algae at this time of year.

Dorie's misgivings had gotten to her. What if Jacqueline Weir didn't want to be found? What if she had a legitimate reason not to see her sister again? What if Mary Browne wasn't her sister? Tess couldn't show up on the woman's doorstep and say, "Heigh-ho, I was hired to find you, any reason I shouldn't?" However, armed with nothing more than a clipboard and one of her plain, tell-nothing business cards, she could transform herself into a pollster and ask all sorts of personal questions that might give her the information she needed. Or she could pretend to be from one of those new computer services that offered to reunite people with lost loved ones, then gauge Jacqueline Weir's reaction to this one-time free offer. She rapped briskly at the door, full of purpose.

No answer, no sound of movement came from within the apartment. Dorie had said Jacqueline/Susan worked from home, but who knew where a consultant might be at midday? She rapped again, and this time heard high heels moving across hardwood floors. Perfect. She stood a little straighter, thinking again of the Banneker monitor and the ramrod spine of Mrs. Nelson. She smoothed her hair with her free hand. Lies crowded her tongue, ready to be told.

They all vanished, every word vanished, when the door opened.

"I'd thought you'd get here a little faster than this," said the woman Tess knew as Mary Browne. "But I guess you did okay, all things considered."

EIGHT

"WHO *ARE* YOU?"

"I'm Jackie Weir," said the woman Tess knew as Mary Browne. Certainly, she dressed like Mary Browne. Today, it was a coral suit with white trim at the cuffs and collars. The white was picked up by her high-heeled shoes, pearl earrings, and a double strand of pearls against her dark throat. All this, just to sit in her home-office, waiting for Tess to come to the punchline of her sick little joke.

"But Jackie Weir is Susan King."

"Right."

"And 'Mary Browne' hired me to find Susan King. You hired me to find *you*." For a moment, Tess wished she were in the habit of carrying her gun. This was crazy, and crazy people made her nervous.

"Yes, which you've done. Congratulations. As I said, I thought you might have been here even faster—it's really not that hard, once you find the name change, and any competent private investigator should have been able to do that. But I'm impressed, nevertheless."

They were still standing in the foyer of Mary's—of Susan's, no, of *Jackie's*—apartment. Tess studied the parquet floors, the other woman's lethal-looking white pumps, her own nubuck flats. They were from the Tweeds catalog and she would have called them off-yellow, but the catalog had labeled them cornmeal. *Why am I thinking about shoes?* Because she was embarrassed and humiliated, and concentrating on her shoes kept her from admitting how angry she was.

"I don't like this," Tess began. "You came to my place of business, you lied to me—"

"I suppose you never lie."

Better to skip past that one. "You wasted my time."

"I *paid* for your time. A new private investigator, starting out—all your cases should be so easy. I know what it's like to start a business. You can't have too many easy jobs. But my next job is harder. You won't have such an easy time finding the person I'm really looking for."

Tess looked up. "What makes you think I'd do any more work for you at all, after the way you dicked me around?"

Jackie's smile was the smile of a businesswoman used to coddling difficult types, smoothing ruffled feathers, working her to way to *yes*. "Look, it's past noon. Can we talk about this over lunch? There's always Clyde's, just across the way."

"No Clyde's," Tess said petulantly, a child saying no just to say no. "I've never forgiven their menu for inspiring that insipid song 'Afternoon Delight.' "

"Let's go into Clarksville, then."

"Clarksville? What's out there, the local Dairy Queen?" Actually a hot dog and a Peanut Buster Parfait would hit the spot. One drawback to city living was the serious lack of Dairy Queens.

"You obviously haven't been keeping up with Howard County real estate. Clarksville is home to some of the ritziest subdivisions around—and one amazing French restaurant. Expensive, but worth it. Come on, it's on me."

"You bet it's on you," Tess said. "After all, you have a stock portfolio worth almost two hundred thousand dollars as of market close yesterday."

There was a small victory in seeing Jackie Weir's eyes widen at that factoid. Good—let her wonder what else Tess might have uncovered along the way.

* * *

CLARKSVILLE HAD CHANGED. TESS REMEMBERED FARMLAND, A FEW simple houses scattered among the trees. Now huge, elaborate homes sat on landscaped lots. These weren't the kind of developments that looked naked and raw in their early years; too much money had been spent for the owners to tolerate anything less than instant perfection. But the very lack of flaws, the absence of anything as spontaneous as a fallen bicycle or an overgrown lilac tree, made the houses forbidding to Tess.

"Mini-mansions, they call them in the trade," Jackie said as they drove west. "The covenant actually specifies a minimum square footage of ten thousand feet and all natural materials."

"But that was a *lavender* stone house. How can that be natural?"

"Closer to periwinkle, if you want to be precise. The owner's Mercedes has been custom-painted to match. Or was it the other way around?"

After seeing the overdone, overlarge houses, Tess assumed the restaurant would be built along the same nightmarish proportions. To her relief, Trouve was a small, fieldstone farmhouse that looked as if it had been moved, stone by stone, from the French countryside. If it weren't for the parking lot full of expensive cars, it might have passed for the working farm it once was.

"Miss Jacqueline, do you have a reservation today?" the maitre d' asked. Tess, glancing at the clientele in the almost-full dining room, suddenly felt underdressed and frumpy. Her warm-weather clothes tended toward things that made as little contact with the skin as possible—a loose, white T-shirt today, and an ankle-length cotton skirt that allowed her to skip pantyhose, but was now badly wrinkled from all her driving.

"I didn't plan ahead, but I was hoping you just might find a place for us, Michel."

"Of course." Tess assumed two women would be hidden away by the kitchen or bathroom, especially when one was so sloppily dressed. But Michel led them to a table next to a large bay window, overlooking a small orchard of fruit trees and, beyond that, a meadow of wild flowers.

Jackie allowed herself to preen just a little. "As I said, I bring a lot of clients here."

"What is it you *do*, exactly?"

"Professional fund-raiser. I started out in development at a hospital in the Washington suburbs, but I found I could make better money on my own, raising money on a contract basis. I do a few good causes to salve my conscience—Advocates for Children and Youth, Health Care for the Homeless, Manna House—but I barely break even on those. The big money is in capital projects."

"And politicians?"

"When I first started. Not so often now. I prefer diseases to politicians."

"Who doesn't?"

Jackie looked at Tess over the top of her menu, clearly puzzled.

"A joke," Tess explained.

"Oh, I get it." But she didn't smile.

At least Jackie—it was still an effort to remember which name to use—had an appetite. She ordered an appetizer, salad, and entree, which meant Tess could follow her lead without feeling the need to explain she had rowed that morning and then run three miles. It was refreshing to be with a woman who ate as much as she did, without apology. So many of the women she knew seemed intent on deprivation, playing some unfathomable game in which the winner was the person who ordered the most pleasureless meal. Her mother specialized in exactly that kind of denial. In Jackie's company, Tess felt she could hang a banner over the table: *Bring on the cream sauces!*

"I really do have legitimate business for a private investigator," Jackie told her after they had ordered. "But I had a bad experience. I hired a guy several months back, and he didn't do anything, just sat on his ass and cashed my checks. Another one gave up when it got hard. So I decided the next time I hired someone, I was going to make sure they could do some rudimentary investigative work. Finding me isn't hard, but you do have to have enough gumption to run my name through a Chicago Title search, then run my name through the MVA to get my address."

"Which name would that be exactly?" Tess asked innocently, slathering butter on a fresh, warm roll.

"The story I told you was essentially true. Susan King got pregnant when she was a teenager, and had a falling-out with her mother as a result. She ended up leaving home and, I'm sorry to say, never quite reconciled with her mother."

"Do you have to speak of yourself in the third person? It's a little on the creepy side."

"Susan King is a third person to me and as dead as my mother."

"Why did you change your name? Were you hiding from your mother after she kicked you out?"

Questions seemed to make Jackie impatient. It occurred to Tess that she had rehearsed this little scene in her head, and now Tess wasn't playing her part as scripted. How she must have enjoyed sitting in her apartment, waiting for Tess to knock on her door.

"My mother didn't kick me out because I was going to have a baby. She was cool with that. After all, I wasn't the first girl in Southwest Baltimore to turn up pregnant."

"Southwest Baltimore? Which part?" asked Tess, a true Baltimorean, forever focused on the precise boundaries of where people lived.

"Pigtown," Jackie muttered. "Pigtown, okay? Anyway, Mama wanted me to keep the baby, so she could raise it, get a little extra AFDC money and food stamps every month. I almost went for it, too. But you know, I had finished high school and I had this nothing job, and I suddenly saw my future. I told myself, 'This is it, girl. You've still got a chance to make something of yourself, but not if you keep this baby.' "

The appetizers arrived—a tart with woodland mushrooms for Tess, some goat cheese thingie for Jackie.

"What about the baby's father?"

"He wasn't interested in being a father. But you know, I give him credit for admitting it up front, for not pretending to be into it and then dumping me as soon as the baby came. I saw that happen often enough to my girlfriends. Anyway, I signed my daughter over to a private agency and never looked back. And when I got a scholarship to Penn, I decided to change my name legally, sort of a symbol of my new life. In the back of my mind, I think I didn't want my baby to come looking for me one day. You see, I figured I was going to be somebody real famous, real successful, and I didn't want any tabloid trash reunion in my future."

Jackie's story was at once impressive and repellent to Tess. How could someone be that calculating at eighteen? Yet the woman's confidence in herself had been rewarded. Here she was, her life tricked out with the material trappings of success at an age when many of her contemporaries were still slacking. Tess knew now she had seized on the issue of "Mary Browne's" age with such glee because she couldn't bear to think that someone just a few years older than herself, someone born without wealth or privilege, could accomplish so much. But Susan-Jackie had tripped over her own age only because that was the one part of her masquerade she hadn't thought out. An uncharacteristic slip, most likely.

"So why did you come to me? Are you worried your daughter is going to show up on your doorstep? Do you want to launch some kind of preemptive strike, make sure it's impossible to find you? It can probably be done, but I specialize in finding people, not hiding them."

"I don't want to hide. I'm not ashamed of my past." Well, well, well. Jackie had a temper, one she couldn't quite control. Hands shaking, she took several long, steady sips from her water glass. When she spoke, she was in control again, her voice steady and smooth.

"As I told you, my mother died within the past year. We had gotten to the point where we had some contact, but I was little more than a human bank machine to her. She'd call to complain about some crisis in her life, I'd send her some money. Once she was gone, I waited to feel bereft. Instead, I felt haunted, as if someone were following me. I found myself blowing off appointments, driving around Pigtown and looking at the young girls there. I kept thinking, *Are you out there? What became of you? Do you hate me?*"

"Your daughter was put up for adoption, probably with some nice middle-class family. She'd have to be an awful ingrate to hate the woman who made it possible for her to have a better life."

"I wish I knew that. She'll be thirteen this summer. I wasn't much older when I met her father. Five years later, she was inside me."

Tess wondered what it was like to be pregnant. She knew only what it was like to fear it, to worry obsessively over failed contraception, to count the days in the calendar over and over again, calculating ovulation and wondering if maybe, just maybe, the pharmaceutical companies of America had let her down. Nothing was 100 percent effective. Then again, what if you couldn't have a baby? What if you spent all this time and money and worry preventing something that would never happen? Could you get a rebate?

"Do you want to be part of your daughter's life again? Because that's not something I'd be party to. I believe your parents are the people who rear you."

"No, absolutely not. I just want to see her, know she's okay. What could I be to her, anyway? I'm a little young to be a mother figure, too old to be a friend. I'll put my name in the state registry and when she turns eighteen, she can find me there if she wants. For now, if I could just see her, even from a distance, and know that it all paid off, I'd be happy. Blood tells. I made so many mistakes when I was younger. I just want to know she isn't making the same ones."

Another lost child, Tess thought, and this one doesn't even have a name. She couldn't imagine where to start.

"Will you do it? Will you help me find my baby?" Jackie had

dropped her detached, professional tone. Her voice was urgent, almost pleading.

"I don't know. What you're asking is pretty hard. Truthfully, I wouldn't even know where to begin."

"There's this Adoption Rights group that meets in Columbia every other week. We could go there first, learn some strategies."

"It's not just the 'how' part that bothers me. After all, I could give it my best shot, earn some money without worrying I was bleeding you dry. I'm still not sure I want to work for you."

"Why?"

"Because you tricked me, you jerked me around. Okay, you got burned by some other detectives. But there were other ways to figure out I'm legitimate. I can't shake the feeling you liked that whole elaborate game, that you really got off on your Mary Browne disguise. I feel like a little mouse, batted back and forth in some cat's paws. Besides, you're bright, you must have connections if you worked for politicians. You can probably find out as much as I can, even more."

"It's true, I'm successful—more successful than you, for a fact."

"Why, thanks for pointing that out," Tess said dryly.

"But when it comes to dealing with people who have power over me—especially *white* people who have power over me—I lose it. I either get all bashful and tongue-tied, or I start screaming lawsuit. Neither approach is particularly effective."

Tess had a strange sense of *déjà vu*, as if she knew exactly what Jackie meant. The principal at Gwynn's Falls Middle School, taciturn Keisha, Beale's uncooperative neighbors, even the Nelsons. They had thwarted her, been less helpful than they might have been, and all because of *her* race.

"Okay, quid pro quo," she said.

"What do you mean?"

"I'll take your case, but I want more than money from you. I want your help, talking to people who won't talk to *me*, on another case I'm working."

Jackie's look was contemptuous. "You mean poor black folks, don't you? What, do you think there's some secret language I speak that will get me by? That some poor black kid is going to talk to a sister, who happens to be driving a Lexus and wearing the kind of clothes I wear?"

"Maybe. I am willing to bet you can convince a middle school principal that you're a particular kid's next of kin, which is something I can't pull off. That's a start. We'll see how it goes from there."

Their entrees arrived and Jackie attacked her *pompano en croute* with a ferocity Tess found admirable, even familiar. She was bent over her meal with the same intensity. But Jackie could concentrate on her food without losing her train of thought.

"So, if I help you on this other case, do I get a discount?"

"Nope," Tess said cheerfully. "The wages of sin, for not being straight with me from the beginning. Consider it a fraud surcharge."

Finally, Jackie smiled, but it was a cool smile, even a little supercilious. "Good for you. You've already learned one of the cardinal rules for the small businesswoman. Don't give it away—unless you have to."

"Did you ever give it away?"

"No. But then I was good from the very beginning."

NINE

THEY DROVE INTO THE CITY TOGETHER, ALTHOUGH IT WOULD MEAN A long trip back for Tess, who had left her car at Jackie's apartment. But she needed to brief Jackie on the names of the children she was looking for, the block where they had once lived, the questions to ask. She also liked the unaccustomed luxury of Jackie's car, the pampered feeling of being chauffered, although she didn't mention this to Jackie.

It was the hottest part of the day and Tess took a perverse plea- sure in sending Jackie off to work Fairmount Avenue in her high- heeled shoes. "I'd go with you, but it would defeat the purpose," she said. "If they see you with me, you'll automatically be less trust- worthy."

"I guess so," Jackie said. "What will you do while I'm out?" Ap- parently Jackie had not achieved her early success by tolerating, much less welcoming, down time.

"I'll think about how we're going to handle our next fact-finding mission," Tess assured her.

She then spent the next hour trying to teach Esskay to fetch, tossing pencils into the corner opposite her sofa. By the time Jackie returned, favoring her left foot as if she might have the beginnings of a blister, Tess had enough pencils stacked in the corner to make a small bonfire.

"I'd forgotten how hot those rowhouses get in the summer," Jackie said, taking the can of Coke Tess offered and holding it against her neck and brow before she opened it. "And how *nasty* some of them are. People who can't believe the way folks live in Third World countries ought to try a tour of East Baltimore some time."

"Did you find any leads on the kids?"

"In fact, I did. Not much, but something." Jackie smiled, pleased with herself. Why not? She had succeeded so quickly where Tess had failed. That's why Tess had recruited her, yet it still needled, this sense of barriers, of places she could not go, people to whom she could never really speak. She turned on her computer and opened up Luther Beale's file. There wasn't much there, just the notes from their initial interview, and a record of yesterday's futile interviews with Keisha, *et al*.

"Tell me what you've got."

Jackie recited her findings as she might have outlined a fund-raising plan for one of her clients: quickly, efficiently, with few wasted words. "Two of the kids were dead-ends. Salamon Hawkings and Eldon Kane. The neighbors don't recall seeing them around here since the shooting, no one knows what happened to them. But the twins, Treasure and Destiny, never really got away. Officially, they're in the care of an aunt somewhere over on Biddle Street, but the neighbors see them around here all the time. The supposition is that they're actually living here."

"Their own place? Who rents an apartment to two teenagers?"

Jackie looked at Tess as if she were too stupid to be believed. It was the same smug expression she had worn when Tess showed up on her doorstep in Columbia that morning.

"They don't pay rent," Jackie said. "They're squatting in a vacant house. Their aunt shows up from time to time and makes them go home. Sooner or later, they're hanging out here again. Treasure has a taste for crack. He's on the circuit."

"The circuit?"

Another look. "He gets his meals at the soup kitchens in the area. Beans and Bread; Bea Gaddy's on the days that Beans and Bread is closed. Destiny doesn't go for that, though. She's a car girl."

"What's that?" Maybe if she admitted her ignorance of things, Jackie wouldn't be so quick to condescend.

"Sort of an apprentice prostitute. A guy comes along, offers her a ride. It's understood that he's asking for sex and she'll get something out of it, but she's not really a pro. Destiny has a taste for Versace, the neighborhood ladies tell me, and fancy leather pocketbooks. But she's got some come-and-go steady boyfriend who provides her with the big-ticket items. The car dates are more for walking-around money. And drugs for Treasure, I'd bet."

"Versace? How does her boyfriend afford Versace?"

"Why, I believe he's what we call a pharmaceutical entrepreneur," Jackie said, raising one eyebrow. "No one seemed to know his name, but they wouldn't tell me even if they did. I don't care who you are, people around here aren't going to go naming names when it comes to the local dealers. People die for that."

"How did you get the neighbors to open up as much as they did?" Maybe Tess could learn something from Jackie.

"I didn't bullshit them. I told them I was trying to find the kids who used to live in the group home, the one where the little boy was shot all those years back. It's funny—people get shot and killed around here every week, but everyone remembers the night Donnie died. I'll tell you this much, they really hate the old man who shot him."

"Luther Beale? What do they say about him?"

"They say he's stuck up, which is about the worst thing you can be in these parts. He thinks he's better than they are, and he makes no secret of it. People will forgive you for a lot, but not for that. Whatever you do, you can't let people know you want more from life than they do."

It occured to Tess that Jackie might be speaking from firsthand experience.

* * *

THE SCHOOL DAY WAS ALMOST OVER BY THE TIME THEY HEADED OUT TO Gwynn's Falls Middle School. Again, Tess coached Jackie along the way. Telling the truth was an okay system, as far as it went, but it had limitations. The tough-cookie principal wasn't going to divulge the whereabouts of her former student, Salamon Hawkings, just because Jackie was a straight shooter.

"I'm to say I'm from Arena Stage?" Jackie asked, puzzled. "I thought I was going to be a relative. If I'm going to make up a story, why not say I'm from the School for the Arts? That's much more plausible."

"Uh-uh. Another school, even one in a different jurisdiction, could track down a student in a single phone call. So you're from Arena Stage, and you're putting on an original work next season, with this really talky part for a teenage boy, reams of dialogue to memorize, and you've heard this Salamon Hawkings is a gifted public speaker."

"What's the name of the play?"

"The name? Jesus, I don't know, Jackie. Improvise."

"I prefer to plan things in advance," she said primly.

I bet you do. "Okay, the play is called—" Tess glanced to the side of the road. They were near the lot where an old amusement park once stood and, just beyond it, the place where her mother had bought produce from a truck farmer in the summers. He had graduated from his truck to a small shop, then added seafood. The store had burned to the ground in a mysterious fire a few years ago, and the family had simply disappeared. Now a small cinderblock church stood in its place. But Tess still remembered the hand-lettered sign that had hung over the fish in their icy beds.

"The play is called 'Fresh Lake Trout.' It's an August Wilson-style drama about a local family scraping by with a produce stand. Lots of tension between the father and son, over whether he's going to stay and help the business, or go to college. How's that?"

"Not very original, but I guess it will have to do. So Arena Stage is putting on 'Fresh Lake Trout,' and it needs a teenager who can handle lots of dialogue."

"Right, and you remember hearing about Salamon Hawkings from one of your cousins, whose daughter competed against him in the state finals."

Jackie looked as if she didn't know whether to be impressed or disgusted. "This is what you do for a living? Make shit up?"

"The truth may set you free, but it doesn't get you much in the way of information. Trust me, when we start looking for your daughter, you're going to appreciate what the right lie can do."

Children were pouring out of the tired-looking school. Tess scrunched down in the passenger seat of Jackie's car, waiting. She didn't want to risk being seen by the principal, who was sure to make good on her threat to have Tess arrested. As it was, the woman was sharp enough that the Arena Stage story might not fly. Tess wished she could be at Jackie's side, ready to provide the additional lies such a situation might demand. Despite the elaborate ruse Jackie had used on her, she didn't seem to have any innate ability for spontaneous prevarication. Successful lying required a certain amount of joy in the act itself. If you focused only on the results, you missed the hang-gliding sensation of simply getting away it. You were out there, high above the landscape where most people lived, feeling the wind on your face. Besides, the Arena Stage story was one of Tess's more inspired lies; she would have liked to deliver it herself.

Fifteen minutes had gone by. The school had emptied quickly and now seemed desolate. Jackie had parked in the shade, but it was hot in the car, the leather seat stickier than a cloth one would have been. Tess rolled down the window, stuck her head out, and panted a little bit, imitating Esskay. She had wanted to bring the dog with them. After all, she had to go all the way back to Columbia to pick up her car, and she could have used the company on the ride back. But Jackie had been appalled at the idea of a dog in her pristine car. Tess wasn't sure she was that keen on having *her* in it.

"That's attractive," Jackie said, coming up behind her.

"I think dogs are on to something. I actually feel a little cooler. How'd you do?"

Jackie walked around the car and slid into the driver's seat. "It was so easy, it was embarrassing. I stayed and chatted with the principal just to ease my conscience about fooling a perfectly nice woman. Turns out Salamon Hawkings got himself a scholarship to some ritzy private school, the Penfield School, up in Butler." She paused. "I'm not even sure where that is."

"The heart of WASP country. You can tell because Butler has exactly two businesses, a saddlery and a liquor store. All the WASP needs."

"What's a black boy doing in a place like that?"

Tess shrugged. "These private schools do care about diversity. Every one I know has at least a few inner-city kids on scholarship. And if Salamon really is a good public speaker, I bet several schools came after him."

"Or maybe they just needed a little black boy to stand at the end of the driveway and hold out a lamp, like one of those old lawn jockeys."

They were passing through Woodlawn, caught in the first waves of Social Security traffic. Tess wished she had noticed what route Jackie was taking; she would have steered her away from this daily snarl of traffic and onto the empty ghost road known as I-70, one of the few interstates in the country that came to a dead-end. People who didn't know Baltimore's shortcuts and back roads made her impatient.

"You still see those jockeys in some parts of Baltimore, I've noticed," Jackie continued. "They painted the faces white, as if that fools anyone."

"Yeah, and you still see ceramic kittens scampering up brick houses. There's one over there. Oh my God, call PETA."

"It's not the same thing," Jackie said stiffly.

"It is in the sense that it's not worth expending energy. Some people are idiots. At least the ones with those lawn jockeys announce themselves to the world. You know what kind of moron you're dealing with up front."

"According to that logic, you must support the special license plates for Sons of Confederate War Veterans. Or do you think that's a freedom of speech issue?"

"I think it's trivial. It's like getting upset over those truckers who have the mudflaps with those big-breasted women on them. What am I going to do, take them to court for hurting *my* feelings?"

"The state didn't issue the mudflaps."

"Maybe they should. They could make a lot more money than they did on the Confederate tags. Look, Jackie, you're my client, I'm your employee. I don't want to argue over stuff I don't even care about."

"I wish I had the luxury of not caring, but I don't. It's my life, it affects me."

Tess sat quietly for a minute. There were a lot of things she wanted to say, a lot of things she was scared to say. Jackie was a client, after all, even if they had acted as partners this afternoon. Besides, such conversations were dangerous under any circumstances. No one, not even best friends, had ever had a truly honest conversation about race. Tess decided to play possum, tilting back the passenger seat and closing her eyes. Reality overtook the pose, and the next thing she knew they were in the parking lot at Jackie's condo. It seemed as if weeks had passed since Tess had arrived here this morning, feeling so cocky about tracking down one Jackie Weir, *née* Susan King.

"The Adoption Rights group meets Monday night," Jackie reminded her, as Tess stretched, stiff from her nap. "You're going with me, right?"

"That was our deal. What kind of person would renege after all you've done for me today?"

"You'd be surprised at what kind of people don't honor their promises." Jackie sounded almost dire. If it were someone else, Tess would have thought the comment an odd joke, but Jackie had made it clear that humor was not her strong suit.

"Another tip for the small businesswoman?"

"A tip for life. One I've known for a long, long time." With that, Jackie was gone, still favoring her left foot in its white high heel. A white high heel that had managed to cover much of East Baltimore without picking up so much as a single smudge.

TEN

EVEN FROM ACROSS THE STREET, IT WAS OBVIOUS THAT SOMETHING wasn't quite right when Tess and Esskay arrived at the office the next morning. The door seemed to sway a little in the summer breeze. Not open, but not quite shut either.

Upon closer inspection, it turned out the lock had been picked. Gouged, really—the deadbolt clawed and hacked from the wood with something sharp, then tossed aside.

"You should get a metal door," said Luther Beale, waiting in the chair opposite her desk.

"Did we have an appointment this morning?" Tess asked, examining the hole where her lock used to be, while Esskay stepped around her and headed for the sofa.

"No, but I thought I would stop by and see if you had made any progress. The door was like that when I got here."

Tess propped a phone book against the door, so she wouldn't end up air conditioning the street until a locksmith could arrive. She had been in good spirits, feeling virtuous about her impulse to stop by the office and do little tasks on a Saturday, before meeting Tyner for a workout and late lunch. But the broken lock had drained all the day's potential. She would be stuck here for hours.

"I didn't do it," Beale added, in the defensive way of a man used to blame.

"I never thought you did," Tess said, looking up her landlord's number in the Rolodex on her desk. She hoped he would have to pay for the new lock. Perhaps she should call the police and make a report first, then summon the landlord, who could file an insurance claim. A tiny, wizened man, he had known and apparently envied her grandfather. He had a way of bringing every conversation back to the fact that he had prospered over time, while her grandfather had failed after a more spectacular start. "Slow and steady, slow and steady," Hiriam Hersh liked to counsel her. "Your grandfather was a hare, I'm a tortoise. You could learn a lot from me." No, she definitely wasn't in the mood for Aesop according to Hiriam Hersh.

"No, ma'am, the door was like that when I got here," Beale said, more to himself than to her.

"I am surprised you just came in and sat here, waiting for me. How did you known I'd be in on a Saturday?" Tess dialed the Eastern precinct, rather than tie up the 911 line. The city had a nonurgent line now, too, 311, but she thought a break-in qualified for a police visit sometime in this millennium.

"I didn't. Just thought I'd drop by and when I saw the door, I decided I better come in and babysit your stuff. This computer wasn't going to last for long, not in this neighborhood."

The desk sergeant at the precinct picked up and put her on hold before she could even get a single syllable out. Tess did a quick visual scan of the room. Nothing obvious was missing—the computer, the scanner, the printer were all still here. The flying rabbit picture was in its place over the wall safe. Perhaps addicts had broken in, looking for metal to sell to one of the scrap yards. A few of the metal dealers weren't too particular about the origins of the copper downspouts, iron grilles, and old water heaters that came rolling up in shopping carts, day after day. But the old stove was still in place, as were the faucets.

Still on hold, she unsheathed her computer and turned it on. Her files were there, apparently untouched. On a hunch, she enlarged the window, checking the "last modified" dates—nothing. Then again, printing a file out didn't count as modifying it. She glanced at the printer. There was paper in the tray, and she only put paper in as she needed it, given that Esskay's hair tended to settle on anything left out. Besides, she was stingy with paper. It was one part of her overhead she could control.

"Do you know anything about computers?" she asked Beale skeptically.

"Huh. I know enough not to buy a Mac, like you did. I have an IBM clone, with 200 megahertz and a gigabyte of memory. Did you know you can read almost every newspaper in the country online? I bet I save fifty dollars a month that way."

"Someone might have made some copies of my files last night."

"Don't you have a password, for security?"

"No," Tess said. If Beale were really so computer-savvy, he should know that. Hadn't he seen her use the computer on his first visit here? "It never occurred to me I'd need one, not in a one-woman office."

"What was in my file, anyway?"

"Not much. Some leads on the twins. You weren't too good on the names, by the way. They're Treasure and Destiny Teeter."

"Never was good with names," Beale murmured. "So where are they?"

"Not sure. According to neighbors, they technically live on Biddle Street, but they're still seen a lot around here." She wondered if she should tell him that, according to the neighbors' description, neither one was exactly college material. But college tuition was only one example of the help Beale wanted to provide. Maybe he could get Treasure in drug rehab, find Destiny a program, something like the Nelsons' school in D.C., only for girls.

"That all you found? That's not much."

Tess, still on hold with the Eastern Precinct, hung up and hit the redial button. Again, she was placed on hold before she could utter a single syllable.

"I think it's pretty good, considering how little information you brought me. Four days ago, I didn't even have the names. Now I know where to look for the twins, and I've pinpointed another one, Salamon Hawkings. He's on scholarship at a private school. Eldon Kane is wanted on a warrant and believed to be far from Maryland, so I guess we can cross him off your list."

"You been to see the Hawkings boy yet? School's almost out."

"Haven't had a chance."

"Moving kind of slow, aren't you? If I pay by the hour, I expect you to make the most of every minute."

Beale was as exasperating as Gramma Weinstein, never pleased, never satisfied.

"I've found it's something of a handicap, having to play Tipton to your anonymous benefactor. Schools don't much like strangers trying to track down their students for reasons they won't divulge. Now I have to come up with a plausible reason to see Salamon Hawkings."

"That's easy," Beale said. "When you get in touch with the school, just tell them there's some money coming to the Hawkings boy, without being too specific. People always go for that."

"You mean like those unclaimed accounts the state advertises every year?"

"Naw, that's too easy to check. Maybe you could be that place that makes kids' dreams come true. Make-a-Wish, Dream-a-Dream, whatever it's called."

"I think that's for sick kids," Tess said. "Still, it's the right idea, at least."

Beale stood to leave. He wore the same brown suit from his first visit, only with a blue-and-yellow-striped shirt this time. He carried the same yellowing Panama in his hands.

"Just don't lollygag," he said. "I am paying you by the hour, as I recall. And that doesn't include sitting here, waiting for a locksmith." Then he was gone, without a "thank-you," without a word of praise for what Tess had done so far. Well, that's what being in business was about. People who paid you didn't have to be grateful, they just had to give you checks that cleared. On that score, Beale was a dream client.

Still on hold at the Eastern Precinct, she hung up and called her landlord instead. Let Hersh deal with the busted door, nattering to the locksmith about how he, tortoiselike, had progressed so far beyond the Weinstein hares. She was going to work out.

TYNER HAD BEEN UNUSUALLY NICE TO TESS AS OF LATE. SHE SUSPECTED he felt guilty for forcing her out of the nest of his office and giving her desk away while her chair was still warm. Certainly, she didn't expect his little kindnesses to last. But she was enjoying the temporary benefits of his guilt, the gifts he showered on her, such as the new watch and this free summer pass to his gym, the Downtown Athletic Club, a place she couldn't afford on her own budget.

The DAC, as its denizens called it, was not the grandest club in Baltimore, but it was easily the largest. Built in an old warehouse on the site where Lincoln's funeral train had passed through, it had its own history. The legendary fights over parking, as the workout-bound folks jockeyed for the spaces closest to the door, determined not to walk one more inch than necessary. The pickup scene that made the men's locker room strictly NC-17 on the weekends. Then there was the apocryphal story about the man who suffered a heart attack during the peak evening hours. While some people had rushed to his aid, other impatient exercisers had used the confusion to sneak ahead in the StairMaster line.

"Oh, c'mon, Mr. Gray," protested the young trainer who was bumping Tyner's wheelchair up the short flight of steps to the main floor as Tyner repeated all these stories to Tess, his stentorian voice jouncing with each stair. "You know no such thing ever happened here."

"If it isn't true, it should be," Tyner insisted. With the attendant's help, he hoisted himself into the Nautilus butterfly machine, pulling on his weight-lifting gloves once he was settled. "What do you have today, Tess? Weights or aerobics?"

"I rowed this morning, a good long one, so all I have are weights. But I'll start with lower body."

"Don't slack. I'll be watching you."

"Watch yourself." Tess reached out and caught Tyner's arm as he attempted to return the weight to its resting position. "C'mon, fight me a little, old man. Press harder. *Harder*. You can do it."

He could, quite easily. Tyner had taken good care of himself. Above the waist, he was as lean and strong as he had been in his early twenties, when he was on the Olympic rowing team. Below— well, below, he was what he had been for more than forty years, since a speeding car had crumpled his legs and ended his Olympic pursuits.

"I've still got much more upper-body strength than you," he taunted her good-naturedly.

The DAC was quiet on a Saturday afternoon. Although school wasn't out, people with weekend shares had already started heading to the shore, or moved their athletic pursuits outdoors while the weather was so fine. Tess would have preferred to be outside herself, but there was no outdoor substitute for weight-lifting.

A stringy, pale man in his forties was on the quad machine. "May I work in?" she asked.

"Only two more," he said, holding up two fingers helpfully. But he just sat there, as comfortable as a man on a barstool, in no hurry to move. Tess decided to work on the leg press instead of waiting, and took the machine next to him.

"What do you think of that?" he asked, still stalling, not anxious to start his next set.

"Think of what?" she gritted out as she released on the final rep, the weight bouncing a little as it hit. She hoped Tyner hadn't heard it, he'd been on her back for such sloppy work.

"The guy in the wheelchair. What's *that* about?"

"I'm not sure what you mean."

"He's an *old* guy in a *wheel*chair, for Christ's sake. What's the point? I do this because I got divorced last year and I'm, you know, out there. Gotta keep the old bod in shape. I hate it, but that's the price you pay. What's he doing it for?"

"You finished on there yet?" Her tone was light, but as sure as Clark Kent slipping into a phone booth, she could feel her secret alter ego emerging. She counted to thirty, but not to control her temper. She was just marking the time of her rest periods, trying to keep them as short as possible.

"Almost." He huffed and puffed through another set much too quickly, his motions fast and jerky, his legs swinging as loose as a little kid. He held up a single finger. "One more set. What's your name, anyway?"

"I'm Tess." *But others know me as the Emasculator.*

She bided her time, patient now, letting him natter on through a long rest period and then his final set, all the while dropping little hints about the things that made him such a great catch. Oh, he was clever enough to weave it into a narrative, an unnecessarily complicated story about how he hated taking his *Range Rover* to the ballpark, but it wasn't so bad when you parked in the *season ticket holders* lot, loved them O's, but didn't eat ballpark food, unless it was at the *Camden Club*, usually went to *Dalesio's* afterwards. None of this was offered as an invitation—Tess could tell he hadn't decided if she was worthy—but she would have the essential information if he decided he didn't have a better prospect for tonight's game.

Finally done, he wiped his nonexistent sweat from the seat in a show of courtliness, then pulled the pin out from the seventy-pound mark.

"Where you want this? I know you gals don't like to bulk up too much."

"Oh, I don't know," Tess said carelessly. "I'm not feeling at my peak today . . . how about 120?"

He laughed, as if this were a wonderful joke, and put the pin where she had asked. With an impassive, bored expression. Tess hopped into the seat and ripped off a set, swiftly, but with good form. Her new friend, now perched on the leg press, paused when he saw where Tess had left the pin. She could tell he was loathe to choose a lighter weight, yet didn't want to get on and find he couldn't lift what she had lifted.

"I guess I'm done, anyway," he said.

Not quite. "The man in the wheelchair?" Tess said as he started to walk away.

"Yeah?"

"That's my boyfriend."

Now he was done.

TESS TOLD TYNER MOST OF THE STORY OVER LUNCH, EDITING OUT THE parts about him. Although Tyner claimed indifference to the idiots of the world, she couldn't imagine that the other man's careless statements wouldn't hurt.

They were at the Point, the run-down tavern owned by her Uncle Spike. It was never clear whether the tavern was simply a front for Spike's bookie operation, or whether this was what kept body and soul together when gambling was slow. June was a slow time for both businesses—basketball and Pimlico winding down, football far away and baseball a sucker bet. To entice people into the bar, Spike had started offering free peanuts in large, shallow-bottomed barrels. But his assistant, Tommy, refused to sweep the floor every night and it was now impossible to walk through the Point without making a constant, crunching sound and raising little clouds of peanut dust around your ankles.

"I'm sure your secret life as the Emasculator keeps you quite busy," Tyner said, "but I'm more interested in how your real work is going."

"It was going fine until someone pried my door open with a crowbar last night. They didn't take anything, but I have a feeling break-ins are going to be a constant worry in my location."

"So it was a junkie?"

"You want some more peanuts?" Tess walked over to the nearest barrel, grabbed two fistfuls, and brought them back to the table, dropping them with a great clattering noise.

"Have you ever noticed how, in every batch of peanuts you eat, there's one that's almost perfect?" she asked, opening a triple pod. "It's roasted a little darker than the rest, has an almost piquant flavor. So you eat dozens more, looking for one that has that same strong, roasted flavor and instead, you find one that's acrid and shriveled, which cancels out the perfect one, so you eat dozens more, trying to regain your equilibrium, and next thing you know you have peanut belly, all swollen and bloated, and you still haven't found that elusive, perfect peanut."

Tyner wasn't the type to be distracted by a monologue on peanuts.

"It wasn't junkies, was it?"

"No," Tess admitted, sighing out loud. "I think someone went into my computer and made a copy of a file. There was paper in the tray, and I never leave it out. I feed it into the printer as I need it."

"Which file was copied?"

"Can't tell, but I assume it was Beale's. He was sitting there when I arrived, said he happened on the scene. Suspicious, I know, but why would he steal his own file? He's entitled to what's in it. Then again, it can't be Jackie. The only person who knows I'm working for Jackie is Jackie."

"As far as you know."

"Yeah, but why would she lie?"

"I haven't a clue, but the one thing we know is that she lied before, right? I mean, even if she had a reason for her elaborate Mary Browne charade, she does lie, and she lies well." Tyner brushed the peanut shells and meal to the floor. "What do you know about the baby's father?"

"Long gone and long forgotten, some guy from the neighborhood. Didn't want to be a father and signed away paternity. Jackie hasn't seen him for years."

"*She* says."

"Again, why wouldn't she tell the truth about that?"

"I don't know why anyone does anything," Tyner said. "My job is to remind you the universe of possibilities is large. Don't take anything for granted, Tess. Someone printed a file out of your computer. There are two files there, Beale's and Jackie's. Beale was sitting in your office when you arrived, declaring his innocence before anyone accused him of anything. Strange, very strange. Jackie has lied to you at least once. Who knows if she lied to you about the baby's father, if there's someone else out there who wants to find the little girl." He thought for a moment. "Do you keep your gun in the office?"

"Yes, in the safe. It was still there."

"You have a license to carry. Maybe you ought to take advantage of it."

"Oh, Tyner, that's so paranoid."

"I'd just feel better about you on Butchers Hill if I knew your gun was a little handier. What are you going to do if you walk in on the burglars next time? Say, 'Excuse me, I just have to get something out of the safe, and then I'll be right with you'? If it is a druggie, you'll need to act swiftly. They're not rational, they might kill you out of sheer stupidity."

Tess didn't say anything, just kept picking through the pile, still intent on finding that perfect peanut.

ELEVEN

ON SUNDAY MORNING, TESS STARTED HER TREASURE HUNT.

Although it was on the hot side, she decided to walk, because that's how Treasure would move through the city, heading west to Beans and Bread, then back east to wherever he was squatting near Butchers Hill.

The Beans and Bread soup kitchen was only a few blocks from her own apartment. Now housed in a former synagogue, the Catholic mission had started in a tiny storefront closer to the water, just around the corner from where Tess now lived. But poverty was one of the few businesses in Baltimore that had never known a slow season, and Beans and Bread had long ago outgrown that small space.

Still, Tess wasn't prepared to see almost fifty men and women waiting outside Beans and Bread's doors at 11 a.m. on a Sunday. A broad-shouldered man in mirrored sunglasses stood with his back to the door, murmuring into a walkie-talkie. Occasionally, the door would open a crack, a woman would lean out and whisper to him and the doorman would then shout numbers to the crowd. Five to ten people would present tickets and be admitted inside. The scene was not unlike one of those New York clubs of the moment, although those waiting here were more polite.

"You can't bring your dog in here, sister." The doorman's voice was firm, but kind. "I'll watch him while you eat, if you like. We've got about a thirty-minute wait right now."

"I'm not here for a meal. I'm trying to find someone who comes around here, though, a kid named Treasure Teeter."

"Treasure Teeter?" The mirrored sunglasses stayed focused on the crowd. "Doesn't sound familiar, but I don't know all the names. Sister Eleanor would probably know him, but she's not here today. Can it wait until tomorrow?"

"If it has to, it has to," Tess sighed.

"You know what he looks like?"

"No, just that he's real young, about seventeen, and he may be using."

"There's one kid who comes in here regular, but I've never heard anyone call him Treasure." He muttered something into the walkie-talkie, listened to the static-y reply. "Joe Lee says the guy I'm thinking of was here when the doors opened at ten. He's long gone by now, though. That's three or four seatings ago."

An old toothless man, who wore a wool hat and heavy coat despite the warm day, sidled up to the doorman and whispered shyly in his ear. He had been on the streets so long that it looked as if dirt and grime had been baked into his skin and clothes. When Esskay tried to sniff the hem of his navy pea coat, the man shrank back in fear and scurried halfway up the block.

"What was that about?"

"Guy says he heard Bea Gaddy is giving away food today, says this kid was headed up there when he left. You know her place, over on Collington?"

The old man had creeped back toward them, rummaging in his pockets even as he kept his eyes on Esskay. Again, he whispered to the doorman, his voice so soft that Tess couldn't make out a word of what he was saying.

"Your dog bite?" the doorman asked.

"Only if you're a hot dog or a rodent."

"See, Howard? Her dog don't bite, and I don't think she does either. Go ahead, ask the sister what you want to ask."

The old man shook his head bashfully, then pulled a can of orange soda from his pocket and held it out to her. The backs of his hands were filthy, but the palms looked recently scrubbed.

"A guy from the Superfresh donated a couple of cases of sodas today, and we're giving each diner a can as they leave," the doorman said. "Howard wants you to take his. Says it's a long walk over to Bea Gaddy's place, and you'll get thirsty on a hot day like this."

Tess looked at the soda can in the gnarled hand, the yellowed, ridged fingernails rimmed with dirt. The bright orange can—America's Choice, the Superfresh's generic brand—was still beaded with condensation. It couldn't have rested in that pea coat pocket for long. She felt the doorman's eyes on her. America's Choice, her choice. She took the can, trying not to flinch when her fingers brushed against his, popped the top and took a long drink.

"Thank you, Howard," she told the man, who began walking away from her backward, then turned and ran up the block.

"You made his day," the doorman said.

"By taking his soda and scaring him with my dog?"

"By letting him do something for someone else. Nobody wants to be on the receiving end all the time, you know. Howard smuggles bread out of here every day, just so he can feed the birds, just so somebody will need him."

Sure enough, Tess saw him standing in the middle of a flock of birds as she turned east on Bank Street. The pigeons and seagulls circled close to him, but he wasn't scared, she could tell. He cooed at them in their own language, crumbling the slices of bread and tossing them into the air like bright white pieces of confetti.

ALTHOUGH SUMMERS WERE A SLOW TIME FOR BEA GADDY, WHO PUT most of her energy into putting on—and promoting—a Thanksgiving dinner for thousands, she kept a table outside her rowhouse for the donations that trickled in every day. Today, the table held only some sweaters and a box of used videotapes. Amazing the kind of junk people sloughed off on the local charities, Tess thought, as if they were tax-deductible dumps.

A young man was examining the videotapes with great care, as if he were at his neighborhood Blockbuster Video and choosing his night-time entertainment. Maybe he had even had a VCR once, but his wasted frame told the story of many pawnshop tickets, of a life plundered of anything that could yield a dollar or two.

" 'Dorf on Golf,' " he said, putting the tape down. "Aw, there ain't nothing here. I heard you had TastyKakes today."

"We did," said a woman watching over the table, making sure people didn't carry off armloads to sell, not that these clothes would fetch much. "You're about ten minutes too late. You know sweets go fast."

"Aw, man." He drew the syllables out in the fretful whine of a disappointed child, stomped his feet a bit. "Did they have Butter-scotch Krimpets? Don't tell me they had Butterscotch Krimpets."

"Why do you care? They're gone. You're not getting any."

"A man likes to know what he's missing. You get me? Now did they have any Butterscotch Krimpets or not?"

"I don't know," the woman said sullenly. "It was mostly Juniors and fried pies."

Tess had hung back politely, waiting for the man to wind up his snack cake inquiry. When he started sifting through the used sweaters, she asked the woman, "Do you know Treasure Teeter?"

"Huh."

The one syllable, although not particularly friendly, was more or less affirmative. "Has he been here today?"

The woman said nothing, just turned her back on Tess and began folding up several brown grocery bags. The man was still picking through the clothes, but he was studying Tess from beneath his heavy-lidded eyes. She took a five-dollar bill out of her jeans pocket and fluttered it ostentatiously in her hand, then began walking away with Esskay. She turned the corner off Collington and waited, out of sight. Soon enough, the man came around the corner, jogging to catch up with her.

"I know that guy," he gasped out when he caught up with her, his breathing ragged from running even that short distance. "Treasure Teeter. He calls himself Trey, though, but there's this girl who comes around sometimes, calls him that. A good-lookin' girl. I don't know what she's doing with him."

"You show me where to find him, I'll give you this five-dollar bill and you can buy all the Butterscotch Krimpets you want." Tess knew he wouldn't, though. With cash in hand, he would forget his sugar craving and start thinking about the junk that made him want sweets in the first place.

"I'll take you right to him for ten."

"Right to him? Deal."

He put his hand out—not to shake and seal the deal, but to take the bills.

"*After* I see Treasure," Tess said.

He took off almost at a trot, heading west, then south onto Chester Street, stopping about midway down the block.

"Here," he said, holding out his palm insistently.

"This is a boarded-up rowhouse," Tess said. "How can I know if Treasure hangs out here?"

"He's here right now." He pounded on one of the windows so the plywood shook and rattled. "Trey, man. It's Bobby. Got something for you. Something good."

The window board swung slowly to one side. The boy whose head poked out looked much younger than seventeen, with a sleep-filled cherub's face like a small child awakened in the middle of the night. There was crust in the corner of his eyes and his hair was flatter on one side than the other. A yellow smear ran down one side of his mouth, lemon filling from his fried pie.

"What you want, man?"

But Bobby had already gone, sprinting away with Tess's five-dollar bills tight in his fist.

"Hi, Treasure. I'm Tess Monaghan. I've been looking for you."

"My name's Trey."

"I'm still looking for you."

"I know you?"

"No."

"I didn't do nothin'," he said automatically.

"I didn't say you did."

"What you want with me, then?"

"Someone asked me to check up on you, see how you're doing."

He was too affectless to evince true skepticism, but she could tell he didn't believe her. "My aunt hired some white woman to come ask me how'm doing? She *knows* how'm doing. I asked her for money last Wednesday, the day Beans and Bread was closed and I couldn't get me no hot meal. Man, she was cold. Said if I was hungry, she would make cornbread for me. That woman can't cook for shit, though. What I want to eat her cooking for?"

"You live with her, don't you?"

"When I wanna. When I have to. Her place is nice in the winter. Other times, I'd rather be on my own."

"What about your sister, Destiny? Does she live there, or here with you?"

"Destiny's gone."

"Gone where?"

"I ain't seen her, but she'll be back soon, and then everything will be all right. That's what she told me, everything going to be cool. We gonna get our own place as soon as she gets back."

"Where'd she go?"

"Dunno." A giggle. "I think she went to Burma."

"Burma?"

"Or maybe she dug all the way to China this time. Yeah, maybe that's it." More giggles.

Junkie humor. An acquired taste. Then again, Tess had always found herself hilarious when stoned.

"When is she coming back?"

"When she done."

"How long has it been since you've seen her?"

Treasure held up his hands, as if to count the days off on his splayed fingers. Instead, he began to laugh again, as if he had glimpsed something hilarious in the palms of his hands. Maybe it was his lifeline. Then he held up his palm, flat, like a traffic cop, and looked over his shoulder, holding the pose for quite some time.

"Treasure?"

"I'm doin' the Heisman."

"What?"

"Doin' the Heisman. You know, like in football." He repeated the movement, and Tess understood then that he was suppose to be the trophy, straight-arming his way through life. "I could run. Man, I could run. I could have had me a scholarship if I wanted one."

"I was asking you about Destiny. I thought twins were close, closer than ordinary siblings."

Treasure just stared at her blankly. "We're close. We're real close. Destiny 'n' me, we always stick together. Look, you want me, or you want my sister? What you doing here, anyway?"

A good question. What could Luther Beale do for Treasure Teeter, besides buy him more crack, perhaps set him up in a nicer place to smoke it?

"You interested in kicking your habit, maybe getting your GED? I know someone who will help you if you are."

"Man, I knew you were full of shit. You're from that clinic, ain't you? The one that sends those social workers out on the street to bring people in. Everybody knows there's no slots for detox now, even if you want to get clean. The state waiting list just goes on forever. 'Less you're a vet. Then the VA has to take you. But I'm no vet. Not officially, anyway." He giggled. Yes, Treasure Teeter sure could crack himself up. "I'd go to war, if they wanted me to. It can't be any tougher than where I been. Yes, ma'am, I'd go to war any time they want me to."

"I could get you in a private hospital. I know a . . . program that will pay the full freight. If you're interested. Private room, good food. Not a state hospital."

Treasure propped his chin on the windowsill. He actually seemed to be thinking about her suggestion. Then he was distracted by a centipede inching its way along the flaking paint. He held out his finger and let it crawl onto his nail, pulled his finger close to his face, staring at the centipede until he was almost cross-eyed. Then he shook his finger, flinging the bug to the ground.

"Naw, that's not for me."

Tess handed him a business card. "If you change your mind, call me. The offer will stand, at least for a while."

Treasure took her card and began picking his teeth with it. "That pie sure was good," he said. "I wish I had taken me two."

KITTY WAS PREPARING TO OPEN THE STORE WHEN TESS AND ESSKAY ARrived home. The dog, who hadn't had the benefit of a homeless man's orange soda, slurped ravenously from the bowl Kitty kept behind the counter, displacing more water than she actually consumed.

"Do you ever feel like there are two Baltimores out there?" Tess asked her aunt, trying to mop up after Esskay's sloppy drinking.

As usual, Kitty understood what Tess meant, even if Tess wasn't quite sure. "More like three or four, maybe five. But it's always been that way, Tesser. Rich Baltimore, poor Baltimore. Black and white Baltimore. Old Baltimore, those folks who can trace their blue blood all the way back to the Ark and the Dove, and immigrant Baltimore."

"I just never thought I'd feel like I was in a foreign land less than a mile from my own apartment. I was scared today, Kitty. Scared of an old man who wanted to do nothing more than give me a soda. Scared to stand in front of a vacant house on Chester Street and talk to some stoned kid inside. The city's dying. It's not going to exist a hundred years from now."

"You're too young to be so disillusioned, Tess. Once you start to think like that, there's no turning back. Remember, in last year's nests, there are no birds this year."

"Say what?"

"You still haven't finished *Don Quixote*, have you?"

Reminded of her literary *bête noire*, Tess scrubbed harder at the floor, although she had soaked up most of the water spilled there. "I finished the first part. It took Cervantes another decade to write the second, so I thought I might take a ten-year break before I read it."

"It's the second part that really matters, more than all that tilting at windmills stuff in the first." Kitty unlocked the store's double doors, where some of the Sunday regulars were already lined up, cups of coffee in hand. These were her devoted customers, the ones who waited until noon each Sunday to buy the out-of-town papers here and then settle into her faded armchairs to read them. Few of them managed to leave without picking up a new book that Kitty had pressed into their hands. Kitty Monaghan, queen of the hand-sale.

"You know, I'm wrong," she said suddenly, straightening a pile of Anne Tyler paperbacks on permanent display by the cash register. It was Kitty's quixotic quest to lure the reclusive local writer to a signing at the store. It hadn't happened yet, but Kitty's hopes never flagged.

"You were wrong about something? Alert the media, I don't recall ever hearing that particular statement come out of your mouth before."

Kitty ignored the dig. "It's not illusions you lack, Tess. It's a Sancho. With Whitney in Tokyo and Crow in Texas, you need a sidekick. There is no Don Quixote without Sancho Panza, you know."

"Whitney will be back. As for Crow—I never think about him."

"Liar."

"Probably. At any rate, Esskay is all the Sancho I need."

The dog looked up at the sound of her name, jowls dripping, chest heaving, tongue lolling from her mouth in an antic grin. One ear stood straight up at attention, while the other flopped forward at half-mast.

"She'll do," Kitty said. "Until the real thing comes along."

TWELVE

"I THINK COFFEE IS GETTING BETTER," TESS SAID, SIPPING A CUP AS SHE and Jackie waited for the Adoption Rights meeting to get under way. "When the prices were raised—when people became accustomed to paying two, three dollars, expectations went up, too. Now places that used to serve that overscorched, underbrewed crap have to offer something decent. Even places like this, where it's free."

Jackie said nothing, just wrapped her arms tighter around her middle and shoved her long legs backward beneath her plastic chair.

"Then again, there's this whole instant coffee mystery," Tess kept prattling, hoping it might calm Jackie down. "I read in the paper that the vast majority of people who drink instant are senior citizens. When asked why they drink instant, they said it takes too long to brew a fresh pot. Takes too long! Like, they have something better to do than wait the ten minutes it takes to make real coffee."

Jackie bent forward at the waist. She now looked like someone with severe abdominal cramps. Tess was beginning to think Jackie wanted her here in case she lost her nerve and bolted from the room. Then again, the Columbia Interfaith Center made her stomach ache, too. The ecumenical, all-religions-welcome-here place of worship was part of the original Columbia vision and the building still had a touchy-feely vibe.

"They're not going to make us form a circle and hold hands, are they?" Tess asked Jackie. "And sing those Jesus songs that sound like bad folk music?"

"Don't be silly, we're just meeting in the community room here, we're not going to a service." Jackie's tone was snappish and impatient, but Tess was happy just to get a response.

Still, Jackie continued trying to fold herself like an origami swan, as if she might be able to disappear if she made herself as small as possible. But Jackie couldn't help being noticed. There was the fact of her clothes, casual for her, just navy slacks and a matching sweater, but nicer than anyone else's here. There was the fact of her beauty. There was the fact that she appeared to be practicing yoga.

And there was the fact she was black, the only nonwhite person in the room.

A brisk-mannered woman with graying sandy hair approached the podium at the front of the room. She turned on the microphone, made all the usual tapping tests, then turned it off.

"I guess I don't really need this tonight," she said in one of those clear, bell-like voices that carry easily. Most of the crowd laughed, Tess included, but Jackie looked impatient and edgy.

"My name is Adele Sirola and this is Adoption Rights, a support group in the best sense of that much overused term. We help re-unite adoptees with their biological parents. We also lobby, at the state and federal level, for increased access to adoption records and more resources for mutual consent registries. Last month, as we do every May, we marched on Washington for 'Open My Records Day.' " She smiled ruefully. "And last month, as they do every May, the media ignored us. We've had what you might call something of a public relations problem over the last few years."

A hand waved down front. "A friend of mine warned me not to come here tonight. She said you were really a radical fringe group that thinks all adoptions should be banned."

Adele sighed. "That's the legacy of Baby Jessica, Baby Richard, and other totally aberrant cases in which a remorseful birth mother wants to reclaim a baby before the adoption is final and some loop-hole in the law—often *her* flat-out lie about paternity—provides the opportunity she needs to take the child back. The television cam-eras gather 'round and record the moment when the screaming, confused child is torn from the arms of the adoptive parents and placed into the arms of virtual strangers. It makes good television, but it's not what we're about."

Adele was pacing back and forth behind the podium, off-script now, but on fire.

"My hackles go up when someone tells me I don't understand something because I haven't experienced it. I like to think of myself as the empathetic type. But the fact is, people who aren't adoptees *don't* get it. They don't know what it's like to have two wonderful, loving parents and still stare in a mirror, wondering who gave birth to you. Why did they give you up? What is their legacy? Given all the ground-breaking research in genetics, how can you not want to know who your biological parents are?"

Another voice piped up from the left side of the room. "The agency that arranged my adoption said I was entitled to medical information, but that if they couldn't guarantee lifetime confidenti-ality, the whole system would fall apart."

"Let me guess, you were placed through Catholic services," Adele said. A few people laughed with indulgent familiarity. *Every group has its own language and folklore, its own private jokes,* Tess thought.

"Yeah, I know that argument," Adele continued. "Kind of out-dated, don't you think? I mean, it rests on the assumption that adoptions result from shameful secrets that can be revealed only at great risk to the parent or the child. Well, last time I checked it was almost the twenty-first century and an out-of-wedlock pregnancy is nothing more than a career move. From Ingrid Bergman to Ma-donna in one generation. When they use the 'shame' argument,

they're saying in essence, 'You're a mistake. You're an embarrassment.' Ridiculous."

Jackie was fiddling with her earring now, opening and closing
the back with a loud snap, over and over again.

"Are you an adoptee?" a woman called from the left side of the
room.

Adele smiled. "I'm a mother of three who works at the National
Institutes of Health and felt I needed to do more with my time."

Tess noticed the women in the group laughed at this, while the
men looked blank.

"Of course I was adopted," Adele said. "I knew that all my life,
but I didn't start looking for my mother until I was in my thirties
and had my own children. That's pretty common, by the way—a
major life change jump-starting the process. I found my mother in
a state nursing home in New York, sick with pneumonia from living
on the streets for much of her life. She died a week later. Let me tell
you, the only thing I ever regretted was not starting the search
sooner. I might have had six months, a year, five years with her. I got
a week. It was better than nothing."

"Why don't you tell us how you found her?" This woman's question sounded rehearsed to Tess's ear.

"Thank you, Terry. Terry's a plant, by the way, she's supposed
to ask that question." Adele's manner was at once so breezy, yet so
practiced, that Tess wondered if she could turn it on for anything.
This crowd was eating out of her hand. She could have sold them
Tupperware or lingerie, timeshares or those magnetic heal-
ing pads.

"I did it the way you're going to find your parents. Start with
whatever you know—the agency that arranged the adoption, any
clues you can glean from the medical records to which adoptees are
now entitled by law—thanks, in part, to groups like ours. Wheedle,
beg, cajole. Get a first name. Get a home state. You'll be amazed at
how far you can get."

Tess, thinking of how hard it had been for her to get leads on four children whose names she actually knew, blurted out: "It's not that simple, finding people. You're making it sound too easy."

The rest of the audience turned back, frowning at the skeptical stranger in their midst. But Adele just shrugged.

"Of course it's hard. That's why we have this twenty-page booklet"—she held up a pamphlet with a peach cover and black plastic ring binders—"which is yours for the unbelievably low price of absolutely nothing. We also have Internet resources and a network of similar groups nationwide, for those of you who trace your parents to other states. Now, if all this help moves you to make a donation, large or small, so be it. Maryland Adoption Rights is a registered nonprofit, and your gifts are tax deductible. Any more questions?"

A few eager hands shot up. "Generic ones, I mean, not about your specific cases." The hands went back down. "Then let's break up, freshen up our coffees, and grab some cookies. Our search consultants will set up at various spots throughout the room, so you can have confidential briefing sessions on how to start your searches. You may also want to talk to some of our folks about whether you're ready to start. But you're here, that's the first step."

Jackie didn't move. Tess went over to the card table, refilled their cups, and filled a napkin with cookies. Pepperidge Farm and those French cookies, Lulus, Sumatra decaf and chocolate almond regular. *Toto, I don't think we're in Baltimore anymore.*

Jackie ignored the coffee and the cookies. Around the room, the one-on-one sessions had started, and the air filled with a hushed, urgent buzz, but she showed no sign of moving from her spot. She was rocking slightly now, holding herself as if she were cold.

Adele walked over and sat down in the chair on the other side of Jackie. Her blouse was half out of her skirt, she had cookie crumbs on one side of her mouth and she was stirring her coffee with a ballpoint. Tess had already been inclined to like her, but something about the Bic pen rattling around the paper cup clinched the deal.

"Feeling a little skittish?"

"*No!*" Jackie said. "It's just that . . . I'm different from the others here."

"Because you're black?" Adele looked genuinely puzzled. Race wasn't supposed to be a factor, not in the Interfaith Center, not in utopian Columbia. It was impolite to even remark on its existence.

"You kept talking about looking for one's parents. I'm not looking for my mother. I was . . . I am . . . a mother."

Adele picked up Jackie's hand. Tess was surprised that Jackie let a stranger touch her. She expected her to snatch her hand back and tuck it under her. But she let Adele hold her hand, while Adele talked to her in a soothing voice, so much softer now, but still as casual and light as it had been during the presentation.

"You were a young one, weren't you? Sixteen? Seventeen?"

"Eighteen," Tess answered when Jackie said nothing. "She's thirty-one now."

"Well, you're right, we don't see as many mothers as we do kids. And we don't see a lot of mothers your age. But that's a good thing, see? Each year, the trail gets a little colder. Did you give birth here in Maryland?"

Jackie nodded, staring into her lap.

"Which part, which jurisdiction?"

"Baltimore, in the city."

"Did you go through a church agency, a private or the state?"

"Private. It was a little office on Saratoga Street."

"You remember a name?" Adele's voice had gotten softer and softer, as if Jackie were a scared, wounded animal she was trying to lure from a hiding place.

"Something Alternatives."

"Okay, Something Alternatives on Saratoga Street. Now I bet you don't think that sounds like much, but I'm going to call Jeff over, and you'll be surprised at what he does with a little piece of information like that." She addressed herself to Tess, as if Jackie were her ward. "Jeff knows Baltimore. I'm more oriented to the Washington suburbs."

She walked over to a thin man with a narrow face and intense brown eyes. If Tess had been noticing such things these days, she would have thought him handsome, but she wasn't noticing such things. Adele and Jeff separated from the group, talking to each other in low, urgent voices. Tess thought she heard a muttered "Jesus Christ," then their voices dropped again. After several minutes, both walked over to where she and Jackie sat. Tess knew from their faces that things weren't quite so easy as Adele had thought.

"It's kind of a good news, bad news situation," Jeff said. "Yes, I know the place. Family Planning Alternatives. It advertised in the yellow pages, pretending to offer a full range of services, from contraceptives to abortions. But they were funded by a radical anti-abortion group. They did some adoptions, but their real purpose was to scare women out of abortions by giving them a lot of misinformation. The state shut them down five years ago."

"What does that mean for me?" Faced with a problem, Jackie was no longer passive. She was a self-made businesswoman again, impatient with all obstacles.

"It means you can't do what we normally advise in this situation, which is to return to the agency and see if you can convince them to offer any leads," Adele said. "And since they've disbanded, it will be virtually impossible to find the people who worked there, much less the records. It's a setback, but it's not the end of the world."

Tess extended her pinkie finger, so the nail was poking into the side of Jackie's thigh. She kept her nails quite short, but there was enough there to dig a little bit. *Remember, that's what you have me for. I found you. I can find a lot of people who are hard to find.*

"So where do I start?" Jackie demanded. "If I can't begin with them, where do I begin?"

"With your own memories," Jeff said. "Agencies often give a little information to mothers, to ease their minds. They've even been known to send out paperwork that reveals information they're not supposed to have. One of our clients got her birth mother's surname on a form the hospital routed to her by mistake."

"They told me my baby's adopted father was a doctor," Jackie began hopefully.

"Shit." Adele shook her head sorrowfully. "I'm sorry, honey, but they tell almost every girl that. It's one of the clichés of the trade."

Jackie looked as if she might cry. Tess dug her nail a little harder into her leg, signaling her to gain control, to have a little faith in the person she was paying.

"This agency," Tess said. "When it went down, did it end with a bang or a whimper?"

"What are you to her?" Adele asked. Not hostile, just a little curious. Tess wondered if she assumed they were lovers.

"A friend," Jackie said, before Tess could reply. It was as good a cover story as any.

"There were a few newspaper and television stories, nothing huge," Jeff said. "I think I've got a file on them back in my office. But there aren't any names that I recall. The clients were protected, the owners of the agency disappeared, along with all their files."

"But I bet there was a little flurry of action down in Annapolis, right? Probably some attempt to draft legislation to prevent this from happening again. Some tearful testimony—distraught clients, maybe a repentant employee or two?"

Jeff looked at Tess as if she were a psychic. "Yeah, that's exactly what happened, only the bill never made it out of committee. How could you know that?"

"Because if some politician can't make a little hay out of someone else's tragedy, what's the point of being a politician?" Tess turned to Jackie. "They keep files on bill testimony, and who testifies, even if the bill goes nowhere. By tomorrow, we'll have a list of names to play with."

"This is more than a scavenger hunt, you know," Adele said earnestly. "This isn't just about finding something and shouting 'Eureka!' You're setting some up some mighty big dominoes, and you don't know how they're going to fall. You really should keep working with us."

Jackie reached into her purse, took out her checkbook and a pen—a Mont Blanc, of course—and wrote Maryland Adoption Rights a check for $250. "Thank you for your assistance," she said. "I'll worry about those dominoes after they fall. Meanwhile—"

Adele looked at her hopefully.

"Could I get a receipt for that, for my tax records?"

THIRTEEN

IT WAS JUST AFTER NINE TUESDAY MORNING WHEN TESS LEFT THE HIGH-way and began working her way north on a narrow country road. The thirty-minute drive to Penfield School had passed quickly, thanks to the woman on the radio explaining a vast government conspiracy, in which all new cars were equipped with computer chips that would allow the federal government to shut them down anywhere, any time. Tess tried to figure out how this would work exactly. If the government disabled her car right now, for example, what would they do with it, or her?

Talk radio, the more paranoid the better, was Tess's entertainment of choice as of late. The cacophony of voices was pretty good company. Unfortunately, the shows where the hosts really seethed were becoming harder to find, replaced by garden-variety blustering conservatives and apologetic liberals who hit the same notes over and over. At the other end of the dial, as well as the spectrum, earnest NPR was the high-fiber cereal of radio: Tess would start liking it, remember it was so good for her, and recoil.

Now a caller was wondering if these new, smaller satellite dishes were really part of a government surveillance program. "Of course they are," the host assured him, going on to explain how pay-per-view events allowed the White House to bug your home. Tess was so engrossed in the details of this elaborate scheme that she almost missed the turnoff to the Penfield School.

It was a balancing act, working for two clients. Jackie had assumed she would head straight to Annapolis this morning, but she had promised Beale to interview Salamon Hawkings. To arrange the meeting, she had called Penfield yesterday, telling the headmaster careful not-quite lies: She was an alumna from Washington College (absolutely true), she was interested in helping the school recruit a more diverse student body (true, not that she'd actually do anything about it), and she had heard Salamon Hawkings was a promising young student, an award-winning public speaker (true). The headmaster had hemmed and hawed, but finally agreed she could meet with Salamon this morning, during his study period.

The plain wooden sign for the school was so small and discreet that she overshot the driveway and had to do a U-turn. The Penfield School, established 1888. It had been a church-run school then, intended for poor, young orphans. In terms of class and background, Salamon Hawkings was actually closer to Penfield's origins than most of the young men enrolled here today.

The headmaster, Robert Freehley, met her in the hallway. *Hello, Mr. Chips*: Tall, thin, prematurely gray, tweedy, he might have come straight from Central Casting. The June mornings were cooler here in the country, Tess thought, but not so cool as to warrant a tweed jacket. With leather elbow patches yet.

"They're waiting for you in the library," he said, leading her through corridors that didn't really look any different than most school buildings, yet Tess could still sense how much richer Penfield was than, say, Gwynn's Falls Middle School. Not to mention the Benjamin Banneker Academy. The differences were small, but telling: The display case, which ran heavily to lacrosse and soccer trophies, was made of oak and the items inside were obviously dusted on a regular basis. Furniture was well-worn, but in that thrifty WASP kind of way. And the building was cool, not just because it had central air conditioning, but because it was made of thick stone that held in the night air. Only the odors were the same from school to school, the smell of chalk dust and adolescent boys being pretty standard everywhere.

Salamon Hawkings sat at the end of a long library table, his head bent over a book. The tables here actually had green-shaded lamps at each place, although the morning sun spilling through the wooden Venetian blinds made them unnecessary just now. A man in a seersucker suit sat next to him. A teacher? The librarian? He was vaguely familiar to Tess, a bland-faced man of thirty-five or so.

"I'll leave you to your business," the headmaster said. He seemed a little nervous to Tess. Perhaps the man at the table was one of his trustees, or a rich alum.

"Miss Monaghan?" The man stood, while Salamon never looked up, just kept reading. "I'm Chase Pearson."

Tess reached for his hand, then realized he hadn't offered it. "Of course. You're in the governor's cabinet. The task force on children and youth, right?" And thinking of a run for lieutenant governor, depending on how the ticket shook out, according to her Uncle Donald's gossip. The Pearson family was rich in connections and blood, if not much else. His first name, Chase, was probably intended to remind people he was distantly related to Maryland's signer of the Declaration of Independence. Very distantly related.

"I'm the special secretary for Adolescents and Children," he said, a little stuffily. Well, it must be disappointing for a politically ambitious man to find out someone didn't know his current title and couldn't recognize his face. "Before that, I headed the task force on young men and violence in Baltimore City, by special appointment of the mayor. People often confuse the two. But I'm here today as a Penfield alum—and as Sal Hawkings's guardian."

The young man kept reading, as if they weren't even there. He probably had much practice in tuning out the world around him, Tess thought, a preternatural ability to concentrate. That was the talent that had gotten him here, as much as his oratorical skills.

"Did the headmaster tell you about Washington College's interest in Salamon?"

"Sal," he corrected, turning a page, still not looking up. "I go by Sal now."

Chase Pearson smiled. Tess saw another problem facing the would-be candidate. His teeth were uneven and yellow, stained with nicotine and brown at the gum line. Good enough for lieutenant governor, but nothing better.

"The headmaster told me what you had told him," Pearson said. "Yet when I called Chestertown yesterday, no one in admissions at Washington College had any idea what I was talking about."

Damn. She knew she should have scheduled this meeting closer to her initial phone call. Even the best lies had a pretty short shelf life. "This recruitment program is through the Alumni Society. The college wouldn't necessarily know about it."

"I don't think so," Pearson said, then picked up a single piece of paper from the library table. "Theresa Esther Monaghan, twenty-nine. Lives on Bond Street in Fells Point, in a building owned by her aunt, Katherine Helen Monaghan. Owns a twelve-year-old Toyota which failed the state emissions test last year and has two outstanding parking tickets, one in Baltimore City, the other in Towson. Former employee of the *Star* newspaper. Now a licensed private investigator for Keyes Investigations. Owns a .38-caliber Smith and Wesson, for which she has a permit to carry."

Tess had wondered what the world's databases had on her, and now she knew. Pearson must have used his government sources to pull this dossier together so quickly. Dorie could have gotten much more, but Pearson had done okay. For an amateur.

He slid the piece of paper toward Salamon—Sal—who never lifted his eyes from his book. "By the way, Washington College was glad to have your new address, as they had lost track of you quite some time ago. You can look forward to a fund-raising solicitation quite soon. Although I have a sense you don't have a lot of discretionary income, not even for your beloved alma mater."

"If Washington College wanted me to donate money, they should have steered me away from majoring in English," Tess said. "Okay, so I lied. Sort of. I represent someone who is familiar with the circumstances of the death of Sal's friend, Donnie Moore. This person, who prefers to remain anonymous, would like to help Sal and the others who witnessed his death."

"You represent Luther Beale."

Tess thought of her office door, loose and swinging in the summer breeze. But she couldn't imagine someone like Chase Pearson going to such extreme measures. He wouldn't have to. Maybe the state police had Beale under surveillance. Maybe another Penfield alum sat on the board of her bank, and knew whose checks she had deposited. Baltimore boards were lousy with Penfield grads.

"There's no database in the world with that information. You have no way of knowing who I represent," she said, curious to see if he would contradict her.

"Whom," Sal said, looking up for the first time. He was a handsome young man, or would have been if he smiled. He had deep-set eyes and strong features, made more prominent by his short, short hair, shaved down until it was little more than peach fuzz on his scalp. "*Whom* you represent."

"Look, someone wants to help you pay for your college education, or take a trip to Europe, if that's what you want. What's the downside to that? Why does it matter who your benefactor is?"

Tess had spoken directly to Sal, but he had turned back to his book, indifferent to the appeal. Apparently, only the rules of grammar and his nickname preference warranted his attention.

"Sal is a straight-A student, with SAT scores above 1300. Almost any college in the country will offer him a full scholarship," Pearson said. "He doesn't need anyone's money. In particular, he does not need anyone's *blood* money."

"Funny, I thought one of your big issues was restitution to victims. Here's someone trying to make restitution, and you want no part of it."

"Luther Beale may have killed one child, but he came close to destroying every child who saw what he did on Butchers Hill that night. I don't want him anywhere near Sal. I don't care how much remorse he claims to feel. The tiger doesn't change his stripes."

"The *leopard* doesn't change his *spots*," Sal amended.

"Don't interrupt, Sal," Pearson said.

"Says so right here," Sal said. "That story is in this book I'm reading right *now*, man." He turned another page, and Tess glimpsed a vivid color plate, a crocodile's jaws clamped on an elephant's nose. Kipling's *Just-So Stories*, how the elephant got his trunk. Not a bad cautionary tale for Tess, with her own insatiable curiosity. But why was a high school junior at an elite school flipping through such a childish book?

"Is Sal so well fixed that there's nothing he needs? Even with scholarships, I would think he could use help with college. Perhaps he needs a car, or a new computer. My client would be glad to help him with that."

At the mention of a car, Sal looked a little pleadingly at Pearson, as if to say, *What's the harm*. Pearson shook his head.

"Easy for you," Sal muttered. "You have a Porsche."

"Penfield is on private property. Sal will be staying here this summer, taking extra credits in math and science to help him catch up. As a courtesy, I'm going to ask that you not return here, and that you never attempt to contact Sal again. If you don't honor my request, I can make it official and obtain a restraining order."

"A restraining order? What do you think I'm going to do? Sit on him and stuff dollar bills in his pocket?"

"Sal is my ward, I am responsible for him. You're not the first disreputable person who has tried to dredge up his past. When Beale was released from prison two months ago, we actually received calls from some tabloid television show, which wanted to stage a 'reunion.' Disgusting. They offered us money, too. Well, I'm determined that Sal's life will not be lived under the shadow of what happened five years ago."

Tess looked at the well-furnished library, at Sal Hawkings in his navy blazer, khakis, and blue Oxford cloth shirt. She thought of Treasure, his face streaked with lemon pie, squatting in a vacant house. "Sal would seem to be the one kid from Butchers Hill who's done pretty damn well for himself. Why aren't Treasure and Destiny enrolled at Penfield? Or Eldon? How come Sal's the only one deserving of your solicitous care?"

"I'm here because I'm *smart*," Sal said, slapping his book shut. "The others were dumb motherfuckers, but I knew enough to want to get out, even if it meant going to a sorry-ass school like this. Now excuse me, but second period is about to begin. I don't have time for shit I don't get graded on."

He left the room, taking the Kipling with him.

"You see?" Pearson said. "Any mention of Luther Beale sets him off. Trauma like that never goes away. Now please leave and be prepared to be arrested if you come back."

As it often happened, Tess was in her car and well on her way to Annapolis before she realized what she should have said in reply. *It wasn't Beale's name that upset Sal, or even Donnie Moore's. It was the mention of the other children, Treasure, Destiny, and Eldon.*

THE LEGISLATURE WAS LONG OUT OF SESSION, BUT ANNAPOLIS WAS busy, swarming with tourists drawn by its over-the-top quaintness. Apparently, the Gap and Banana Republic became much more exotic when fronting on narrow, cobblestone streets. Tess pulled into the public garage off Main Street, although it always hurt her to pay for parking—hence, those two tickets—and walked up the hill to the Senate office building.

She had never covered the General Assembly as a reporter, but she knew the basic civics lesson of how a bill became law. Jeff from Adoption Rights had told her that the failed bill targeting operations such as Family Planning Alternatives was Senate Bill 319, offered by a senator from Carroll County, a once-rural area now considered part of the Baltimore metro area. Tess had found it odd that someone from outside the city had sponsored the bill, especially an old pro-lifer like this senator. There must be a wounded constituent somewhere in the mix. If the committee files proved useless, she could always check with the senator's office and see what kind of material he had kept. But changing the law apparently hadn't been all that important to the senator. Over the past five years, he had never attempted to reintroduce the bill.

Tess walked into the empty Senate building and climbed the broad double staircase to the third floor. The secretary who handed Tess the file seemed almost grateful for any distraction.

"What are you trying to find, anyway?" she asked.

"Looking for some folks who testified on this bill, see if they can give me any leads on the adoption agency that inspired it all." Tess pulled out the sign-in sheet that was put out before each hearing. In order to testify, one had to sign in. The list for SB 319 had just five names: the senator himself, someone from the Department of Human Resources, the state agency that oversaw all adoptions, a couple, Mr. and Mrs. John Wilson of Baltimore, and a woman, Willa Mott. The senator and DHR had filed written versions of their testimony, but there was nothing in the file from the Wilsons or Willa Mott.

"Is this everything?" Tess asked.

"If that's all there is, that's all there is. You know, I've been in this office for ten years and I've got a good memory for most of the controversial stuff that comes through, but I don't remember this one *at all*. What's the big deal?"

"No big deal, but I'd like to find the people who testified. I just wish I knew what they said, or where they fit into the whole debate."

The secretary shrugged. "There's always the tapes."

"Tapes?"

"Senate records every committee hearing. If you know the date and the time—and it's right there, so you do—you can go over to

Legislative Reference and listen on a pair of headsets, just like it was an old radio show. Only even more boring, if you know what I mean."

"Can I do that right now?"

"Sure. But I feel sorry for someone who can't think of something better to do on a nice June day than listen to one of our hearings. Whyn't you go down to the dock, have a meal at one of the seafood places? There's this one place that serves the best crab dip. And if you're on expense account, the Cafe Normandy does a real good rockfish."

Tess, trying not to shudder too visibly at the idea of crab dip or rockfish, thanked the woman and headed across the street to Legislative Reference.

Although tempted to fast-forward through the testimony, she listened dutifully to the entire tape. The senator's dull, rambling introduction, with all its little formalities, the agency's defensive posturing—DHR didn't seem to have anything against the bill, it just wanted to make clear it was not to blame for aberrations such as Family Planning Alternatives.

The law itself, as described, was trivial, requiring that such services disclose in their advertising whether they provided abortions. The pro-lifer senator seemed to be trying a preemptive strike, offering a weak, ineffective bill that would keep the government from scrutinizing other agencies that might be pulling the kind of bait-and-switch Family Planning Alternatives had tried: luring women in with promises of abortions, then using all sorts of propaganda to talk them out of the procedure. (One woman, for example, had been told an abortion halved her probability of ever becoming pregnant again and increased her risk of gynecological cancers tenfold.)

The testimony droned on and on. Tess almost nodded off, then the tenor of the voices changed and she snapped to, rewinding the tape.

The Wilsons were a couple who had started an adoption through Family Planning, then broken off the relationship because they had been disturbed by a worker's offer of a steep discount if they would take a biracial, disabled child. "It was like she was running a tag sale, wasn't it, Mike?" the woman appealed to her husband. " 'Would you take a baby like that if we knocked a thousand dollars off the fees? How about two thousand? What if the baby isn't disabled, just biracial?' "

Again, Tess stopped the tape and played it back. Yes, the woman definitely said Mike, despite the fact that she and her husband had signed in as Mr. and Mrs. John Wilson. Unless the woman tripped up again on the tape, and gave their full names or hometown, finding them would be impossible.

Willa Mott, according to her testimony, had been a worker at the agency for ten years and now ran a day-care center in Westminster, the senator's home county. Bingo! Tess thought, writing down the name. Assuming the woman hadn't moved out of state, she'd be easy enough to find, with a name like that. In a nervous, thin voice that suited her spinsterish name, she described the scare tactics her former employers had used, and how she had finally leaked the story to a local television station. A clerical worker, she had sat in on most of the interviews and seen the files on every client.

"Why did you wait so long before telling anyone what was happening?" one of the committee members asked.

Willa Mott stuttered from nervousness. "I myself do not believe in abortion, because of my religious pr-pr-pr-principles. I thought it was right to counsel young women against it. But I began to see that they were hurting the women who came in, and some of them just went someplace else, anyway. It didn't seem Christian to me, what they were doing. I and one of the clients called a television reporter. I didn't go on camera—they shot me in the dark, with one of those machines that makes your voice sound funny. But before the report even aired, my supervisors closed the office and disappeared. I showed up for work one day and the place was locked."

Another senator, a woman, asked a question: "The adoptions they arranged—were those legal and aboveboard?"

"Oh my goodness, yes. If they could have just kept doing that, without trying to coerce the women who came to see them, I would have been proud to work there. But they had a cause, you know? They honestly believed in what they were doing."

The testimony ended there and before Tess knew it, she was listening to a debate over a different bill, something about the state's private adoption laws. She turned her headset in and walked outside, blinking in the bright sun on Lawyers Mall, the square at the center of the State House complex. Tourists were gathered around the statue of Thurgood Marshall, snapping pictures, posing alongside the bronze version of the Supreme Court justice as if he were one of those life-size cutouts of the president or a popular sports figure.

Marshall was a relatively new addition to the State House grounds, added as a way of soothing the hard feelings engendered by a statue of the other Marylander to sit on the Supreme Court, Roger Taney. Taney's claim to fame, alas, was that he had written the Dred Scott slave decision, helping the nation set course for the Civil War. Inevitably, people in the bury-the-past nineties had wanted to tear Taney's statue down, as if that would make everything better. The state, in a rare burst of Solomon-like wisdom, had countered by adding Marshall's likeness. The compromise had worked in ways few imagined. For while Marshall stood in this open square, literally embraced by tourists, Roger Taney sat high on a hill on the other side of the State House, lonely and ignored.

Back in her car, Tess turned on the radio and punched the buttons until she found a man talking about the media conspiracy to conceal some Washington scandal. It was a liberal media conspiracy, of course, an allegation that always made Tess smile. The media was one of the most conservative forces she knew.

A traffic announcer broke in, warning of a back-up along the streets west of her office. A rowhouse fire had Fayette and Pratt blocked, traffic snarled in every direction. She would have to swing to the east, approaching the city through the Fort McHenry tunnel, although the tunnel always made her claustrophobic and she resented tolls almost as much as she resented paid parking. But most of all, she hated the idea of all that water beyond the white-tiled walls, hated the moment when the radio went out, leaving her alone in her car, without even the mattering voice of a conspiracy buff to keep her company.

Maybe she should call in to one of the talk shows before she hit the tunnel, share her revelation about the two Supreme Court justices. Most of the shows were desperate enough for callers that they paid for cell phone calls. But she didn't want to talk to some pompous baritone. Tess realized she had been speaking to Jackie in her head about the two statues, imagining what they might talk about when they drove to Westminster looking for Willa Mott. She had always done this, putting away anecdotes she knew would amuse someone close to her, looking forward to the chance to provoke Tyner, make Kitty laugh.

Only Jackie wasn't a friend, she reminded herself, merely a client. Once Tess found her daughter, she'd be gone.

FOURTEEN

"DOESN'T CARROLL COUNTY STILL HAVE AN ACTIVE CHAPTER OF THE KKK?" Jackie asked, looking nervously around the bagel shop where she and Tess had stopped, killing time before their 10 a.m. appointment with Willa Mott.

"Uh-huh. In fact, they've got a recruiting flier up on the wall over there," Tess said, pointing with her chin toward the bulletin board. "I've heard it's a great way to meet men. Want me to write down the number?"

"You know, some things are not funny."

"I'll concede that if you'll concede some things *are*."

Jackie broke off a piece of her bagel, then looked at it as if she couldn't remember what she was supposed to do with it. She wasn't quite as tense and nervous as she had been at the Adoption Rights meeting, but she was definitely rattled. Was it possible to want something so much that it scared you?

"Remind me to check my teeth in the rearview mirror before we head out," Tess said. "I don't want to interview someone with poppy seeds in my teeth."

"You should have ordered something without seeds, then." Oh so prim.

"What, like that banana nut thing with *blueberry* cream cheese you're toying with? I have news for you, Jackie. That is not a bagel.

If the local KKK came in here right now, they'd take one look at what you're eating and say, 'At least she's a Gentile.' Then they'd drag me out of here by the braid like the cossacks who used to come calling in my great-grandmother's village."

"Really? Did things like that truly happen to your ancestors?"

Tess shrugged. "We only have Gramma Weinstein's word for it and she's never been above a little embroidery. Especially if it's in the cause of trying to get one of her grandchildren to eat liver."

"But you're not really Jewish, right? Your last name is Monaghan."

"Judaism comes down through your mother."

"Is that how it works?" Jackie seemed genuinely curious. "I mean, if your father was Weinstein and your mother was Monaghan, you wouldn't be Jewish?"

"I'd be exactly what I am, a nonbelieving mongrel, but I wouldn't qualify for citizenship in Israel." Tess pulled her lips back in a gumbaring grin. "Any seeds?"

"One, up near the pointy tooth. No, other side. You got it."

"Let's go meet Willa Mott."

H. L. MENCKEN, NEVER A LOOSE MAN WITH A COMPLIMENT, HAD DEscribed Carroll County as one of the most beautiful places in Maryland. In some undeveloped pockets, you could still see the soft hills and long, tapering views that had inspired him. The older towns—Westminster, New Windsor, Union Mills—had the nineteenth-century red brick houses, more like the old German and Mennonite homesteads on the Pennsylvania side of the Mason-Dixon line. It was a place out of a time. Then you rounded a curve in the highway and found a seventies-ugly development hugging the land like a family of jealous trolls, determined to keep anything beautiful at bay.

Willa Mott lived in one of the oldest, ugliest subdivisions south of Westminster. A faded sign in the front yard advertised "Apple

Orchard Daycare," but the only tree Tess could see was an ailanthus that no one had tried to chop down until it was too late. The bastard tree had struggled through a crack near the driveway and was now a spindly twelve feet.

"The kids are watching a video," Willa Mott said, opening the door before they were up the walk. "So we have exactly eighty-eight minutes. Although they sometimes like me to sing along with the hunchback."

It was hard to imagine Willa Mott singing, or doing anything vaguely joyful. She looked just as Tess had imagined her while listening to the taped testimony: a plain woman of little distinction. She wore a denim skirt, polyester white blouse, and navy cardigan. Her hair was a dull brown, her eyes a duller brown. The only color in her face was her nose, red with a summer cold. She found a tissue and blew the way children do, one side, then the other.

"Allergies," she said. "The pollen count is 150 today."

"Is that high?" Tess asked.

"Terribly. But I guess you didn't come here to talk about my sinuses." She squinted at Jackie. "I can't say as I remember you. But I guess you've changed some, since back then. Do you recognize me?"

"I think so. Maybe." But Tess could tell Jackie was lying, especially to herself. In her yearning, she was prone to say what she hoped was the right answer, even if it wasn't true.

"Jackie came to the agency thirteen years ago, under the name of Susan King. She would have been just a teenager then, not much more than eighteen. Does that help?"

"Not really. We saw a lot of young girls. Gosh, is that real gold?"

Willa was looking at Jackie's hands, clenched almost as if she was praying, and the watch on her left wrist. Ornate, with diamond chips encircling the face, it was an unusual piece, but not, in Tess's opinion, so unusual as to distract from the topic at hand.

"This? Yes, I suppose it is."

"I like old things like that," Willa said. "There's an antique pin in a consignment shop, down in Sykesville. I've had my eye on it and as soon as I get a little bit ahead, I think I'm going to get it. I thought maybe with my tax refund check, but that always seems to be spent before it comes, doesn't it?"

Tess looked around the small split-level house. Life as a daycare center was hard on any home—juice stains along the baseboard, sticky handprints on the wall, grimy traffic patterns worn into the carpet were to be expected. But even without the toddlers' decorating touches, Willa Mott's house would have looked tired and run-down. Judging by the noise, there were five, maybe six kids in the next room. Willa Mott pulled down six hundred, maybe nine hundred dollars a week. Tess didn't know exactly what daycare cost, come to think of it. Not subsistence wages, but not a lot of money left over for antique pins.

"When I called yesterday, Ms. Mott, did I mention that it's customary to pay people for their time? I mean, I understand we're keeping you from your work and I wouldn't want you to think we didn't value that."

"Miss Mott," Willa corrected with a nervous laugh. "And goodness, I don't think I could take money, not when I can't be much help. Although—" she studied Jackie's face. "You're thinner than you were, aren't you? That's why I didn't recognize you at first. You're so much thinner."

"Of course I'm thinner," Jackie said. "I was pregnant when I came to the agency."

"No, it's not just that. Your face was fuller then, and you had big glasses, which you kind of hid behind. You looked a lot older than you were, didn't you? Yes, it's coming back to me now."

Tess remembered the photo that Jackie had brought her when she thought Jackie was Mary Browne and the photo was her missing sister, Susan King. Willa was right, or making an uncanny guess. Jackie had been heavier as a teenager, and the weight had made her look older than she was.

There was a loud thud in the next room, then a childish wail. "Miss Mott! Miss Mott—Brady says I look like Quasimodo."

"Chrissie looks like Quasimodo. Chrissie looks like Quasimodo." All the children were chanting it now.

"Excuse me," Willa said. "I think I'll go give them some juice packs I have in the big freezer, out in the garage. That might help to keep them quiet."

As soon as she was gone, Jackie poked Tess in the calf with the toe of her high heel.

"Give her some money."

"She said she didn't want anything."

"She's full of shit. Everyone needs money. You stopped at a cash machine on the way out here. It's all part of my tab, right? Give her some money."

Willa came back from the garage and passed through the room with her arms full of juice packs. Distributing them caused much whining and shouting, then another brief ruckus about who had the best flavor. She ran back to the garage for another grape one. Almost ten minutes had passed by the time she returned to the living room.

"Yes, now I'm remembering," Willa said, as if there had been no break in their conversation at all. "There was something about the father of your baby, too, something unusual there, but I can't remember quite what it was."

"The father of my baby's not important," Jackie said. "I know who the father was. I want to know who adopted my girl."

Willa furrowed her brow and pressed her lips together, making a great show of thinking hard. Tess half-expected her to hunch forward, chin in hand, as if sculpted by Rodin. Eventually, she did just that. Sighing, Tess pulled her billfold from her knapsack and dropped a twenty-dollar bill in Willa Mott's lap.

"Oh goodness. I don't want you to think I'm doing this for money." Tess dropped another twenty, then a ten in Willa's lap. She dropped her business card, while she was at it. Willa waited a beat, in case any more bills were going to fall, then folded the ones that were there and put them in the pocket of her cardigan, along with Tess's business card. Preferably not the pocket with the wadded-up tissues, Tess hoped, although she really didn't care if Willa Mott ended up blowing her nose on a twenty.

"Really, I don't know so very much. You had a baby girl, right? I think the adoptive father may have been an executive at one of those plants out in Hunt Valley. Could have been McCormick, Noxell, the quarry. One of those places. I remember he made real good money. You had to make good money to adopt a baby from us, it cost more'n ten thousand dollars. His wife was a schoolteacher, but she was going to stay home when they got a baby. The name was kinda common. Johnson or Johnston. They wanted a girl, and they were going to name her Caitlin."

Jackie looked skeptical. "How did you remember all that, all of a sudden?"

"Oh, I remember all the girls who came through, to tell you the truth. It just takes a little time to jog my memory is all, to hook up the face with the circumstances."

"If I took off this watch and handed it to you, would you remember anything more?"

Willa Mott looked truly affronted. "I'm grateful you compensated me for my time today, but the money didn't have anything to do with my remembering. It took me a minute there to connect you with the way you used to be, that's all. You know, when you were fat."

"I was *not* fat." Jackie's teeth were gritted.

A child's shriek. "Miss Mott! Miss Mott! Cal keeps poking me with his shoe."

"Am not," a boy's voice retorted.

"You are! You are!"

"I guess I better go check on my little ones," Willa Mott said. "Nice to meet you both. If I remember anything else, I promise I'll call you first thing. I've got your card right here."

With that, Willa Mott waded into the melee in the next room, picking up the offending Cal by the collar of his T-shirt the way a mother cat might grab her kitten by the scruff of the neck, then turning off the video with the toe of her navy blue Ked.

"No more *Hunchback*, until everyone in this room starts behaving," she proclaimed. "This means all of you—Cal, Brady, Bobby, Chrissie, and, yes you, Raffi."

Tess suppressed a laugh.

"What's so funny?" Jackie asked. She seemed angry that Tess could find anything to laugh at.

"Maybe it's a coincidence, but every kid in the Apple Orchard Daycare Center is named for someone in the Orioles' starting lineup from the year Cal broke Lou Gehrig's record. Cal Ripken, Chris Hoiles, Rafael Palmiero, Brady Anderson. It's got to be—that would have been just about the time they would have been conceived."

"White folks are crazy," Jackie said with a snort.

THEY WERE ALMOST BACK IN BUTCHERS HILL BEFORE JACKIE SPOKE again.

"You paid her too much."

"Excuse me?"

"That wasn't worth fifty dollars, what she told us. You paid her too much and she thinks we're suckers now. I bet she knows more than she's telling."

"First you tell me to pay her, then you say I paid her too much. But she did remember what you looked like. That seemed genuine enough. I saw the photo, remember. You were a . . . big girl. What was that stuff about the baby's father, anyway?"

"Nothing." Jackie was gripping the steering wheel so tight her knuckles looked like they might pop out of her hands.

"No secrets, Jackie, and no lies. That was our deal, remember?"

"Okay." Small sigh. "My baby's father was white." Then, before Tess could react in any way, "Don't look so surprised."

"I'm not looking anything. But you told me he was a boy from the neighborhood."

"There were white boys in my neighborhood."

"I know. I know Pigtown." Tess liked seeing Jackie squirm at the mention of her inelegantly named old neighborhood. "I wonder why Willa thought that particular detail was so memorable, though. The agency she worked for definitely did biracial adoptions. I know that much from listening to the taped testimony."

"What do you expect from some Carroll County cracker? Forget about her. Where do we go from here?"

"Got me. Looking for someone named Caitlin Johnson-Johnston in metropolitan Baltimore is definitely needle-in-the-haystack time."

"Well, *I* have an idea. Can you work tonight?"

"Sure."

"Meet me at your office at seven tonight, and I'll show you how to do what I do for a living. I'll even bring dinner."

"What are we going to do?"

"I'll tell you when we get to your office. You have one phone line, right? We can use my cell phone, I guess. Not the cheapest way to go, but it will take too long without it."

When they pulled up in front of Tess's office, Martin Tull was waiting in his unmarked car.

"Gotta talk to you," he said without preamble, then looked at Jackie behind the wheel of her white Lexus. "Privately."

"Now?"

"Right now."

"That's okay," Jackie said, looking from Tull to Tess. "I'll see you here at seven. It won't take more than fifteen minutes to explain my idea to you."

Esskay jumped down from the sofa, stretching as if bowing toward Mecca, then began her ritualistic treat dance. Tull usually asked if he could give Esskay her bone, but today he barely seemed to notice her. Tess found a biscuit in the cookie jar, one of the homemade ones from a South Baltimore bakery, threw it to the dog, and put her gun back in the wall safe.

"I thought you didn't like to carry your weapon."

"Tyner felt I should, because of the break-in."

"That's right, you had a break-in over the weekend. Police report said nothing was taken, though."

Tess decided not to ask why a homicide detective knew about her little burglary. She hadn't filed a police report, but the landlord might have. She hoped Tull wasn't getting protective on her. That was all she needed, yet another person fretting over her safety and well-being. "You want a Coke? It's got caffeine at least."

"Lots of bad things happening on Butchers Hill these days. There was a fire in the neighborhood yesterday afternoon," he said, ignoring her offer. "Right around the corner from here."

"Uh-huh. The radio said it was a vacant rowhouse on Fayette." She got herself a Coke, wandered back to her desk, checked the counter on her answering machine. No calls. Keyes Investigations, always in demand.

"The radio was wrong on two counts. The fire backed up traffic on Fayette, but the house was on Chester. And it was vacant, but it wasn't unoccupied." Tull tossed an envelope on her desk. "They found a body in the basement. Guy looked like he was smoking a crack pipe and he dropped it."

Tull seemed to expect her to reach for the envelope. When she didn't, he took it back and opened it, extracting a pair of Polaroids.

"That happens, of course. I'm surprised it doesn't happen more often. These pipeheads take over abandoned buildings, use them to smoke or shoot up. Accidents will happen. But according to the medical examiner, this guy was dead *before* the fire started. Someone bashed his head in and set the place on fire. We might not have been able to identify the guy, except he had dental records from when he was in foster care. State makes all the kids in its custody get at least one medical checkup."

"Awfully decent of the state." Tess's stomach clenched. She capped the bottle of Coke, put it down next to her computer.

"Kid's name was Treasure Teeter." Tull flicked a Polaroid at her, like a playing card. Tess let it skim past her shoulder and fall to the floor, but she couldn't help seeing the charred human shape at the center as the image flew by.

"You heard of him, right? You were looking for him, as I hear it. Looking for his sister, too. Destiny? I'm guessing you never found her, though. Big break for you—I did."

He flipped the second photo on the desk. Tess saw the yellow crime scene tape at the edges, the body lying on the bright green grass, the gash in the throat, a ghoulish echo of the mouth above. Except it was impossible to see the mouth, impossible to make out any features in a face that had been battered to the bone.

"Meet Destiny Teeter," Tull said. "You may know her better as the prostitute at the pagoda."

FIFTEEN

LUTHER BEALE WAS SCRUBBING HIS MARBLE STEPS, A CHERISHED VISUAL cliché in Baltimore. Even if he hadn't been out front of his house, Tess would have known instantly where he lived. In a block where the other brick rowhouses looked wilted and unloved, Beale's home was painted a soft yellow with white trim. A tub of yellow daisies sat next to the marble stoop. The paint job appeared fresh to Tess's eyes, which admittedly were not expert in matters of home improvement. At any rate, it did not look like Luther Beale had been planning to leave this house any time soon.

Plans change.

"Pretty flowers," said Tess. Sometimes, being furious made her absolutely banal.

"Those are my second ones this season," Beale said, never looking up from his task. "Someone stole the first tub. I expect someone will steal this one as well, although God knows why. I can't imagine you can get more than a dollar selling flowers." Beale dipped his brush back into the aluminum pail and attacked another spot, rubbing at it fiercely and methodically, determined to eradicate it.

"Can we go inside? I need to talk to you."

"Then talk to me while I work. I got started late today. I'm behind."

"This isn't a conversation we can have out on the street."

She wished he looked more surprised, that he would resist a little more, or pepper her with insistent questions. Instead, he dropped the brush back into the soapy water and stood, knees creaking.

"I'm on the third floor," he said, unlocking the outside door, then another inside the vestibule, a wooden one polished to a high sheen and smelling of lemon furniture oil. "I used to rent out the first two floors, but I don't anymore. I'd rather have my privacy than the money."

Beale's apartment looked like the kind of place where the occupant spent a lot of time sitting in the dark. Clean, which Tess had expected, but also quite bare. She thought old people always had a surplus of stuff, the way her grandmother did. Beale's apartment, with its empty white walls and clean taupe carpeting, felt like a gallery waiting for an exhibit to be installed. She followed him through the living room, which had only one chair, a computer, and a television set, into the kitchen. Here, at least, there were two chairs, vinyl padded ones that matched the yellow-topped formica table.

"You want a cold drink?" Beale asked. She had asked Tull the same question not even a half-hour ago. Perhaps it was instinctive, this offering of beverages to forestall unpleasantness.

"No, thank you," She paused, and still couldn't find a place to begin. "Your place is pretty spare. I like it, though."

"People broke in while I was in prison, stole what they could and broke the rest. Once I got the walls painted and the new carpet done, it seemed easier to keep it simple." He looked at her sternly. "You didn't come here to talk about my interior decorating. What do you want?"

"Why didn't Destiny matter?" It wasn't where she had meant to start, but it would have to do.

"Destiny?"

"Destiny Teeter, the girl twin. You said she didn't matter, that it was okay if I couldn't find her. Was it really because she was just a girl? Or was it because you knew she was dead? Knew she was dead because you had killed her."

"The girl's dead?" He sounded more confused than surprised. He rubbed his temples, as if his head suddenly hurt.

"She's the one whose body was found in the park a few weeks back, before you hired me. Her brother, Treasure, was killed in an arson fire yesterday. Someone hit him over the head, then set a fire, hoping to make it look like an accident. When the cops ID'ed him through the dental records, they had the inspiration of trying to match Destiny's records to the dead girl."

She had hoped her torrent of words might provoke a similar stream from Beale. He merely looked thoughtful. "Well, that's a shame. But the others are still alive, right? Didn't you go out to the skinny boy's school yesterday? How's he doing? Besides, the fat one still might show up. Those boys don't stay away forever when they run. They always come home. They don't have the imagination to start over somewhere else."

His coldness, his obtuseness, infuriated her even as it gave her new hope. If he had killed the twins, wouldn't he be stammering excuses or alibis by now?

"Mr. Beale, I don't think you understand the significance of what I've just told you. Destiny and Treasure Teeter were murdered, and the police are going to be here with a warrant for you real soon."

"Me. They always blame me. Doesn't anyone else in this city ever do anything? It doesn't make much sense, paying money to find children just so I can kill them."

"The police believe you killed Destiny in a rage—that you didn't plan it, but when it happened, it felt good, cathartic. So you decided to kill the others, too, to punish them for testifying against you. But you didn't know how to find them, did you? That's where I came in. I would find them, thinking I was doing a good deed, and then you'd kill them."

If Tull was right, Beale's plan had been ingenious and multilay-ered. After his chance meeting with Destiny, he had sought Tess out to locate the others. He had insisted on not meeting the children face-to-face, so he could then have plausible deniability when the bodies started turning up. According to Tull's theory, Beale had broken into her office and stolen his own file, in order to find out what she had learned while still declaring his ignorance. But the file he would have printed out early Saturday morning had only the information about the Teeter twins. She hadn't had a chance yet to summarize Jackie's findings about Sal and his scholarship to the Penfield School. Lives often hinged on such coincidences. So Treasure Teeter was dead and Sal Hawkings was alive. He would have been harder to get to, anyway. Beale would have needed to think long and hard about finding a credible death for Sal.

"The police are going to arrest you today," Tess said. "They'll be here any minute with a warrant. But I wanted to talk to you first, see what you had to say for yourself."

Beale walked over to a wall calendar hanging by his kitchen door, the kind given out at hardware stores. This month's picture was a covered bridge, the reminder beneath it was to buy gardening supplies. Each day in June so far was X'ed, except for yesterday. He took a black pen and carefully crossed off that square as well.

"Forgot to mark my calendar. Like I said, I got a late start this morning. I've been out of prison for sixty-seven days now. Do you know how many days I was in prison?"

Tess was pretty good at doing math in her head, the by-product of having to know her checking account balance almost to the penny over the last few years. "Five times 365, for a total of—1,500 plus 300 plus 25, 1,825."

"You forgot the leap year, so 1,826. I figure I have to live to be seventy-two to get all those days back. And I never really get them back, do I? You never get anything back in this life, once it's taken from you. My wife Annie, the babies who died inside her. We tried five times to have children, but she just couldn't carry a baby. She was all messed up inside. Nowadays, you're like that, the doctors can do things, as long as you got money. Isn't that a fact?"

"Yes, I guess it is." Tess hadn't known how this conversation was going to go, but she surely hadn't envisioned discussing modern obstetrics.

He sighed. "Children, children, children. Truth is, I was disappointed only for Annie's sake. The way I see it, children are one of the shakiest investments you'll ever make. You spend all this money on 'em, spend all this time and there's no way knowing how they're going to turn out. Now that boy Treasure, he was a cute little boy once. Mouthy, in with bad company, but a real good-looking boy. The girl was pretty, too, or would have been if she had worn nice clothes. All those children, always dressed so shabby. I'm sorry they're dead, but I didn't kill them."

"But you never intended to help them, did you? This was never about helping these children at all."

"I believe I'll have some iced tea. You sure you don't want some?" When Tess shook her head, Beale took a jar of presweetened, instant powder from the top of the refrigerator and stirred it into a tall, amber glass filled with tap water. He took a long time stirring, as if making instant iced tea required a great deal of precision.

"You ever listened to a child tell you the plot of a picture show?" The teaspoon was still hitting the sides of his glass, tap, tap, tap. "You know how they get all mixed up, forget the important parts, double back to the beginning? And no two children will tell the story quite the same way. It likes to drive you crazy, listening to them."

Tess waited. It seemed to her that Luther Beale wasn't a much better storyteller himself.

"Now the children who saw Donnie Moore die all saw the exact same thing. They all told the jury the same story, almost word for word. Me, standing there with my gun out, looking like the devil. The girl saw it, although she was around the corner and heading up the alley before Donnie went down. Her brother was right behind her, but he saw me, too. The fat one saw it, although his back was to me. Yet they all told the same story, almost word for word. Now isn't that something?"

"Their testimony had probably been rehearsed to some degree,"

Tess said. "They were children, after all, the prosecution had to prepare them for taking the witness stand. You'd expect a certain similarity."

"Which would be fine, except for one thing. I *didn't* kill Donnie Moore, Miss Monaghan."

What had Tull told her, when they watched the moon rise over Locust Point? *He wanted to take the witness stand in his own defense. Luckily, his lawyer wasn't that crazy.* How had she ever gotten involved with such a crazy old man?

"You mean someone else with a gun just like yours happened to be on Fairmount Avenue that night and just happened to shoot Donnie after you opened fire and it just happened that no one heard the other shots? You'll have to do better than that."

"I heard two shots. At the time, I thought it was a car backfiring. Later, I realized they were gunshots, probably came from the car I saw coming round the corner."

"But the bullet they found in Donnie matched your gun, right?"

"The bullet passed through Donnie. They never found it. But then they weren't looking for it. They didn't need to find any bullets. They had me, they had my just-fired gun, they had four children saying I did it."

"It still sounds pretty incredible to me. But okay, I'll play along. Someone else shoots Donnie Moore. Why?"

"It wouldn't be the first time a child was shot when some drug dealer was trying to hit someone else. See, it's gotta be drugs, because if it wasn't, why didn't the folks in that car slow down? Why didn't they call the prosecutor and offer to testify, too? And if there was someone else there they were trying to kill, that person's not going to help me out. He's just going to run. The children say it was me because they don't want to go against the drug dealers."

"But after Donnie died, the other children were separated. They were put in different foster homes. They couldn't have conspired to tell the same story even if they wanted to."

"I'm going to tell you again. I didn't kill Donnie Moore, Miss

Monaghan. It's true, I told you a little lie at first. I didn't think you'd be able to find the children if you weren't dangling money in front of their noses. Once you found 'em, I planned to tell you the truth. But all I ever wanted to do was to talk to them, to find out why they lied, why they didn't mention the other gunshots, or the car that turned onto Fairmount just as Donnie died."

He finished his iced tea in one long swallow, then immediately took the glass to the sink, rinsed it out, and put it in the rack on the drainboard. Watching him, Tess struggled with her own feelings. She wanted to believe him, if only because she didn't want to be implicated in Treasure's death. But she couldn't let him off the hook just to get herself off the hook.

"Are you still going to work for me?" he asked.

"The police told me you had a PBJ for agg assault. So you're not quite the righteous man you hold yourself out to be. You hurt someone once, almost killed him according to the cops. Why wouldn't you do it again?"

Beale pulled a long, gold chain from his pocket, worrying it between his fingers the way Tess's Monaghan relatives manipulated their rosary beads. "I told you about my Annie, how she wanted children. But her body wasn't kind to her. It killed the babies she wanted, and then it killed her, the female parts turning against her. She was dying, no way around it, and I rushed over to the hospital from work each day, wanting only to be with her when she finally slipped away. One day, the boss kept me late after work, some stupid thing. When I got there, an orderly was pulling the sheet over her face."

Tess waited.

"So I pulled it down to look at her, one last time. She was so thin at the end, she had lost most of her hair, she didn't even look like the woman I had married, but she was my Annie. I looked at her, and I saw her neck was bare. The orderly, his fist was clenched, he was trying to back out of the room. I knocked him down and I sat on him, and I beat his head against that hospital floor until he opened his hand and gave me back my Annie's locket. Then I pounded his head on the floor until he was unconscious and had to be admitted to his own emergency room. When the judge heard the whole story, he gave me PBJ."

He flipped open the locket at the end of the chain in his hand and showed Tess the faded photo there. Luther Beale, the young Luther Beale that Annie had known.

"He had her wedding ring, too. But it was the locket that made me crazy."

"It's a nice picture. You were a handsome young man." He was, although there was something severe and cold in his face, even as a young man. Luther Beale looked like he had come into this world feeling righteous.

"I always wonder if I should put Annie's photo in there now. I mean, should it be the way it was, or is it my locket now, my way of remembering her?"

Tess couldn't begin to answer that question. How do you remember your dead? Light a candle, unveil a stone, sit in the dark and drink tequila. Although she had tried only the last of these three rituals, it was something she had been struggling with for almost a year, since she had seen Jonathan Ross run down by a taxi on a foggy morning in Fells Point. She drank tequila and went through the dreary litany of what-ifs. *What if they had slept in that morning. What if they had left by the front door instead of the side. What if, what if, what if.*

She assumed Luther Beale had his own version. What if Annie had lived? What if they had had children? Then they might have moved, in order to find better schools, and then Luther Beale would have been long gone from Fairmount Avenue.

"I didn't kill Donnie Moore, Miss Monaghan. I didn't kill those twins. And if I didn't, someone else did. I'm too damn old to serve more time for a crime I didn't do. You still working for me, Miss Monaghan? You believe me now?"

"I believe you didn't kill the twins," Tess said slowly. "And I believe you didn't mean to kill Donnie Moore. Is that good enough?"

"It's better than what most people think of me."

And they sat in the kitchen, waiting for the cops to come.

SIXTEEN

THE COPS CAME FOR LUTHER BEALE LATE THAT AFTERNOON. THEY HAD A search warrant, but he wasn't being officially charged, not yet, just taken in for questioning. Tyner suspected they had waited until late in the day hoping Beale would be tired, presumably easier to wear down during the interrogation. Tess thought the cops should know Luther Beale better than that.

"But this is good for us," Tyner told Tess, when she telephoned to say they had taken Beale away and started searching his apartment. "I bet they don't have any physical evidence or eyewitnesses to link him to the twins' deaths."

"They want my files, though, and they want to interview me. The homicide detective in charge of the case tried to tell me my files aren't privileged because Beale hired me before he was a suspect. When that didn't work, they brought back Tull, who went all moral on me, saying he just wanted me to do the right thing for myself, so my conscience could be clear."

Tyner laughed. "Good effort. But we have my paperwork to show that Beale came to you as a referral. I'll be at police headquarters if you need me. Luther Beale and I have a long night ahead of us, but I'll have him out eventually."

* * *

TESS HAD HER OWN LONG NIGHT WAITING FOR HER. GIVEN THAT SHE FELT about three weeks had passed since that morning, she was less than enthusiastic about meeting Jackie at her office. But a promise was a promise, and a client was a client, even if the search for Jackie's daughter now seemed mundane alongside the Butcher of Butchers Hill, the Sequel.

Jackie met her at the office with a current telephone directory, a criss-cross directory, a sheaf of photocopies, and a brown bag of little cartons.

"Chinese food?" Tess asked, her spirits lifting a little bit.

"Fresh Fields," Jackie said. Tess made a face, although she had never actually been inside that earnestly good-for-you grocery. Fresh Fields was too far afield for her. Besides, she had heard it specialized in healthy stuff, low-fat and organic. She boycotted the place on general principle, on the grounds that grocery stores should not be in picturesque old mill buildings with a Starbucks next door. Still, Jackie's haul of containers looked pretty good.

"Vegetable pad thai, sushi, chicken curry salad, smoked couscous, focaccia, pasta salad," Jackie said. "Eclairs for dessert."

"Pad thai? Isn't that a fish thing? And sushi is a *raw* fish thing. I might have to eat both eclairs." Tess peered into the empty bag. "No wine?"

"We're working, remember? You can't afford to have any of the edges blurred."

"What are we doing, anyway?"

"We're going to do an easy little telephone survey, not unlike something I'd set up for one of my clients. You take the Johnsons, A through M, I'll take Johnson N through Z. Then we'll move on the Johnstons. You check the current phone book, then cross-reference it to these pages I photocopied from a thirteen-year-old phone book. If the name doesn't show up on the photocopy, put an asterisk next to it, then move on. If it shows up, you call."

"There are almost a dozen pages of Johnsons in the phone book. This will take forever."

"Not once you control for longevity and location." Jackie patted the county criss-cross. "Remember, we know our Johnson-Johnston lived in North Baltimore County. Call only those listings that show up in the old phone book with an address in that area. That should narrow it down considerably."

Tess was impressed, but determined not to let Jackie know it.

"So we're just going to call this people and say, 'Yo, is Caitlin home?' "

"No, because then there's a chance we'd get a Caitlin who's the wrong age, or whose parents don't fit the profile. Caitlin was the WASP name of choice for a while there. Instead, we say we're doing a survey about popular children's names, specific to the Baltimore metro area. In exchange for the person's time, tell them they might win a twenty-seven-inch color television in a drawing. Ask how many kids they have, what their names are. Then ask the ages. If we find a thirteen-year-old Caitlin, zero in, ask for the exact date of birth. By the time we're finished, we should have at least a few possibilities."

"Assuming they haven't moved. Assuming Willa Mott was right."

Jackie's world held no room for doubt. "Let's not concede defeat before we've started, okay? Now eat your supper, then we'll start calling about seven-thirty so we won't catch people at their dinner tables."

"You mean I finally get a chance to be a telemarketer and I'm *not* going to interrupt people while they're eating? They're going to know we're imposters."

Jackie was setting up work stations for the two of them, arranging piles of photocopied phone lists alongside two maps, so they could cross-reference each listing. Apparently, she was going to work from her cell phone, while Tess would use her office phone. But *two* maps, Tess thought. Couldn't they share the map at least?

"Part of the reason I'm so good at what I do is that I don't call people at supper," Jackie said. "I also stop promptly at ten o'clock. People don't like to hear a phone ring after ten. They always think it's going to be bad news, and you never get past that first little buzz of fear they feel."

Tess, who had started with the eclairs and planned to work backward to the couscous, didn't say anything. Her mouth was full.

JACKIE HAD WRITTEN A SCRIPT, WHICH SHE STUCK TO WITH ALMOST grim determination, rattling off her lines into her cell phone. "We're not trying to sell you anything . . . just doing a survey for a local publisher on Baltimore's favorite baby names . . . for answering our questions, your name will be entered into a raffle for a twenty-seven-inch color television set . . . May I ask what you and your husband do for a living? Do you have any children? Their names are? Their ages? . . . Thank you. Have a nice night."

Tess tried to vary the pitch, partly to keep herself interested, partly because she didn't want to admit even to herself how clever Jackie's plan was. But she quickly learned it was inefficient to try the spiel extemporaneously and resorted to the script Jackie had made for her. But where Jackie had a talent for making each call sound fresh and spontaneous, Tess's voice became deader and deader as the evening wore on. How did anyone do this for a living?

By ten, Jackie's witching hour, they had worked through about half of the names. And Tess, despite her slow start, had ended up reaching a few more families than Jackie. They had found a five-year-old Caitlin, an eleven-year-old Caitlin, and even one thirty-two-year-old Caitlin, a woman whose parents obviously were ahead of their time. But not a single thirteen-year-old Caitlin, not in North Baltimore County.

"You may have a future at this," Jackie said, studying Tess's list. "If the private detective thing doesn't work out, you could always come work for me. Although then you really would have to ask people for money, and that's a different skill altogether."

"Can I have a drink now, boss, as it's quitting time?"

"Sure, but I didn't bring anything like that."

"We can always go down to the Korean's. He sells beer. 'The Korean's.' Listen to me. I'm beginning to talk like everyone else on Butchers Hill."

"I'm not much of a beer drinker," Jackie said, wrinkling her nose. "I prefer wine."

"Now that's a problem. Mr. Kim stocks more kinds of Doritos than he does of wine. I know, we'll go over to Rosie's Place. It's around the corner from here."

"Aren't these neighborhood taverns kind of rough?"

Tess laughed. "Not Rosie's. You'll understand when we get there."

FROM THE OUTSIDE, ROSIE'S LOOKED LIKE ANY OF THE CORNER BARS IN East Baltimore. A neon sign advertising Budweiser on tap, a pair of porcelain fisherman in one window, two of the Marx Brothers in the other, Harpo and Chico. The inside was nothing more than a long bar, with a television set turned to some sitcom, and a set of pale green booths along the far wall.

"People are looking at us," Jackie whispered to Tess as they seated themselves in a booth. "Is it because I'm the only black woman in here?"

"Well, you're better dressed than everyone else. They don't see a lot of Chanel suits in Rosie's. But they probably don't see many interracial couples, either."

"You mean . . . ? "

"You were quick to notice it was all-white, but you missed it's all-female as well," Tess said. "Can you imagine a more tolerant group than working-class lesbians? I think I'll have a mixed drink, after all, something different. You know what I want? A mint julep."

"Do you think they have white wine?" Jackie was still whispering.

Tess whispered back. "Of course they have white wine. They even have decent white wine. But have a julep with me. The bartender makes the syrup from her own mint plants, which she grows out front. They're fabulous."

The juleps were served in ten-year-old Preakness glasses, commemorative cups used at the track, usually with a vile concoction of vodka, grapefruit juice, and peach schnapps known as black-eyed Susans. The bartender at Rosie's was wise enough to keep the glasses and avoid the drink.

"Spectacular Bid, Sunday Silence," Jackie read from the side of the glass. "You know, I've never even been to a horse race."

"It's fun, as long as you keep it in perspective." This batch of juleps was syrupy, and served over so much cracked ice that it was like a snowball with an alcohol kicker. "You can't go to the track expecting to win, not unless you're willing to do the time to become a real handicapper. I got lucky my first few times out, hit an exacta and a dollar triple, total beginner's luck. Then I got cocky and thought I could make real picks, began trying to calculate speed figures and use the past performance charts in the *Racing Form*. I lost every time. Now when I go, I think of it as an interactive entertainment, like a play in which I have a vested interest in the outcome."

"A kind of performance art."

"Exactly. I make goofy bets, but educated goofy bets. If it's not too crowded at the betting windows, I like to watch the post parade, pick out the horse who looks like he's ready to run a good race."

"How can you tell a winner, just by looking?"

"Well, as I said, nothing's foolproof. But I like the ones whose ears are straight up, and look kind of prancey. My favorite race of all is the very last one on Preakness Day."

"Isn't that the Preakness?"

"Uh-uh. Preakness is the penultimate race. The last race is just a little stakes race, no big deal. Half the paid attendance has already left. But I've always had good luck at that race. Hit an exacta there just this year."

"I thought you said the exacta was a sucker's bet."

"It is."

Jackie actually smiled, although she tried to hide it behind the rim of her glass.

"So you *do* have a sense of humor."

"Who said I didn't?"

"You don't laugh at most of my jokes."

"Did it ever occur to you that most of your jokes aren't very funny?"

Tess pretended to clutch her heart. "What perfidy."

"Truthfully, it's good to hear you cutting up the way you usually do. You seemed a little distracted this evening. Is everything all right? What was the deal with that guy who wanted to see you this morning?"

"I've had some . . . unexpected developments on another case."

Jackie hesitated, then said as if reciting a phrase from a foreign language handbook: "Do you want to talk about it?"

"It wouldn't be ethical. You wouldn't want me chatting about your case with another client, right? Besides, if the cops do come after me, I can't maintain I'm entitled to client-attorney privilege if I've been blabbing about the case all over town."

"Could that really happen?"

"It's possible."

"Could it happen any time soon?"

Tess had to laugh at Jackie's worried face. "Don't worry, Miss Weir. I'll be here tomorrow night, ready to continue the survey of Johnson-Johnstons of North Baltimore County."

She signaled the bartender for another round, but Jackie covered the rim of her glass. "I have too long a drive home."

"Not me," Tess said. "Did you know James M. Cain had a snow-ball machine and used it to make mint juleps? I bet they weren't half as good as these, though."

Some people she knew could have talked about that single detail for hours. But Jackie's imagination wasn't engaged by long-dead writers, not even ones who knew the secrets of every hash house waitress and insurance man.

"You always want more, don't you?"

"Huh?"

"I was thinking of that photo back in your office. More juleps, more rides on the flying rabbit, more chocolate malts."

"I did love malted milkshakes. I always asked for an extra teaspoon of malt. Poppa would give it to me, Gramma wouldn't." Suddenly, the second julep didn't seem so delicious. Second helpings never did. "Gee, isn't it shocking that I developed an eating disorder, what with one grandparent urging all those treats on me, and the other one always trying to take them away?"

"An eating disorder. Now that's real white-girl craziness. Anorexia?"

"No, just a little garden-variety bulimia. An occasional binge, followed by an occasional purge with the help of Ipecac. Exercise was my coping mechanism. I was running ten miles a day when I was in high school, doing endless sit-ups in my room. By the time my parents finally figured out I wasn't even on the track team, I had shin splints like you wouldn't believe."

"Then you just stopped?"

Tess was thinking about the food they had left in her office. She had eaten quite a bit, yet there was still so much left. They had wrapped it up and put it in the refrigerator, except for the pad thai, which Jackie would take home. There was a time when even that would have been too risky. She would have thrown it away, or forced Jackie to take it. She wouldn't have trusted herself to behave responsibly around so much food.

"Overeating is like alcoholism, except that you don't have the option of going cold turkey. Everyone has to eat, right? On top of that, I have to exercise, because I'm addicted to the endorphin rush. I just brought both activities into almost-normal limits. I started rowing, which isn't as hard on the knees, and I alternate my runs with weight workouts. I also resigned myself to life as a mesomorph. Women think I should lose ten pounds, men think I'm fine the way I am." She grinned. "That's better than the obverse, isn't it? Unless, of course, you're a regular customer here."

"You look fine. As I said before, white girl craziness."

"Really? Then why did you get so upset when Willa Mott kept saying you were fat?"

Jackie made a face, as if repelled. It wasn't clear if the face was intended for Willa Mott, or the girl she used to be. "When I got pregnant, I spent the first four months eating like crazy, thinking no one would notice I was carrying a baby, they'd just think I was fat. It wasn't the most inspired plan, I admit. By the time I accepted what was going on, there was nothing to do but carry the pregnancy to term."

"You look so different now." Tess was seeing the photograph again, the shapeless girl with the flash of camera caught in her myopic eyes.

"Not so different."

"You do. It's not just the weight. It's the glasses—"

"I wear contact lenses now. You've heard of them?"

"And the hair—those two little tails sticking straight out from your head, the ends looking as if someone chewed on them."

"Hey, not everyone can wear the same hairstyle for their entire life. As I said before, you haven't changed much. You have one of those faces that will never change. When you're fifty, people will be able to match you to that photograph. Is that something in the genes, you suppose, having a face that never changes?"

"I've never thought about it much, but I guess it is, at least on my mother's side. The Monaghans start out with these round little marshmallow faces that get sharper and frecklier every year. Not too long ago, I was walking downtown and someone I went to fourth grade with recognized me and said, 'You haven't changed a bit.' I wasn't exactly flattered."

"You should be," Jackie said fervently. "To have that kind of continuity in your life, to have people know you that way—that's a wonderful thing."

"An interesting observation from a woman who changed her name, ran away from her family, and did everything she could, short of going to a plastic surgeon, to alter her appearance."

Jackie said nothing, just played with her empty glass, running her fingers over the painted surface.

"Ready to go?"

"Absolutely."

Outside, the night air was muggy, as if a storm might be near. Tess and Jackie were moving slowly up Collington Street, when a skeletal woman pushing a baby carriage approached them. Although the woman looked as if she hadn't eaten in weeks, the sleeping baby was pink-cheeked and healthy looking.

"Ladies, ladies, do you have any spare change tonight, ladies? My baby needs a prescription, and the food stamps are late this month, and the doctor says I have to start on this new medication, and my husband, he just wrote from Georgia that he can't find work—"

Jackie started to reach inside her purse, but Tess laid a hand gently on her wrist.

"We're down to living on plastic until our next pay day," she told the woman, politely but firmly. "Sorry."

The woman looked at them resentfully, muttered something under her breath, and pushed the stroller forward accosting a group of people gathered on a stoop several houses down.

"She had a baby," Jackie said. "She's not some druggie or alcohol trying to get money for a fix."

"It's not her baby and that's exactly what she is."

"How do you know that?"

"She's famous in the neighborhood. You see, she kept coming back. Some people tried to help her, get her a place to live. They found out that she volunteers to babysit when she's hard up, then wheels the baby around, using him as a prop to get more contributions. One of the *Blight*'s columnists wrote about her. The details give her away. Lies demand details, lots of them. People pay her to shut up as much as anything. She's one of the women who walk."

"Who?"

"The women who walk, the lost souls of Baltimore, the ones who talk to themselves and wander through the city. I see them on buses, down in the harbor, even up at the Rotunda shopping center. Some of them panhandle, some don't. Not that long ago, I used to worry I was going to become one of them."

"Bullshit," Jackie said softly.

"What?"

"I said *bullshit*. You were never really in danger of falling through the cracks like that. You have parents, family. There was always someone to catch you if you really fell."

Tess wanted to argue, but Jackie was right, she had caught her in her lie as surely as she had caught the woman with the stroller. Oh, she might have felt as if she were scraping bottom at times, but there had always been family to help her out. When she had lost her job, Aunt Kitty and Uncle Donald had rallied, finding work for her. And if she hadn't been so proud, her father would have squeezed her on the city payroll somehow.

"You're right, I was being glib. I always had support. I guess you really didn't."

"I had one person. Now I don't have anyone. I'm all I have."

Tess wanted to contradict her, say something soothing, but what was there to say in all honesty? Her mother was dead, her daughter was someone else's daughter. Jackie Weir was about as alone as anyone could be in this world.

SEVENTEEN

TESS YEARNED TO GO STRAIGHT TO TYNER'S OFFICE THE NEXT MORN-
ing, but it was her turn to take Gramma Weinstein to the hair-
dresser, one of Gramma's many codependent rituals. Unlike some
older folks, who clung to the steering wheel long past the point of
prudence, Gramma had announced on her sixtieth birthday that
she would not drive any more. She had taken it for granted that her
husband and, after his death, her children and grandchildren would
gladly pick up the chauffeuring duties.

But the rotation, as maintained by Gramma, was far from foolproof.
Today, as Tess pulled into the parking lot behind Gramma's apartment building, she saw her mother getting out of her blue Saturn.

"Free at last," she said to herself. Now she could check in with
Tyner, find out where things stood with Beale. But something in
her mother's face kept her from throwing her car into reverse and
peeling out of the parking lot. The tense lines on either side of her
mouth, the anxious look in her eyes. She reminded Tess of herself,
on her way to visit Judith.

"Hey, Mom. Looks like Gramma double-scheduled again. I
thought it was my turn."

"Great. I had to take a personal day to get the morning off.
Unlike you, I can't make my own hours. The federal government
isn't quite so flexible."

"Nor is the state government, yet here comes Uncle Donald. Triple-teaming—that's a new one even for Gramma. Is she getting senile, or does she just not care what else we do with our lives?"

"Don't be disrespectful of your grandmother," Judith said automatically. "She won't be with us much longer."

"*You* wish," Tess said, and her mother looked stricken. *By the joke, or the reality behind it?* Impossible to tell.

Uncle Donald strolled up, whistling a show tune, "Younger Than Springtime." He was Gramma's favorite, if only because he had never married and his loyalties were clear. Even his fall from political grace, in the scandal that had sent his senator boss to prison, hadn't shaken Gramma's affection for him.

"Good morning, Sis, Tesser. How do you want to resolve this? We can toss a coin, or cut a deck of cards that I happen to have in my car. High card wins. Loser takes her to the Beauty Palace."

"I'll do it," Judith said. "I took the day off, I might as well."

A reprieve, Tess thought. Yet when she looked at her mother's dutiful, unhappy face, she couldn't just walk away.

"Let's all go. Make it a family outing. My mom and my favorite uncle. And Gramma," she added, when Judith gave her another look. "We could go to S'n'H afterwards, like we used to do with Poppa."

"Why not?" Uncle Donald replied.

"Why not?" Judith echoed weakly, but she looked as if she might have several reasons.

THE PIKESVILLE BEAUTY PALACE SAT IN AN OLD SHOPPING CENTER ON Reisterstown Road, near the synagogues that had been built as Baltimore's Jewish families began moving to the north and west. Although the neighborhood was less and less safe as time went on, the Beauty Palace had scores of loyal customers like Gramma, who wouldn't dream of going anywhere else for their weekly sets and periodic root touchups.

"Mrs. Weinstein!" the receptionist said with the chirpy insincerity common to those who dealt with Gramma. "We're all ready to take you back to the shampoo girl."

"You didn't give me one of those Russians, did you? I hate it when they talk that gibberish around me."

"We have you with Lisa today."

"I've never had her. Isn't she the one who snaps her gum?"

"She won't," the receptionist said, her smile becoming more and more of an effort. "I'll speak to her about it."

"Why can't I have Wanda?"

"She's with another customer."

"Then put me with Francie. I always liked her."

"She left to work at a salon in Mount Washington."

"Probably running for her life," Tess said under her breath.

"Don't mutter," Gramma said. "If you have something to say, say it."

"Be nice, everyone," Judith pleaded. A whistling Uncle Donald wandered away, as if he didn't know this trio of querulous women, and developed a sudden fascination with the hair accessories in the display case by the front door.

"Let's just forget the whole thing," Gramma said suddenly. "I don't like the idea of someone new touching my head."

"But you've had Lisa," the receptionist said, a little desperately.

"Put me down for next Wednesday. And make a note: no Russians, no strangers, no gum-snappers. I want Wanda, you understand. Wanda for shampoo, Michael for my set. Donald, bring the car around. We'll just have an earlier lunch than we planned at S'n'H."

Uncle Donald jumped, as if he were a twelve-year-old boy again. Judith smiled feebly at the glaring receptionist, while Tess stared at the ceiling. *One big happy*, she thought.

* * *

EVEN WITH GRAMMA ALONG, IT WAS NICE TO BE BACK AT S'N'H, AS THE old-timers all referred to the Suburban House restaurant. S'n'H was a sanctuary, a windowless, timeless place with desserts to die for and placemats with supposed-to-be-funny Yiddish translations. Oivay, for example, was translated as April fifteen, a bris was "getting tipped off," and a goy was defined as one who buys retail.

Her breakfast long forgotten, Tess ordered chicken noodle soup with kreplach. ("Kosher-style ravioli," according to the menu.) Gramma decided on a potato pancake, while Uncle Donald chose cheese blintzes and a side order of herring. Judith wanted nothing more than an iced tea.

"That's right, Judith," Gramma said approvingly. "You'll keep *your* figure."

That was the cue for Uncle Donald, who acted as the peacemaker in those rare moments when he realized there was peace to be made. "Has your lawyer finalized the division of that property yet, Mama? If you have any trouble with any of the government agencies involved, you just let me know."

"Not to worry, it's almost done. I'm having a crab feast next Wednesday night and we'll have a little celebration then, sign all the papers together." Even kosher Jews ate crabs in Baltimore, as if there were some unwritten exemption in the dietary laws. "That's why it's important for me to go back to the beauty parlor before then. Can you take me next week, Donald? I know how hard it is for you to get away from work." Not for Judith, Tess noted, who actually did work at work. Hard for Donald, who didn't really do anything.

"A crab feast in your apartment?" Judith asked. "But crabs are so messy, Mama, you really need to do them outdoors, with picnic tables and newspaper."

"I know. I thought we'd do it at your place. You have such a nice yard. And if we do it outside, you won't have to clean. Working as you do, I know it's hard for you to keep on top of the house cleaning."

Time for Tess to jump into the cross-hairs. Conversation with Gramma was a little like running through a sniper's alley, each family member taking a turn as the target.

"Did you subdivide the land so each one has his or her own parcel, or are you transferring the deed so we're all listed as the owners?"

"One piece, so it's all for one, one for all. My children and grandchildren are going to have to learn to get along eventually."

A new complaint. Hand it to Gramma—at an age where most people declined to take on anything different, she was always open to new grievances.

"We all get along okay," Tess said tentatively. Gramma was spoiling for a fight this morning. The skirmish at the Beauty Palace had only whetted her appetite.

"You're hard on Deborah, Theresa Esther. She thinks you don't respect her because she's just a full-time mother and you're Miss Big Britches Private Eye, getting written up in the newspaper."

"Did she *say* that?" Tess was surprised. She thought she and Deborah, intense competitors during childhood, had agreed to an adulthood truce. They may not approve of one another, but they didn't call attention to it.

"No, but I can tell. I have a sixth sense about these things."

"Right. And I bet you tell Deborah that I'm, I don't know, jealous of her because she has a husband and a baby, while I'm 'just' a spinster with a struggling business. Does your sixth sense pick that up as well?"

"Mama, did you see Hecht's has a sale on the hose you like so much?" That was Judith, trying to get Gramma's scope trained on her and away from Tess. "Would you like me to pick some up for you this afternoon? As long as I've taken the day off, I might as well put it to good use."

Gramma held her hand up at her only daughter like an impatient traffic cop, her eyes still fixed on Tess's. What had Treasure Teeter called that move? *Doin' the Heisman.*

"There's still time to take your name off that deed, Missy. What do you say to that?"

Tess had much she wanted to say to that. *Go ahead, take it away from me, you bitter old woman. Give my share to one of your beloved china springer spaniels. You can't hold me hostage with money. You're mean and you're petty. Poppa probably died because he couldn't take living with you any more.*

Uncle Donald started whistling another show tune, "Some Enchanted Evening." Judith simply looked miserable, even unhappier than she had when Tess had glimpsed her in the parking lot outside her grandmother's apartment building. But was the cause of her unhappiness her mother or her daughter?

"I say"—Tess took one last glance at Judith's face—"that I'm sorry if I sounded impudent and of course I'm grateful for your generosity. Can I bring anything Wednesday night?"

A PLUMP, VAGUELY FAMILIAR WOMAN WAS WAITING ON TESS'S DOOR-step when Tess returned to her office.

"Miss Monaghan?" She wore a kelly-green suit with a red silk blouse. Merry Christmas, Tess thought, but she was touched at the same time. The woman, whoever she was, considered visiting Keyes Investigations important enough to dress up.

"That's me." Tess unlocked the door. The moment the key was in the lock, she could hear Esskay unfurling herself from the sofa, rushing across the floor with a great clatter of toenails. The dog sounded pretty impressive—she could be a Rottweiler or a pit bull, except for the lack of bark—and the visitor cowered behind Tess.

"The only thing my dog will do is lick you to death," she assured her visitor, who edged through the door, trying to keep Tess between her and the dog. "Now, what can I do for you?"

"Don't you remember me?"

Tess hadn't, at first. She had made the mistake of looking at the clothes, not the woman's face. "Keisha Moore. Donnie's mother. Where's Laylah?"

"My sister-in-law's looking after her."

There was an awkward silence, Tess waiting for Keisha to say why she had come, Keisha apparently waiting for Tess to start asking her questions.

"Is there something I can help you with, Keisha?"

"I heard, on the news, that the man who killed my boy may have killed some other children. The ones you were looking for."

Shit. Tess had counted on the television stations not catching wind of the police department's suspicions unless Beale was officially charged. Either they had more evidence than Tyner thought, or someone at the police station had leaked the story, hoping to turn the heat up on Beale. As a convicted killer, he was a tough man to libel, alas.

"That's just speculation, Keisha."

The green suit was much too tight, and when Keisha sat down, her shiny red blouse seemed to surge out of the top. It was hard for Tess to believe that all this show was just for her.

"Well, if those other ones are dead, who gets their money?"

She certainly was focused. For five years now, Keisha Moore had tried to find a way to turn her son's death into a payday, and she hadn't given up hope there was some cash to be squeezed out of it.

"I regret to tell you there isn't any money for anyone. I thought there was, but it turns out things were not quite as they seemed."

"I heard the girl got her money. It's all over the street."

"You didn't know anything about her when I stopped by your house," Tess pointed out.

"Yeah, well, I just didn't make the connection, you know? I was thinking of some little girl. How much she get, anyway?"

"All Destiny got was a pretty ugly death."

Without realizing it, Keisha was holding the tip of her tongue between her teeth, as unselfconsciously as a child. The tongue disappeared, and her eyes suddenly looked sly.

"Did you help him kill her and her brother, the one who burnt up?"

"Jesus, no. What a horrible thing to ask."

Keisha was unrepentant. "Well, you asked me some pretty rude things when you came to my house. Why was Donnie in foster care, as if that had anything to do with anything. What did I do to lose him? You were worse than any cop or social worker. That's the worst thing about being poor, having to answer people's goddamn questions all the time. *'You own a car? You got any money in savings? You got a man living with you? Who's your baby's father?'* I get sick of it, okay?"

"I can understand that."

"Huh. Like you ever had to answer some nosy bitch's questions."

"I was on unemployment for a while. Trust me, I answered my share of questions."

Keisha didn't seem mollified. She slumped in her chair, chin lowered to her scarlet chest, glaring at Tess.

"Do you need money, Keisha?"

"You know anyone who doesn't?" she countered.

"It's early in the month to be running short."

"I had some . . . unexpected expenses. There's a dining room set I put money down on. If I don't make a payment today, I'm going to lose it." So the Christmas finery was for the guy at the furniture store. Tess didn't want to think about what Keisha might do in lieu of payment. Jackie was right. She had never really known what it was like to scrape bottom, or even how far down the bottom was.

"I might be able to help you out. But first, I want to ask you some of the same questions I asked you before. Only this time, I'd like some answers."

Keisha's eyes were amber, Tess noticed. A cold, hard amber with a swirl of green at the center of the iris.

"I'll get my dining room set?"

"You'll get your furniture," Tess assured her. "Now why was Donnie in foster care?"

"I went off on an errand, up to Atlantic City. I thought I'd be home that night, but there was, like, an accident. When his teacher found out Donnie had spent the night alone, the Social Services came and took him."

"A car accident? A breakdown?"

Keisha squirmed a little in her chair, but said nothing.

"If I call a friend in New Jersey, am I going to find out you have a record?" Tess didn't actually have any friends in New Jersey, but Keisha didn't know that. It was plausible. Someone must have a friend in New Jersey.

"I was a mule, okay? I was a mule and I got popped."

"A mule?"

"I carried drugs for a man. I was taking them to Atlantic City on the train, and they picked me up the second I got off. The public defender up there got me off—he asked for a lab test and it turned out the stupid-ass motherfucker had put me on the train with a case of powdered sugar and quinine. But by the time I got home, I'd been gone for a week, and they had taken Donnie. He had to go to school and flap his big mouth about how he didn't have no mama and he was living off cereal. Social Services told me he couldn't come home until I took some class about how to be a parent. I had two more classes to go when he was killed."

"The man you carried the drugs for—was he Donnie's father?"

"No." Keisha's look told Tess that she found the question incredibly stupid. "He was just some guy I was with for a while."

"What was his name?"

"Look, he's dead. What you need to know his name for? He was a stupid, stone-ass junkie and he ended up the way most junkies do. I may have tried to help him sell some drugs, but I never took any."

"The guy you're with now, Laylah's father—he's not part of that life, is he?"

"Don't worry. I'm not planning on being the same fool twice." Keisha stood, her curves shifting again. She was like a big, walking Jell-O mold of a woman. She opened her purse, a bright yellow bag bigger than some suitcases. "You got any more questions, or can I go get me my dining room set now? I owe $119 on it. You can just round it up to $120 if you need to go to the ATM to get it."

"I said I'd get you furniture. I didn't say it would necessarily be the furniture you had paid down on."

Keisha's mouth was a round little O of rage, although no sound came out. If she hadn't been wearing her Sunday best, she might have flown across the desk at Tess. Instead, she snapped her purse shut, stamped her feet, stamped her feet some more. Tess ignored her dramatics, scrawling a set of numbers on a piece of paper.

"There's a man named Spike Orrick," she said, passing the paper to Keisha. "Call him at this number, and say Tesser sent you. It's important that you refer to me as Tesser, that's how he'll know I gave you this number. He'll get you the furniture you need by nightfall and some food, too. He may even throw in a new television set, or a stereo, if he has one handy."

Keisha looked at the piece of paper skeptically. "We talking new furniture, or some secondhand shit?"

"It will be as nice as whatever you picked out, probably nicer," Tess assured her. "And Keisha?"

"Yeah?"

"Why don't you have Spike throw in a changing table? On me."

EIGHTEEN

THE BUTCHER OF BUTCHERS HILL WAS BACK. WITH A VENGEANCE. ONE might say. Certainly, that was what every single television reporter in Baltimore felt obligated to say, as if they were all working from the same handbook of tasteless clichés.

Tess and Kitty watched the six o'clock news together that night in Kitty's kitchen, clicking from channel to channel in order to see the same five-year-old footage unspool again and again. As Tyner had predicted, the police didn't have enough evidence to charge Luther Beale. As Tess had suspected, that didn't keep the media from going hog-wild with the story. On each of Baltimore's four early evening newscasts, another solemn face beneath another fluffy head of hair recounted the same scant details: Beale questioned in murders of teenage twins who had testified against him. No charges filed. At least one resourceful reporter then resorted to the time-honored punt of journalists everywhere: the man on the street, live and uncensored.

"I think we need more people like Luther Beale," said a balding white man identified as Joe of Remington, a scrappy, lower-middle-class neighborhood. "I mean, who did he kill? Three punks. A delinquent, a whore, and a druggie. This city could use a few more Luther Beales."

Words to warm Martin Tull's heart, Tess thought. He wasn't the primary on the case, thank God, but she knew he wouldn't give up on trying to get her to talk to the police. Tull had a zealot's conviction when it came to Luther Beale, and the case seemed to become more personal for him every day.

On camera, Joe kept speaking, his features pinched in an uglier and uglier rage, but with voice-over narration from the anchor substituting for his other thoughts on the case. You didn't have to be a particularly good lip-reader to make out the non-FCC-sanctioned words flying from Joe's mouth, along with a few choice racial epithets. Another drawback of doing man-on-the-street interviews. Sometimes, the man said what he really thought.

"Now what's the point of giving air time to someone like that?" Kitty asked, genuinely puzzled.

"Don't you know, that's their version of providing 'both' sides of the story," Tess said. "On the one hand, killing is wrong. On the other hand, what if you kill the right people? Jesus Christ. Have you noticed no one is entertaining the notion Beale didn't do it? At least Tyner was smart enough to keep Beale away from reporters. If it gets out he doesn't think he killed Donnie Moore, he's going to look like a lunatic."

"How can you work for him if you don't believe him?"

"I believe he didn't kill the Teeter twins. I believe he saw a car and heard something the night Donnie was killed. Did someone else shoot Donnie Moore? I don't know and it's not important. For what it's worth, I believe *he* believes in his innocence, but Luther Beale is a man who likes to be right. Over the past five years, he may have gone over and over that night in his mind until he's found a way to clear himself. It doesn't matter. They're not going to try him again for the death of Donnie Moore."

"It seems to me everyone is overlooking one possibility in this," Kitty said, switching the television to a cooking show on one of the cable channels. Kitty didn't like to cook any more than Tess did, but she liked to watch. "This could be a coincidence. A hideous, totally random event."

"What do you mean?"

"Destiny had a habit of getting into strange men's cars, right? Treasure just had a habit. They lived high-risk lives. If you have a sister who hang-glides and a brother who sky-dives, would it be so unusual if each died within a few weeks of each other? It would be strange and stunning, worth a story in a newspaper, but it wouldn't be unheard of. You read about leukemia clusters, strange concentrations of cancer cases in certain places, like the one up in Massachusetts, but they can never quite prove the link. I think there are sorrow clusters, too, unexplained critical masses of tragedy."

Tess considered this. Kitty's logic was screwy yet appealing. But she didn't buy it, even if a Baltimore jury might.

"I think the two deaths *are* connected. Treasure said Destiny had gone somewhere, and when she came back, they were going to be rich. He said she had gone to Burma. Maybe that's some new street term for selling drugs."

"I think Burma's called Myanmar now."

"Do you expect some kind of geographic exactness in the local drug trade? Look, Keisha Moore told me today about being a 'mule,' an unwitting delivery woman for some dealer. I wonder if Destiny got caught up in something like that, and someone killed Treasure, thinking his drug-addled brain could hold onto enough details to be dangerous."

"I like my theory," Kitty said stubbornly. "Sorrow clusters."

"So it does," Tess said. "Shit, look at the time. If I'm late for my second night of telemarketing, the boss will have my head. I thought having my own business meant not answering to anyone. But clients expect far more than my bosses ever did."

"It helped," Kitty said, "that you worked for me and Uncle Donald."

Tess provided dinner for that night's round of calls, carry-out from a storefront more notable for its ambitions than its accomplishments. Butchers Hill Hot Food Hot served pizza, Italian entrees, subs and burgers—"American sandwiches" in the parlance of its menu—along with passable Indian food. It was the latter Tess had chosen, ordering an array of samosas, nan, and a double portion of rogan josh. She also had asked the delivery boy to tuck four bottles of Kingfisher Beer in with the order.

"Look, I need a beer tonight, okay?" she said, when she caught Jackie's disapproving look.

"I didn't say anything," Jackie said, examining the foil containers, the plastic lids fogged over from steam. "From Fresh Fields to the Grease Pits in twenty-four hours. For all you know that's greyhound meat in that so-called lamb dish."

Esskay whimpered, not because she understood Jackie's slur, but because she adored rogan josh and seldom got more than a smear of sauce and a few grains of rice.

"It's better than that fish-and-tofu abomination you brought in here last night. Do you really like that food? Or do you just think you should like it?"

"You know, I think I'll have one of those beers after all. But whatever you do, don't eat or drink while you're on a call. It's too tacky."

THEY HAD STARTED WITH A SENSE OF EXCITEMENT, BUT THE HOURS dragged slowly this time, each call putting them further away from the possibility of an answer. Twenty-four hours ago, victory had seemed so imminient. Even skeptical Tess had become convinced that Jackie's systematic approach would lead them to her daughter. But tonight's calls yielded no new clues. Not a single Caitlin. Not even a thirteen-year-old Kate or Katie. With the end so tantalizingly close, the work became dull and frustrating. Tess raced too quickly through her rehearsed lines, only to repeat them for bewildered listeners. Jackie become impatient and imperious, bullying her Johnsons as if she suspected them of lying about their children's names.

At 9:55, when Tess punched in the number for Wyler Johnston

and heard the quavering voice on the end of the line, she simply hung up.

"That's it," she said. "She's not out there."

"You didn't even ask that household any of the questions," Jackie protested, reaching for Tess's sheet of numbers.

Tess grabbed the paper back from her, tearing it, not caring that she was tearing it: "He sounded as if he was ninety-five. According to the criss-cross, he's lived at that address for forty-five years. Do you really think he's your daughter's adoptive father?"

"He could be her grandfather. And there are still people we haven't made contact with." Jackie began shuffling through her papers. "Maybe we should broaden our search to the whole metro area, canvass anyone with a name close to Johnson and Johnston. Or it could be Jones. Willa Mott's memory isn't perfect, you know, you said so yourself. No one remembers everything just right."

"Jackie—"

Jackie put her hands over her eyes, although Tess suspected it was her ears she really wanted to cover, like a child who chants over words she can't bear to hear.

"Maybe someone else can help you." She tried to sound kind and caring, instead of just tired and frustrated. "I don't know. But I feel like I'm taking your money under false pretenses at this point. We're not getting anywhere here, and I don't know where else to go. Sure, there was a chance that Willa Mott remembered the name right, that the family who took your daughter in was right where they always were, and that they named her Caitlin. But it was always a long-shot. People don't stay in the same place for thirteen years anymore. Maybe the people at the Adoption Rights group have some ideas, but I'm fresh out."

"They don't, you know they don't. The agency was the only lead we have."

"Then you need a private investigator who knows more about this kind of work than I do. The truth is, the other case I'm work-ing on is going to take more and more time. There might be criminal charges, and I'm in pretty deep. You'd be better off working with someone else, someone who can give you first priority."

"No. I want *you* to help me."

They had saved two of the Kingfishers, planning to drink them in a triumphant toast. Tess opened both now and began to pour one in Jackie's glass, but Jackie took the bottle from her and drank straight from it, just as Tess always did.

"Look, it's great that you wanted to give a break to a new businesswoman. But there's got to be some other female private investigator starting out on her own. Go to her."

Jackie had already downed more than a third of her beer. She stared into the bottle as if her daughter might be at the bottom. Tess was remembering how adamant Jackie had been that first day, how sure of herself. *Why did you choose Keyes Investigations? You were in the paper, weren't you? Something about shooting someone or someone shooting you?* Yes, she had been in the paper quite a bit, but not for being a private detective. The announcement of the agency's opening, a paragraph in the *Baltimore Business Journal*, had been a brief item, using the more formal version of her name, Theresa Esther Monaghan. You had to be paying close attention to link the two articles, to know that Tess the near-shooting victim was now the near-entrepreneur.

And you had to be paying really close attention to know of Tess's fondness for chocolate malts, a detail Jackie had known before Tess mentioned it. How can you know what kind of dark smear a kid has on her face in a black-and-white photo? You can know it's chocolate, perhaps, but you can't know it's malt. Yet Jackie had always known.

"It wasn't just a woman you wanted, was it? It's me. It had to be me. Why Jackie?"

Jackie Weir raised her eyes from the bottle and looked at Tess helplessly, as if she could no longer speak. Then she shifted her gaze to the wall, to that photo. The crying girl on the flying rabbit.

"I knew you," she said at last. "When we were younger."

"Were we at Western together?" Jackie could have been a senior when she was a freshman.

"No, at the drugstore," she said, pointing her beer bottle at the photo. "Not that one, the big one, the one on Bond Street."

"The Weinstein flagship on Bond and Shakespeare? That's my Aunt Kitty's bookstore."

"It wasn't then. Not when I was eighteen. Not when you were fifteen. Not when you used to come in after school and drink choc-olate malteds, and talk to your grandfather about your day. Your hair was usually in a long, shiny plait down your back and you were so thin, then, almost scrawny. That must have been when you were running all the time."

"It was. But I don't—" She stopped, embarrassed.

"Don't remember me? There's no reason you would. I was just the girl in the back, flipping burgers. I wore an apron, and a hairnet, and those big glasses. But I could hear you. You told your grandfa-ther about the good grades you were getting and the parties you were going to and what this boy or that boy had said to you. It was like watching a rerun of those old Patty Duke shows, listening to your life."

"Funny, my adolescence seemed more like a sitcom based on Kafka to me."

Jackie heard her, but she wasn't having any of it, any more than she had let Tess see herself as some poor frail female about to plunge through the tattered safety net. "Then last March, I read about you in the paper. Your picture was there, with that dog. Like I said, you look just the same. Later, when I saw you had opened up a private detective agency, I knew I had to hire you. I knew when it became difficult, or rough, you couldn't drop me, like the first de-tective did, or spend my money without getting results, like the second one did. You had to help me. You had to."

"Just because you once worked for my grandfather, because I was out front sipping sodas while you were in the back, making burgers?"

Jackie looked frightened, as if the words she were about to utter were so forbidden, so long unspoken, that she wasn't quite sure what they might do once let loose in the world.

"You have to help me because Samuel Weinstein was my baby's father."

NINETEEN

AS MANY TIMES AS SHE HAD BEEN THERE, TESS ALWAYS NEEDED THE marker of the wheelchair ramp to find Tyner's house in Tuxedo Park. It was so dark in his neighborhood on a summer night—darkness being the perogative of truly safe places as well as the really dangerous ones—and the shingled houses were virtually indistinguishable. Hard enough to find the street, St. John's, much less the house itself. Once she did, she waited on his front porch, drinking from the international six-pack she had assembled at Alonso's Tavern, where they allowed you to mix-and-match the beers. A Red Stripe, a Bohemia, a Royal Oak, a Tsingtao, a Molson, and an Anchor Steam. Around the world in eighty beers.

It was past eleven. The velvety voices of television anchors drifted from open windows, filling the night with authoritative sounds. So emphatic, so sure. You didn't even have to hear the words to know how a story was supposed to make you feel. The pitch told you everything you needed to know. *Bad thing had happened. Important thing had happened. Funny thing had happened. Weather had happened.*

Shit happened. *Where was Tyner, anyway?* Tess drained the Red Stripe. She was halfway through Mexico by the time his van pulled up out front. She called to him as he came up the ramp, so he wouldn't be startled to find her on his shadowy front porch. But nothing ever really surprised Tyner. Lucky him.

"Not a very good training regimen," he observed, looking at the glass bottles at her feet.

"Depends on what you're training for. Where have you been, burning the midnight oil on Luther Beale's case?" She couldn't help sounding a little petulant, as if Tyner should know she would be waiting on his front porch.

"Luther Beale is safe at home, where I expect him to stay unless the police come up with something significantly more substantial than the circumstantial bullshit they threw at us all day. I had a date."

"A date?" She had known women found Tyner attractive, but she hadn't known he actually did anything about it. "Who is she?"

"Another lawyer. No one you know."

"How old is she? Or should I ask, how young is she? Young enough to be your daughter? Young enough to be your grand-daughter?"

"What an odd thing to say."

"Not so very odd."

And she told him everything. She began with her conversation with Jackie, veering off into wild digressions about Willa Mott and Adoption Rights and the leather seats in Jackie's Lexus. Somewhere in the middle of her rambling story, Tyner reached for the Anchor Steam and the bottle opener, but he never spoke. By the time Tess's voice wore down, the street was silent, the televisions long turned off, all the windows dark.

"So I'm looking for my aunt, I figured out," she said. "What's that stupid West Virginia joke, the one about the song. 'I'm My Own Grandpa?' I'm looking for my thirteen-year-old aunt."

"Lots of people have aunts and uncles younger than they are. Given the imperatives of biology, it's not that unusual."

"Jesus, Tyner, there was a fifty-year age difference."

"So?"

"So that's sick."

"It was legal, though. She was of age to give consent."

"He was her boss, which makes it sexual harrassment. And adultery. Which isn't legal in the state of Maryland, no matter how old you are."

"Does Jackie think she was sexually harrassed, or is that your take on it?"

Shrewd Tyner. He always did have a way of knowing what truly bothered her. She was the angry one, not Jackie. The man Jackie remembered—a man she called Samuel, in an affectionate voice that made Tess's skin crawl—had been kind to her. If it hadn't been love between them, it had been a genuine fondness, two lonely, unhappy people finding solace in one another's company. He had given her gifts, encouraged her to think about life beyond the grill at Weinstein's Drugs. When she told him she was pregnant, he had given her money for an abortion, which she had pocketed, knowing she was too far gone for the procedure. He had even offered to help her with college, but his business troubles had kept him from honoring that pledge. Still, Jackie had nothing unkind to say about him. He had never promised to leave his wife for her, she had told Tess. He had never promised anything, except to provide her a corner of warmth and regard in a world that had given her so little of either.

"She's crazy," Tess muttered.

"That's a possibility. Or she could be lying. Remember she lied the first time you met her."

Tess had not thought of this and it was a tempting out. Would Jackie tell such an outlandish story to keep Tess working for her? True, she had known much about Weinstein Drugs, but it was possible she had worked there without being bedded there. Perhaps she had hated her employer and waited all these years to punish his descendants. Tess allowed herself the fleeting pleasure of embracing this theory, then just as quickly discarded it. Not even Gramma Weinstein could have provoked someone into seeking such a convoluted revenge. Besides, there was definitely a daughter out there somewhere, Jackie had convinced her of that much. It suddenly occurred to her that the strange detail Willa Mott had remembered about the father of Jackie's baby was not his race, but his advanced age.

"I'd give anything if I could prove this was all some sick lie, but I can't."

"Why not?"

"Because in my heart of hearts, I know it's true." Tess opened the Royal Oak.

"So what are you going to do?" Tyner asked.

"I don't know. Even if the whole thing didn't make me nauseated, I still maintain she'd be better off with a more experienced investigator. Being related to her daughter doesn't make me any more qualified to find her. Besides, I wasn't bullshitting her. Luther Beale has to be priority one, right?"

She looked at Tyner hopefully, but he had no intention of letting her off the hook.

"Nothing's going to happen with Beale, unless a witness comes forward, or some physical evidence links him to one of those bodies. It was kind of sad about Destiny, actually. One of the reasons they didn't make the ID was because her body looked so used up. They were carrying her as a Jane Doe, twenty-five to thirty-five, and she was only seventeen."

"Well, as long as she looked twenty-five, right?"

"Jesus, Tess. When you turn on someone, you really turn, don't you?"

"I looked like a grown woman when I was fourteen. Do you know what that's like? I couldn't make it the six blocks from the bus stop to home without fielding at least three offers to climb into someone's car. Some of them left me alone when I told them my age. Some of them, especially the geezers, just got a lot more interested. Gee, I wonder why Poppa didn't invite *me* into the back room?"

"Just because a man would want to be with a young woman

doesn't mean he would go after his own granddaughter. Give your grandfather that much credit."

"Sorry, Poppa's account is closed. Gramma's, on the other hand, suddenly shows a huge balance. Maybe that's why she's such a sour old woman, because her husband was diddling the help all those years. I bet Jackie wasn't the only one. Who knows how many undiscovered aunts I have throughout Baltimore?"

Tyner reached for the Molson. "You know, I'm probably as old as your grandfather was when you were a teenager, right?"

"Thereabouts."

"What would you say if I told you my date tonight was twenty-five?"

"You said she was a lawyer."

"There are twenty-five-year-old lawyers."

"Well . . . that's different."

"Why?"

"Because she's older and because—well, it's not like you're having sex with her."

"No, but only because it was our first date. I'm too much of a gentleman to make my move so early. Or did you think we didn't have sex because I'm in a wheelchair?"

"Of course not." Tess's voice was vehement, for that's exactly what she had thought. Sure, older men had sex and men in wheelchairs had sex, but surely the combination disqualified Tyner. She couldn't be more grossed out if her parents had started talking about their sex lives in detail.

"Tess, tell the truth."

"Okay, that is what I meant. But I'm drunk. Book me for TWI—talking while intoxicated." She held up her wrists as if to be handcuffed, and noticed her hands were shaking.

"Meanwhile, there's Kitty," Tyner said, ignoring her outstretched hands. "How old is her current boyfriend? Or how young, I guess I should say. Certainly, she's been with men young enough to be her sons."

"It's not the same. He was in his sixties, she was a girl who *worked* for him. I don't care if she's not angry with him. *I'm* angry. I'm furious. There was a person I loved, and now he's not who I thought he was, and I can't love him anymore. I wish Jackie Weir-Susan King-Mary Browne had never walked through my door."

Her words exploded in the night, as loud and sudden as a car backfire. Someone shouted from a nearby house, "Keep it down out there. This isn't Hampden, you know."

"And this isn't Roland Park, although I bet you tell people it is," Tess called back. She was suddenly sick of Baltimore's little hierarchies, as reflected in the rigid neighborhood system. Roland Park looked down on Tuxedo Park, which felt itself superior to Evergreen, where people fretted they would be mistaken for Hampden-ites, whose feelings were hurt by the suggestion they lived in Remington, where people sneered at Pigtown. On and on, down and down the social ladder. Say you lived near the water tower on Roland Avenue and old-timers asked: Which side? How silly people were, how stupid.

"Well, you're right about at least one thing," Tyner said, when the night was quiet again.

"Yeah? I must have missed it."

"You've had too much to drink. You better bed down in the spare room here, lest you add a DWI to your TWI. At least the latter isn't a felony."

"Why not? It can be just as dangerous."

THE PATAPSCO LOOKED DECEPTIVELY INVITING THE NEXT MORNING, WITH only a few oily spots along the surface. Although Tyner had told Tess to stay close in during her workout, she had ignored him and headed down a narrow tributary, where she knew she would be alone. Few other rowers wanted the hassle of passing beneath the low bridges here, which forced you to bring in your oars, duck your head and use the pilings as hand-holds to get to the other side.

She had not slept well. The beers, the strange night, the strange bed, which made her realize how seldom she slept anywhere except her own lumpy mattress. There had been times in her life when Tess slept around, but she had never slept *around*. She was a homebody.

Yet Jonathan Ross had found her anyway.

Your nightmares always know where to find you, and Tess had been traveling with this particular dream for almost a year now. At first, it was just Jonathan in flight. Lately, though, he had begun to get up, brush himself off and talk to her. He seemed nicer, now that he was dead, and she didn't think it was because she romanticized his memory. She remembered all too clearly what Jonathan had been like alive—arrogant, self-centered, impeccable in his work, duplicitious in his life. Emotional quicksilver. Not that she had absolved herself from responsibility for the unhealthy bond between them. If he were alive, she'd probably still be beating on that sick little triangle of theirs, Jonathan running back and forth between her and his fiancee, trying to stave off being a real grownup for a few more years. Tess, wary of her own adulthood, had been a willing accomplice.

But Jonathan had gotten pious in death. He lectured her, he hectored her. Not that she remembered much of what he said in these dreams. Jonathan's appearances were like hangovers, dull aches that left her feeling she really must behave better next time, even if she didn't quite remember what she had done.

You mustn't be afraid of the truth.

She came to another bridge, but instead of pushing her way through, she held onto the pilings, listening to the humming tires of the cars above her bowed head. Truth. If she had been interested in truth, she would never have gone into journalism, much less the detective business. She was a fact-gatherer, not a truth-teller.

Here was a truth: she loved the little lies she told as a detective, the license it gave her to nudge people along with harmless falsehoods, a practice presumably forbidden in journalism. Assuming there was such a thing as a harmless falsehood. Little white lies. Could you say that now? Or was that non-PC as well, implying as it did that white was better than black.

Little white lies. Big white lies. Poppa Weinstein, kind as Jackie insisted he was, had sent her on her way with cash for an abortion, soothing his own conscience. Now Tess wanted to do the same thing, more or less—send Jackie on her way, the balance of her retainer refunded to her. All for her own good, of course. There had to be better detectives, people with more experience who knew how to do these kinds of things.

But Jackie wanted her. She was—did Tess dare say it, say it out loud, whisper it here on the water—family. There would be time enough to deal with how this fact made her feel. For now, the important thing was finding Jackie's daughter. Poppa's daughter. A thirteen-year-old time bomb sitting out there somewhere, ready to detonate with a blast that could destroy her family. Tess had to find her, if only to protect everyone else from the fallout.

Maybe that's what Jonathan Ross was trying to tell her. Maybe he simply wanted her to go ahead and become a real grownup, seeing as he wasn't going to get the chance.

A MEDIUM-SIZED MEDIA CLOT WAS OUTSIDE TESS'S OFFICE WHEN SHE arrived that morning. Fucking Jackie. She had sold her out, gone public with her daughter's paternity, decided to destroy the whole family.

"Have you spoken to your client today, Miss Monaghan?" asked a breathless young brunette.

"My dealings with clients are confidential," she snapped, unlocking the door and jerking on Esskay's chain. Although the greyhound had already received more than her share of media attention, she was always eager for additional exposure. She faced the cameras delightedly and opened her mouth as if ready to issue a statement.

"But Luther Beale is your client, isn't he?" a man's voice called after her. The pack stayed on the sidewalk, savvy enough not to trespass.

"Luther Beale?"

"The Butcher of Butchers Hill, now a suspect in the deaths of two twins."

"Two twins? As opposed to three triplets or four quadruplets?" Tess was smiling, and not just because of the reporter's redundancy. *Luther Beale.* Thank God. She had forgotten most of the tele-weenies were so new to Baltimore that few of them knew there had ever been a Weinstein's drugstore chain. The only way her grandfather could make news today was if he fathered Madonna's baby.

"Again, that information is confidential," Tess called back. "I'm sure you can appreciate that. After all, you wouldn't want me to tell you if the spouse of one of your general managers had hired a private investigator to find out why he's spending so much time cruising prostitutes. Word is, he's been tooling along Patterson Park every night. And it's not even sweeps month."

"Are you saying—?"

Tess walked back to the door, mindful that she might be able to get some free publicity out of this. "I'm saying Keyes Investigations is a discreet firm, where all clients are assured of absolute confidentiality. As I'm just an associate here, it's impolitic for me to speak for the firm in any event. I do know Tyner Gray is representing Mr. Beale. As for any questions about the agency, you should probably call the owner, Edward Keyes."

"How do we get in touch with either of them?"

"Well, as seasoned investigative reporters, you probably have your own methods. Me, I'd try the phone book." Tess smiled and waved at the cameras, while Esskay poked her nose around the door, wagging her tail in best "Hi, Ma!" fashion. They probably wouldn't make the news—it would have been a much better shot if Tess had ducked her head and run past them. But if they did use the sound bite, viewers would know that Keyes Investigations was scrupulously tight-lipped, pathologically smart-assed, and equipped with a re-markably friendly watchdog.

Tess tried Jackie's pager number and got the voice mail. "I'm in," she told the empty air. "I don't know how I'm going to help you, but I am going to try. But it's a new deal, a new contract, according to my specifications." She then dialed her Uncle Donald's number. Another machine. Underemployed as he was, Uncle Donald made it a point to never answer his phone and to carry a clipboard with him as he roamed the halls, from coffee pot to men's room and back again. It was more important to look busy than be busy, as he had once explained to his niece.

"Favor time," she told the machine. "A big one." Uncle Donald would understand she was going to ask him to do something that was, technically, illegal. He just wouldn't know it involved his own father. That was her new deal. Instead of charging Jackie a fee for her services, all Tess wanted was the guarantee of her silence. Once the girl was found, Jackie had to get out of her life forever.

Esskay's ears, more sensitive than hers, suddenly stood straight up. Tess heard it, too, a creaking sound from the bathroom. Nothing unusual there. The old building often sighed and moaned as it settled. But this sound was unlike any she had heard before. Quietly, she slid her gun out of her knapsack. Perhaps her burglar had come back. Just as quietly, she started to slide her gun back into her knapsack. What if the burglar were bigger than she, or better armed? The gun might provoke him to shoot when he had no intention of doing so. People burgled because they disliked confrontation. Otherwise, they'd be robbers.

She took a dog biscuit out of the cookie jar on her desk and threw it down the hall, just past the bathroom door. Esskay took off, sounding suitably ferocious. She heard a muffled, involuntary cry, the sound of something falling in water, the whine of a window opening too quickly.

A brown topsider was floating in the toilet and a pair of khaki-clad legs was about to disappear through the window when Tess caught her intruder by his sodden ankles. He twisted and fought in her grip, but succeeded only in bumping his head, first on the window sash and then on the old-fashioned bathtub. The second hit gave Tess the opportunity she needed to grab his backpack, which she used to flip him over and straddle him.

"Am I bleeding?" Sal Hawkings asked.

TWENTY

THERE WAS, IN FACT, QUITE A BIT OF BLOOD ON SAL HAWKINGS, WHICH made Tess nervous. What if she had knocked out a tooth or two in the mouth of Maryland's best extemporaneous speaker? But the blood came from a gash on his forehead and although there was a lot of it, the wound was superficial. She gave him a wad of paper towels to stem the flow, but it was too late to save his white shirt and navy blazer.

"Shouldn't you wash it?" he asked worriedly. "That bathroom floor was pretty dirty. I could get an infection."

"What do I look like, the school nurse?"

"No, she's fat, wears bright red lipstick, and spends most of her time smoking on the loading dock behind the dining hall."

Very charming. Or would be if Tess was amenable to being charmed just now. She folded up another wad of paper towels and passed it to Sal.

"I could take you to a hospital emergency room if you like. After I call the police, of course, and Penfield. You're AWOL, I assume?"

"Why would you drop the dime on me?" Must be hard, keeping up with the current slang while ensconced at Penfield. Tess wondered if Sal tried to impress his well-heeled classmates by playing the part of the savvy street kid. If so, he really ought to be a little more current. *Drop the dime.* She figured if she knew a term, it was long out of date.

"You broke into my office, second time in a week that's happened. Someone was in here over the weekend, too. Maybe it was you."

"I didn't even know you existed until you came to my school Tuesday morning."

"Chase Pearson knew who I was, though. I wonder—is it possible he started working on my little dossier before I called him? He pulled together quite a bit of information in a short time."

"You'd have to ask him."

"Perhaps I will. But for now, you're here and he's not." Sal's knapsack was sitting on her desk, a much nicer, newer version of the one she carried. Its leather wasn't as scarred or stained. She pulled it into her lap and undid the shiny brass buckle.

"That's illegal search and seizure."

"Only if you're a cop." Tess pulled out a notebook, two pens, a small leather case that carried a set of screwdrivers, and an old, thick book bound in faded green cloth. The letters on the spine had almost been rubbed off over the years. *The Kipling Compendium*, the book Sal had been reading in the library.

"What are the screwdrivers for? Just burglary, or boosting cars, too?"

Sal scowled. "I take wood shop. The screwdrivers were a gift from Mr. Pearson. Besides, I told you, I wasn't here this weekend. You can check with Penfield if you don't believe me."

"You definitely were here this morning." Tess gestured to his soggy topsider, dark with water, drying in a patch of sun on the windowsill. "Quite a little Cinderella act."

"I wasn't breaking in exactly."

"No, you appeared to be breaking *out*. Which raises the question of how you got in to begin with. I didn't go to Penfield, but I think that follows logically. What goes out must have come in."

Maryland's best extemporaneous speaker, middle school division, was briefly silent. Tess picked up the telephone and dialed 311. Busy, of course, so she faked getting a connection. "Eastern District—I have a burglary I'd like to report on—"

Sal reached over and depressed the disconnect button. "Mr. Pearson came to school the day before yesterday and told me they were going to take Luther Beale in."

Going to take—Chase Pearson had good sources. He had known about Beale's arrest before it happened. Tess said nothing, just put the phone back in the receiver and waited, hoping Sal would keep talking if she didn't.

"I know Beale hired you to find all of us. You found me. You found Treasure. You couldn't find Destiny because Beale had already killed her."

"That hasn't been established, Sal. Far from it."

"Sure." He gave her a superior look, as if she were hopelessly naive. It was strange to be on the receiving end of a look like that from a seventeen-year-old kid, but Sal almost carried it off.

"What do you want, Sal?"

Here came the charm again—the bright eyes, the eager smile. "I was wondering if you know where Eldon is. Of all us who lived at the Nelsons', we were the closest. I mean, everybody was close, living in a three-bedroom house like that, but Eldon was my special buddy, you know. We were tight. I wrote him letters for a while, after they split us up, but he never wrote back. Eldon wasn't much for writing."

Sal Hawkings looked so rueful that Tess almost felt sorry for him. After all, she knew what it was like to have a best friend who didn't write. Whitney was given to beautiful gifts and the occasional hour-long phone call out of the blue, but she wouldn't sit down and compose a letter with a gun pointed at her bright blond head. The written lines of communication between Bond Street and Tokyo had been decidedly one way.

"Eldon's trail is pretty cold," she said. "According to records, he's wanted on a bench warrant because he failed to show up for a hearing. That was about seven months ago. My guess is he left the state. He's probably taking great care not to be found."

"Eldon's only seventeen, two months younger'n me. How'd he end up in the adult system?"

"I guess he was so precocious they skipped him ahead."

Sal Hawkings wasn't amused. "Hey, Eldon's good people. If he ran, it's probably because he didn't even do it, but doesn't know how to get anyone to believe him. He just doesn't know there's any other life, okay? He's just trying to get by."

"You learned there was another life, though. Think about it, Sal. Five kids living in the Nelsons' house on Fayette Street. One was shot. One took drugs, one turned tricks, and now one is a felon on the run. You got out because Chase Pearson helped you, but Pearson wouldn't have helped you if you hadn't started winning all those public speaking awards. What made you different, Sal? What separated you from the others?"

Sal scowled, folding his arms tight across his chest as if to keep Tess from peering into his heart, his soul. "Now you sound like the psychologist at Penfield. Everyone always poking at me, wanting to know why, why, why. Some dude from the University of Maryland even wanted to write a paper on me. 'Sal H. A Success Story in Spite of the Odds.' "

"Did he?"

"Hell, no. Mr. Pearson said he wasn't going let them turn me into some damn syndrome. I'm just a kid, just myself, you know. You can't take me apart and find the answer to all the world's problems. They made me feel like some freak." Sal put on a Massachusetts accent, in apparent mimicry of someone, and stroked his chin. Was he playing the social worker, the psychologist, or just some generic busybody? "My God—a black male who thinks! Who wishes to better himself! What could it possibly mean?"

"They meant well," Tess said, somewhat defensively. After all, she had been asking the same thing in a slightly different fashion. "If they can figure out why you succeeded, maybe they can help other kids."

"Sure." He gave her the superior look again. "Maybe I succeeded because I'm special. Isn't that an option?"

"Oh, you're very special. Public speaker, star student, and a little burglar in training, hanging halfway out my bathroom window."

"I told you. I wanted to know where Eldon was."

"Yes, but did you come down here to ask me, or to search my office for that information? If you really wanted to see me, you could have made an appointment."

"I don't think Mr. Pearson would let me see you."

"Probably not. How did you get away from Penfield, anyway?"

"We had a field trip to the National Aquarium and the Columbus Center this morning. I grabbed a cab and came over here. When I saw all those reporter types out front, I decided to go around the alleyway."

Good story, smoothly told. But that was Sal Hawkings's particular talent, wasn't it? Thinking on his feet, making things sound smooth and plausible.

"Tell me about the car, Sal."

"It was a Checker cab, nothing special. Polish dude at the wheel, barely spoke English, had some lame-ass radio station on."

He couldn't be that dense. It was almost as if he knew the question was coming, and had a dodge prepared. "Not the car that brought you here. The car that was turning onto Fairmount Avenue the night Donnie was killed."

"I don't know what you're talking about." The answer was prompt, too prompt. It was if Sal had learned a part so well that he could still slip into it on a moment's notice, the way Tess could recite the memorized dialogues from junior high French class after all these years. *Bonjour Jean, comment vas-tu? Dis donc, ou est la bibioteque?*

"Luther Beale told me there was a car and two shots, shots he didn't fire. Yet none of you mentioned the car, or any other gunshots. You all told the same exact story, with the same details. But Luther says Destiny and Treasure had already rounded the corner, and even Eldon's back was still to him when he started firing. You couldn't have all seen the same thing."

"He's a damn liar. We wouldn't do that, okay? We were a posse, we stuck together, we wouldn't abandon one of our own. We ran afterward, after Donnie was dead, because we were scared. Who wouldn't be? He was going to kill us, too."

"And there was no car?"

"No car, no second shooter, no O. J. Simpson, okay? That's why the old man's killing the rest of us, you know, because once we're all dead, there won't be anyone to contradict his sorry lies, and he wins. But he did it. He's just gonna have to learn to live with that, the way we had to live with Donnie's death and the way they broke us up, sending us to new families."

Sal grabbed his knapsack and began throwing in the items Tess had spread out on her desk. Tess let him have everything except the Kipling, which she hugged to her chest. She suspected it was the one thing he wouldn't leave the office without, and he did look anxious when he saw it in her hands.

"You don't see a lot of kids reading Kipling these days, although in my day, we had to memorize reams of it. But I guess Penfield is kind of old-fashioned."

"Gimme that. It's *mine*."

She flipped through the pages. The old color plates were quite beautiful, if a little worse for wear. There was the female of the species, so much more deadly than the male, the road to Mandalay and, of course, good old Gunga Din. "*Merry Christmas, Love, Grand-mere,*' " was inscribed on the frontispiece. Tess guessed that faded, cursive inscription had not been written to Sal. Both the book and the handwriting were at least forty years older than he was.

"That's mine," he repeated, his voice a childish whine. "It's the first book I ever owned, it was a gift from Mr. Pearson. At Penfield, the poetry is all those modern guys, Kunitz and Cummings and Merwin and shit. I'd rather read this."

"I'm not sure I'd agree with your assessment of modern poets, but I am impressed if you read Kipling for pleasure. You're a better man than I am, Gunga Din."

Sal looked at her sullenly, hand outstretched. Probably he thought it was a racial slur, non-PC at the very least, likening him to the faithful water boy. She handed him the book and he brushed its spine before putting it back in his knapsack, as if her touch had contaminated it in some way.

"How will you explain the cut on your head when you join up with your class at the aquarium?"

"I'll think of something," he said, shouldering his book bag, checking the brass fastener to make sure the Kipling was safe inside, then taking his shoe from the windowsill.

Tess had no doubt of that. It was all too clear that Sal Hawkings could think on or off his feet. She watched him go, his right topsider still squishing a bit.

TWENTY-ONE

UNCLE DONALD WORKED FAST WHEN HE HAD SOMETHING TO DO. TESS and Jackie were instructed to meet him Monday morning at his office in the Department of Human Resources. The destination made Tess nostalgic, for the agency was housed in the old Hutzler's, once the city's grandest department store. Ten stories high, so full of things to buy and covet that it had a second building to the south to catch the overflow. Tess had bought her first makeup here, cutting school and taking the #10 bus downtown. By today's standards—department stores with grand pianos and marble floors and espresso bars—the old Hutzler's wouldn't seem quite so grand. But something caught in Tess's throat when she saw what it had been reduced to, just another state office building with flimsy walls and little warrens of offices.

"Let's take a walk," Uncle Donald said when he met them in the lobby, clipboard in hand.

Glancing at his watch, he led them to the Light Rail stop around the corner and sat on the benches, the ones designed so homeless people could never stretch out along their length.

"As soon as I started making inquiries, I was told there was a judge," Uncle Donald began. "He does this for a fee, usually."

"How much?" Jackie asked.

"Ten thousand dollars."

"I have that." And Jackie actually took out her check book and her Mont Blanc pen. No ordinary Bics for Jackie. Uncle Donald put his hand over hers before she could start filling it out. Tess could just imagine what she might have written there. *Pay to the order of judge-so-and-so. Ten Thousand Dollars. For: just a little bribe.*

"It's strictly a cash business, dear. Besides, I said he usually does this. When I told him of your situation, he said he can't help. See, all he can do is unseal the original birth certificate. But you know what's on that, right? And there's nothing that connects the original birth certificate with the second one issued."

"Another dead-end," Jackie said bitterly. "From everything I've learned, it sounds as if my daughter could find me pretty easily, but I'll never be able to find her."

The Light Rail train pulled up just then, half-empty as usual. A tall, broad-shouldered man with curly blond hair poking out from beneath the brim of a Yankees cap got off and sat down next to them, studying the sports pages of the *New York Post*. He wore a denim shirt, untucked, faded jeans and dirty-white Chuck Taylors. Normally, wearing a Yankee cap in Baltimore was akin to sporting a "kick me" sign, but it was hard to imagine anyone bothering this man. It wasn't just his size. He carried himself with an assurance as formidable as it was irritating to Tess. She disliked natural self-confidence, given how much she had to work at faking it.

"If you're headed to Camden Yards, you're about six blocks too far north," Tess told the man, put off by his invasion of their personal space. What kind of creep sat down right next to you when there were plenty of benches free? "If you're heading for Yankee Stadium, that's two hundred miles to the north."

"Believe me, I know where I can go when I want to watch some real baseball," the man said in a quiet voice, his eyes focused on the box scores. "The Yankees are only three back in the all-important loss column. Only three back in the loss column, five out of first place. You know baseball? You understand the significance of that?"

"We're sort of having a private conversation here, and it's not about baseball geekery."

"Donald, you might want to tell this woman who I am. Well, not who I am, but why I'm here."

"Tess, Miss Weir, call this gentleman Mr. Mole."

"What, are we playing *Wind in the Willows* all of a sudden?" Tess asked. "Dibs on being Mr. Toad."

Mr. Mole studied her, but not with the squinty, sun-averse gaze of his namesake. He had bright blue eyes, eyes that burned so bright they seemed freezing cold. He easily won the stare-down.

"Mr. Mole works in the Health Department," Uncle Donald said. "He has access to birth certificates, which are private under Maryland law. As I said, we know what's on the original birth certificate, because Jackie filled that out herself. What Mr. Mole proposes to do is go through all the birth certificates in the eighteen months following the birth of Jackie's daughter."

Tess didn't see how this would work any better than everything they had tried. "How can you match the new certificate to the old? At this point, we're not sure of any of the clues we started with—not the name, not the parents' names, not their location. For all we know, everything we were told was a lie, or just flat-out wrong."

"I don't need a name," Mr. Mole said. "I can immediately narrow my search to any certificate that has a different issue date than the date of birth. That's the tip-off, you see, it indicates there was an adoption. Otherwise, the two dates are the same."

"How broad a field of possibilities are we talking here?" Tess asked, still skeptical.

"Pretty small, actually. The certificate had to be issued through the city, because that's where the adoption took place. It has to be a girl. I'm going to go through the county records, just in case, but I'm confident I'll find it in the city records. This baby was biracial, right?"

"Right," Jackie said, glancing sideways at Tess, checking to make sure she was allowed to give this much information. She had immediately understood and accepted Tess's condition that the Weinstein family be sheltered from the exact details.

"Once you have the parents' names and the kid's name, you'll be amazed at how easy it is to find them. Computers today—"

"I know all about computers today," Tess said. Even to her own ears, she sounded like a cranky, know-it-all child.

Jackie was pulling out her checkbook and Mont Blanc pen again. "So how much do I owe you for this?"

Mr. Mole shook his head. "No money."

Now Jackie was the skeptical one. "Then why do it? What's in it for you?"

"I'm adopted. When I started at the Health Department, they showed me how to pull birth certificates and I found the original of my certificate, with the name of my mother on there. It was supposed to be under seal, but it's a bureaucracy, you know? It involves people and people fuck up. I found my mom. She had lived two miles from me the whole time I was growing up. It didn't change my relationship with my 'real' Mom and Pop, but it made me feel as if some question had been answered. Why shouldn't I give other people a shot at the same deal?"

They could hear the rumble of the next Light Rail train approaching from the south. Mr. Mole stood and tossed his newspaper in the waste bin.

"I need to know what the original birth certificate says, just in case. Donald told me it was a baby girl born August eleventh, thirteen years ago this summer, right? What does the certificate say for mother and father?"

Tess looked anxiously at Jackie. They hadn't anticipated this question.

"Mother, Susan King," Jackie said. "Father unknown."

The Light Rail's squealing brakes covered the sound of Tess's relieved sigh. She didn't know if Jackie had told the truth or not about the father being listed as unknown, but she was keeping her end of the bargain. Mr. Mole wasn't searching for the original birth certificate, anyway. And if he should see it, Tess knew he would be discreet. Mr. Mole wasn't someone she could like, but she had a feeling he was someone she could trust. He boarded the train without a backward look.

Uncle Donald stood, clipboard at the ready. "Back to work. I have many corridors to roam, many cups of coffee to drink before this day is through."

"How long before we hear from Mr. Mole?" Jackie asked.

"No idea. He'll signal me with a coded memo. Truthfully, I think he likes making this a little more mysterious than it has to be. It's not that exciting, you know, working at the Health Department."

"How did you find him, anyway?" Tess thought Mr. Mole looked vaguely familiar, like an old *Star* reporter who had gone to work as a Public Information Officer for the state when the paper folded, then later dropped out of sight completely.

"A guy who *doesn't* charge for information? Oh, honey, he's famous in my little network. Scares the piss out of people. A few more like him, and the whole system collapses." Whistling to himself—"Hey, There" was today's selection—Uncle Donald headed back into DHR and another long day of underemployment.

TESS AND JACKIE WERE IN UNSPOKEN AGREEMENT THAT IT WAS BAD luck to be too optimistic. They had thought they were close before, only to find themselves completely stymied. So they did not discuss Mr. Mole when they stopped for lunch at the Women's Industrial Exchange, or anything about the case at all. Which left them with very little to say.

"I can't believe this place almost closed down," Jackie said, for the second time since they had been seated.

"It's okay, if you've got a thing for tomato aspic."

"I have to admit, I always feel cheated when I don't get Miss Marguerite as my waitress." Jackie was chattering, as Tess had once chattered to her, trying to get a response. "Do you think they re-serve her for the big shots, like Jim McKay, since she had her little cameo in *Sleepless in Seattle*?"

"I don't know," Tess said listlessly. "Why would you want to be waited on by a ninety-seven-year-old woman, anyway? Besides, she's retired."

"It's all part of the experience."

"It just reminds me to start a retirement fund so I'm not waiting tables at ninety-seven."

"You haven't done that yet? Girl, you really need to get with it. I hate to be the one to tell you, but this is your life. You may be waiting for something to happen, but it already has. Your life is here."

They fell silent, Jackie fiddling with her tomato aspic, Tess eating a Charlotte Russe, because it was what she really wanted and she didn't see the need of faking her way through a BLT or a tuna salad for the privilege of dessert. She was a big girl now, she could eat what she wanted, when she wanted.

"You sure you don't still have an eating disorder?" Jackie asked.

"This is proof positive that I'm cured."

Another awkward silence. She and Jackie had just been getting to the point where they could almost speak, instead of fencing clumsily with one another. But since Jackie's revelation—was it really just four nights ago?—Tess could barely make eye contact with the other woman. Long disdainful of the modern mania for apologies, she now saw some sense in it. She wanted to apologize to Jackie for everything—for her grandfather, for being born poor and black, which had led to her job at Weinstein's Drugs and her treat-ment at the hands of Samuel Weinstein. That Jackie didn't see her-self as a victim was further proof she was, to Tess's way of thinking. Like someone with Stockholm Syndrome, she had fallen in love with her oppressor. Well, not in love, but something like it. A form of bondage she had confused with love.

"I always forget," Jackie said, putting down her fork. "The Women's Industrial Exchange is famous for its tomato aspic, so I order it. But I don't actually like tomato aspic."

Tess picked at her Charlotte Russe. Either it wasn't as good as she remembered, or else everything was beginning to taste like sawdust.

AT LEAST THE MEDIA CIRCUS HAD FINALLY DECAMPED OUTSIDE TESS'S office. With no charges immediately forthcoming against Luther Beale, the television reporters had decided to pursue other scenarios, all tricked out with libel-proof question marks. Is there a serial killer in East Baltimore? Tess had heard that rhetorical question posed just this morning, as she dressed for work. The answer, of course, was no, unless one wanted to change the definition of serial killer, but no one actually cared about answers in the case of Luther Beale.

It was a relief to sit quietly at her desk in the twilight, to be free for a few minutes of the endless visitors who had paraded through here over the past two weeks. Beale, Jackie, Detective Tull, Keisha Moore, Sal Hawkings. So many people desiring her help, so few willing to pay for it. At least Beale and Jackie had given her money.

But they hadn't been much more honest than anyone else. Beale and Jackie had revealed their true motives only when necessary. Sal had wanted to find Eldon, but she still didn't understand why that involved coming in through her bathroom window. Well, he wouldn't be visiting again any time soon. The bathroom window had a spanking brand-new deadbolt and was now nailed in place. Tess believed in overkill.

Now Keisha Moore, she had been straightforward. She had wanted money. For a new dining room set. She had even been precise about the amount, $119. But then, lies were always precise. That was one of the secrets of "the women who walked," piling on the details until you were dizzy, or just bored enough to pay them to leave you alone. They really wanted cash, and not for the things they claimed to need. Maybe Keisha had been so angry at Tess's bait-and-switch with the furniture because there was no dining room set, no down payment coming due. Maybe it had been another ploy to get cash, quick. But why? She had been dressed up, and the oversized purse she had carried was big enough to be an overnight bag.

Keisha had come to Tess because she had heard something, something about Beale and Destiny and money. It always came back to that for Keisha: My son is dead. What's it worth? But what had she heard? How much did she really know?

Tess grabbed Esskay's leash off its peg by the door and tucked her gun in the outside pocket on her knapsack. It wasn't the safest ten blocks between Butchers Hill and Keisha's rowhouse, but the almost-summer sky was still light and Esskay could look intimidating from a distance. They took off at a semitrot, although the dog kept slowing down to enjoy the strange smells of an unfamiliar route.

TESS COULD HEAR LAYLAH'S CRIES A BLOCK AWAY. THE BABY SOUNDED frantic, but exhausted, as if she had been screaming for hours and no one had come. Great. Keisha was back to her old ways, despite all her promises and assurances.

"She ain't been crying that long," said an old woman sitting on the stoop next door, as Tess charged up Keisha's steps. "It's good for her. Keisha spoils that baby something awful."

Laylah was having trouble catching her breath now, so her cries came out in little stutters, weaker and weaker. Tess pounded on the door, then brought her leg up and kicked it, flat-footed. It buckled slightly, but held, apparently the best-made door in all of East Baltimore.

"You got a warrant?" asked the Dr. Spock of the stoop. Tess ignored her, running around to the alley in back. Keisha's house had a small square of concrete for a backyard, surrounded by a chain-link fence. The gate was fastened with a padlock, but the fence was only waist-high. Tess hooked Esskay's leash to the gate, then climbed over it. The kitchen door was open, the storm door pulled to and locked. Tess glanced through its murky panes, seeing nothing. She thought she could force it by sheer will, but this door also held fast, no matter how she yanked at it or kicked. She ended up using her gun to break the lower pane of glass and reached in to depress the button that held the door in place.

She found Laylah in a small room at the top of the stairs, sitting in a wooden crib from the fifties, the pre-Consumer Safety kind with wooden slats and toxic decoupages of pastel animals with lunatic grins and silky eyelashes. Tentatively, Tess reached for her, thinking a stranger might make the baby more hysterical. But the little girl dug her tiny fingers into her arms, as if Tess were a log floating by in a flash flood.

Still, she kept crying. No wonder. Laylah stank. Tess held the baby at arm's length, looking at her dubiously. She hadn't changed a diaper since her baby-sitting days, almost fifteen years gone. But how hard could it be? She found a fresh diaper and a box of wipes in the bathroom, then looked around for a place to change her. There was the changing table, Keisha must have called Uncle Spike after all. Diaper-changing was easier than Tess remembered. Thank God for disposable diapers with sticky tabs, one of the great technical innovations of the age.

Laylah continued to cry, although the tenor had changed slightly. She wasn't as panicky, now she sounded adamant, demanding. It was the same tone Esskay's whining noises took on when supper was overdue. Tess carried Laylah downstairs—there *was* a new dining room set, she hadn't noticed it in her mad rush upstairs—and rummaged through the kitchen. A can of formula, which she didn't have a clue how to prepare, a bottle with what she hoped was apple juice sitting in the refrigerator. Laylah sucked, temporarily appeased.

But what to do now? If she called Social Services, Laylah would be in foster care within hours. Surely, that would be preferable to leaving her in Keisha's "care." Still, maybe Keisha had a good excuse. She hadn't been lying about the furniture. Maybe she had left the baby with someone who had wandered off, her careless sister-in-law, or some neighborhood kid. Tess paced the empty dining room, rocking Laylah. Her repertoire of baby-care skills was pretty much depleted. If Keisha didn't show up soon, she'd have to call DSS or the cops.

Laylah's skin seemed cold and clammy. Was the early evening air too cool for a baby? Holding the baby on her hip, Tess headed back upstairs in search of a T-shirt. Nothing in Laylah's room except a pile of dirty clothes in a small hamper. The bathroom held only the diaper pail. Using her foot, she pushed open the final door, figuring it was Keisha's room.

She had not figured on Keisha being in there.

Her amber eyes were open, a little stunned looking, as if she had just enough time to register what was happening to her. The man lying across her—had he tried to shield her, or was he trying to bolt from the bed when the shots came? His gun was on the floor, just inches from his stiffening fingers, his back ripped out by the gunshots, which must have passed through Keisha, too, judging by the blood. Quite a bit of blood, but it wasn't enough apparently. The killer had fired twice more—through the back of the man's head, and then into Keisha's forehead. Just to be sure.

Tess was suddenly aware of Laylah, still balanced on her hip and cooing, reaching her pudgy baby arms toward her dead mother.

TWENTY-TWO

"THIS IS FAMILIAR," MARTIN TULL SAID. "YOU, ME, A MURDER SCENE."

Tess was sitting in Keisha Moore's kitchen, still holding Laylah, who had finally fallen asleep in her arms despite the excitement around her—the police and technicians wandering through the house, the medical examiner loading up her parents' bodies. Looking down, Tess realized she never had found a T-shirt for the baby. She held her a little closer.

"I suppose you think it's Beale," she said.

"I suppose you don't." He was stiff and cool, much less friendly than he would have been if she had been a stranger. She knew, she had been a stranger once. She remembered how kind he had been to her the first time they had met, how empathetic. He hadn't believed a word she had said, but he had listened to her babbling without condescension.

"Are you going to take Luther Beale in again?"

"Someone's headed over there right now." Something in Tull's face seemed to give a little. "But you know what? I don't think this has anything to do with him. Looks like an execution. I'm sure we'll find the boyfriend was involved in the local business."

Not going to be the same fool twice. "Keisha Moore said he wasn't."

"You coming over to my side, now? Ready to talk to me about your client?"

Tess sniffed the top of Laylah's head. It smelled sweet, as if the apple juice she had downed was coming through her pores.

"Well, the death of Donnie Moore's mother is as good an excuse as any to bring Beale in, see if he has anything to say. Or to confess."

"He's tougher than you are."

"Yeah, he is," Tull said, and she looked up from Laylah's head, startled that he would grant Beale any credit, no matter how grudging. "You know how tough you have to be to kill three kids in cold blood? Damn tougher than me, that's for sure."

"He didn't kill three kids."

"How many did he kill, Tess? How many does it have to be before you admit he's everything I told you he was? Is one not enough? Try two. What if it's five? You tell me. Do you really believe he didn't shoot Donnie Moore, or just that he didn't shoot him on purpose? Do you believe he killed Treasure but not Destiny, or vice versa?"

Esskay cried mournfully off in the distance. She had been locked in the back seat of Tull's police car to keep her from wreaking havoc on the crime scene. "Or what's left of the crime scene," one lab tech had muttered, as if Tess should have known she was in a house with two fresh corpses as she changed diapers and scrounged for apple juice.

"Did anyone hear the shots?" she asked Tull.

"Neighbors say now they think they did, but they didn't call it in because they thought it was back in the alley. They don't always call in shots, not around here."

"Whose fault is that?"

"Theirs for shooting at each other all the time. See, I can play ugly cop as good as anyone, Tess. Is that what you want? Is that what you think of me?"

"It's the way you've been acting for some time now."

"It's the way I've been acting since you got mixed up with Luther

Beale. And I was right about that, wasn't I, Tess? Look at it this way. If you hadn't taken Luther Beale's case, you wouldn't have ever talked to Keisha Moore and you wouldn't be here right now. Wouldn't you like to have been spared that, at least? I mean, bad enough to have the death of Treasure Teeter on your conscience—"

"Are we done here?"

"Not quite."

A policewoman came in and held her arms out to Tess. For a moment, she wasn't sure what she wanted. When she realized it was Laylah, she held the baby tighter.

"Don't worry," the policewoman said. She was startlingly young, even by Tess's standards. She couldn't be more than twenty-one or twenty-two. "The baby's going to be fine."

The policewoman had a large diaper bag, packed and ready to go. Apparently she had been able to find the clothes that had eluded Tess. But Tess still wasn't ready to admit she could be more competent than she.

"What are you going to do with her?"

"We'll put her in a temporary placement tonight, then figure out if one of her family members can take her in."

Tess thought of what she knew of Keisha's family—the addict Tonya, the never-seen sister-in-law who had dumped her children on Keisha as the mood struck her.

"And if they can't?"

"She'll stay in foster care. Don't worry, we know how to do this."

"Jesus, it's like there's a procedure or something."

"There is, Tess." Tull's voice sounded like the old Tull, the one who was her friend. "You think this little girl is the first baby in Baltimore to have her parents murdered?"

"No, I guess not." With that, Tess reluctantly passed the baby to the policewoman. Laylah slept through the exchange, never opened her eyes through what might be the most momentous event in her young life. Everything that would happen to her would come back to this night, to the decisions made here. What would she think, when she woke up in a strange place, with strange faces all around? How much did babies know, what did they remember? Would she wait one day for her mother to come find her? Was Jackie's daughter waiting for her, did she have some primal memory imprinted upon her that could never be erased? Tess tried to imagine her life without Judith. Infuriating, maddening, critical, wonderful Judith, the eternal martyr. And there was no Judith without Gramma Weinstein.

"Let me give you and your dog a ride home," Tull urged. "It's dark now, I don't like to think of you walking back to Butchers Hill by yourself."

"Esskay looks scary. No one will bother us." Tess felt as inept as Tull, incapable of allowing him to show her any kindness. If he hadn't made that crack about Treasure Teeter, she might have been inclined to take the ride, to make a move toward making up. But he was the one who had asked if she was ready to come over to his side, the clear implication being that his side was right, and hers was wrong.

"Well—call my pager when you get there."

"Okay," she said, softening a little. "Is there any way I can check up on Laylah?"

"Laylah?"

"The baby."

"I'll keep tabs for you, follow up with Social Services, how about that?"

"Okay, I guess. But what if she has to go into foster care? What will happen to her then?"

"I don't know, Tess. I just don't know."

"Yeah."

"I hate to tell you how many guys would have killed the baby, too, just for the hell of it. These guys were pros at least. That little girl is lucky."

"Sure. She's poor, she's an orphan, and she's about to go into the same system where her brother died. How lucky can you get?"

TWO BLOCKS FROM KEISHA MOORE'S HOUSE, TESS BEGAN TO REGRET turning down Tull's offer to drive her home. It was past nine now, and Fayette was emptier than she had thought. She picked up the pace, and Esskay trotted happily beside her, always glad for an outing. Tess listened to their footsteps—the dog's light clatter, like castanets, the slightly heavier tone of her nubuck loafers. She thought she heard another set of footsteps in just the same cadence, but one tone deeper, suggesting bigger, heavier shoes.

She stopped. Nothing. Probably just the echo of her own steps.

She started again, stopped again. The noise stopped with her. If someone was following her, the person was swallowed up in the shadows behind her, perhaps crouching behind a stoop right now, or in the alley she had just passed.

"I have a gun," she announced to the night air, to the seemingly empty street.

Good for you, the night and the street seemed to respond. But no one else had anything to say.

Had someone watched Keisha Moore walk this same route last week? She would have been hard to miss, in her red and green outfit and strappy red heels, not quite the same color as her blouse, but close enough. And the bright yellow bag, so awful it was fabulous. What had she carried in that big pocketbook? Obviously not money, and probably not something worth much money, if she was trying to shake Tess down for $119. What had Keisha Moore known? What did she have in common with Treasure Teeter, other than the fact that she had talked to Tess?

Sometimes your own mind manages to give you a quick goose. *Other than the fact that she had talked to Tess.* She had talked to three people in connection with Luther Beale's case, and two of them were dead. At least two of them.

She started to run then, not bothering to listen for footsteps, ran as if her life depended on it, and if it didn't, perhaps another life did. With Esskay setting the pace, they didn't slow down until she reached her own block in Butchers Hill.

She looked behind her one more time, gun drawn, then felt silly. No one was there. She let herself inside the office, wishing she could simply stick her head in a bowl of water as Esskay did. Instead, she sat at her desk and tried to catch her breath. When she had stopped panting, she dialed the number for the Penfield School.

"Is Sal Hawkings there?"

"Who's calling?"

"Tess Monaghan."

"Ma'am, we don't allow our boys to take calls this late unless it's urgent. And we have strict instructions not to take calls from you at all."

"Yes, from Chase Pearson. Look, I don't want to talk to Sal, I just want to know if he's okay, if he's accounted for."

The voice sounded insulted. "Of course he is. We are not in the habit—"

"Would you just please fucking check or I'm going to call Baltimore County police and report him missing."

There was a long silence. Tess would have thought the phone had been disconnected, except for the series of clicks in the background, possibly an old-fashioned intercom system, and some murmured voices. Finally, someone came back on the line. It was a different voice, a familiar voice.

"Sal is fine," Chase Pearson assured her. "Is there some reason he shouldn't be, Miss Monaghan?"

"Donnie Moore's mother was killed tonight."

A pause, as if Chase Pearson couldn't quite remember who Donnie Moore was. "I'm sorry, but Donnie's mother always did keep bad company, didn't she? As I recall, that's how her son ended up in foster care in the first place. What could this have to do with Sal?"

"I don't know he—" But Tess decided not to share the news of Sal's visit with Pearson. "I don't know, I panicked, I guess."

"Indeed."

"Are you usually at the school, Mr. Pearson?"

"I'm not sure what you mean. I'm an alum, I have my ward here, I sit on the board—"

"I mean, are you usually at the school past nine o'clock on a Monday night?"

"I was at a country club function in Phoenix and thought I'd drop by."

A *function*. Whatever she did with her life, Tess hoped it wouldn't take her in the direction of attending any social event so dreary it had to be called a function. "You're worried about Sal, too, aren't you, Mr. Pearson? You're worried that the person who killed Destiny and Treasure may come for him, and you're staying close by."

"Miss Monaghan, everyone in Baltimore knows who killed the Teeter twins. It's only a matter of time before police find a way to charge him with the crime. Until that time, yes, I am worried about Sal. It will be harder for Luther Beale to get to him, but not impossible. He's proven to be quite a shrewd man, hasn't he?"

"If Luther Beale didn't kill the Teeter twins, then someone else is coming for Sal, Mr. Pearson, someone infinitely more dangerous because you're not looking for him."

"Why would anyone besides Luther Beale have murdered those poor children?"

"Because they know something. They saw someone the night Donnie Moore was killed. Perhaps it was a drug dealer who threatened Sal and the others if they testified, and they gave him their promise of silence. But if they made such a promise, it's obviously no longer good enough. With Luther Beale out of jail and determined to prove his innocence, the real killer has to get to the only witnesses before he can."

"Miss Monaghan, do you listen to talk radio?"

The question caught her off guard. "Yes, sometimes. But I don't see—"

"I thought so," Pearson said, his voice edged in disdain. "You sound just like one of the paranoid types who call those shows." And with that, he hung up.

TWENTY-THREE

A WEEK WENT BY, A WEEK IN WHICH NOTHING HAPPENED. OH, THE SUN came up and the sun went down, Tess went through her daily workouts and Kitty finally dumped Will Elam, which provided about five minutes of drama. He cried, he said he would never forget her, he tried to steal her first edition of Anne Tyler's *A Slipping Down Life* and Esskay nipped him on the ankle. Luther Beale stayed out of jail, and no one else died—at least, no one that could be linked to Tess. Inertia was too strong a word to describe the state she was in. All was waiting. Every time the phone rang, she assumed it would be the announcement of Sal Hawkings's death, or perhaps the discovery of Eldon Kane's body, bobbing to the surface in the harbor or turning up beneath the ice skating rink in Patterson Park.

But when the phone finally did ring, it was Uncle Donald, summoning her and Jackie to his office, a week to the day after their meeting with Mr. Mole.

"It has to be good news, don't you think?" Jackie asked, as they waited in the lobby of DHR, maybe ten feet from where the Hutzler's cosmetics counter used to stand.

Tess, who was beginning to buy into the no-news-is-good-news concept, tried to look optimistic. "Well, it's too soon to throw in the towel."

"That's exactly what I was thinking." Jackie was almost bubbling over in her excitement. "It's like when you ask for a shoe in a certain size. The longer they stay in the back room, the greater the likelihood they don't have it at all. But if they get right back to you, they always have a box in hand. Not that I'm comparing my daughter to a shoe. But you know what I mean."

Tess rubbed her forehead. She had a killer headache, right at the bridge of her nose, sinuses most likely. And although she didn't want to rain on Jackie's parade, much about this hastily called meeting bothered her. The arrangement with Mr. Mole had been covert and unofficial. So why were they inside the agency, waiting to be summoned to the office of the general counsel? Uncle Donald had been strangely terse on the phone, choosing his words carefully. Tess had the distinct impression that someone was monitoring the call. They had broken the law. Maybe they were going to be reprimanded and interrogated until they gave up Mr. Mole.

One of the three elevators opened and a stout, middle-aged woman beckoned to them. "They're ready for you."

"They? How many people are we meeting with?" Tess asked, as the elevator climbed to the tenth floor.

"Just the general counsel, the head of the Social Services Administration, your uncle, and some private attorney, David Edelman."

"Why is there a private attorney involved?"

"I'm sure I don't know," the woman said placidly. She was short, with a broad chest that reminded Tess of a pigeon. The woman even had something of the same dim, self-satisfied air that such birds had. "I didn't keep my job here for almost twenty-five years by asking about things that were none of my business. But they're agitated, I can tell you that. They've been dithering around all morning."

This intelligence only made Tess more anxious, but Jackie was still obliviously blissful. Jackie was allowing herself to hope again, and she was almost giddy with expectation. And when they entered the general counsel's office, Tess felt her own spirits lift slightly.

These folks may have been dithering all morning long, but they were nervous and deferential, as if Jackie had all the power in this equation. So why did Uncle Donald's spaniel brown eyes look so sorrowful?

The general counsel was an Asian-American woman in her thirties, while the head of the Social Services Administration was a tall, thin black man. They looked at the private attorney, Edelman, as if to say, *Who goes first here?* He shook his head. *Not me. Not us*, they shook back.

"Is anybody going to say anything?" Uncle Donald demanded. "For God's sake, *I'll* start. Jackie, you know how sometimes when you're looking for something, it's right under your nose?"

She nodded, still beaming.

"Okay, so you were looking for your daughter, but you assumed she had a different name and a new birth certificate, because that's what happens when a kid is adopted. But what if she wasn't adopted?"

"I don't get what you mean," Jackie said, her joy ebbing away.

"There was no birth certificate that could be traced back to your daughter. My . . . friend had the idea to run your name and your daughter's birth name through the files here, after he came up empty on the original search. The funny thing was, it kicked out, in no time flat. She was right here all along, Samantha King."

"She was right where all along?"

"She's in foster care," the general counsel said. "She's in the state's custody and has been for almost all of her life."

"How can that be?" Tess could see all the emotions battling inside Jackie—the exultation at knowing her daughter had been found, her puzzlement that she was in foster care, her concern that there was another shoe yet to drop in this conversation. Tess shared the last feeling.

"The adoption never happened," the general counsel said. "According to our records, Family Alternatives turned your daughter over to the state when she was fourteen months old. Whatever arrangements they made fell through, and they couldn't find another set of adoptive parents. So she went into foster care."

"Is she okay? Can I see her? Is she in some group home, or living with a family?"

"She's fine," David Edelman said. "She's doing great."

Jackie turned to look at him. "What would you know about it?"

"I'm her foster father."

Awkward was inadequate to describe the silence in the room. Jackie and Edelman eyed each other. Edelman looked wary and defensive, while something hateful crept into Jackie's face.

"You look like you're doing pretty well, in your nice suit and your Bally shoes," Jackie said at last. "Why do you have to take kids in for money?"

"We didn't take Sam in for the money, we took her in because she needed a home. My wife and I wanted to adopt her, but we can't. Policy prohibits a white couple adopting a biracial baby in Baltimore City."

"Policy does not prohibit it," the SSA director broke in. Robert Draper, according to the name plate on this desk. So this must be his office, even if he had given his desk chair to the general counsel. "Each jurisdiction is allowed to set its own standards on adoptions. In Baltimore City, the social workers elect to follow the recommendations of several prominent groups, that believe such placements are harmful to the child."

Edelman glanced at the SSA director. "Fine, Robert. So do you want to explain how Samantha King ended up in permanent limbo in my home, or shall I?"

Draper nodded stiffly, indicating Edelman should continue.

"Did you ever hear of a lawsuit called *LJ v. Massinga*?" the lawyer asked Jackie and Tess. Jackie shook her head. Tess thought it sounded dimly familiar, or at least the name Massinga did.

"Wasn't she the secretary of this agency at one point?"

"Yes, more than a decade ago, when the foster care program was in a crisis state. Workers were juggling huge caseloads, there was virtually no oversight. It was a catastrophe. Social advocacy lawyers, working with private attorneys like myself, brought a class action lawsuit against the state on behalf of seven children, who had been taken from their own parents only to be placed in homes that were more abusive. LJ was a boy, the lead plaintiff."

"Was my daughter one of the seven?"

Edelman smiled at Jackie. "Sam was one of the lucky ones, actually. Not long after the suit was filed, I got a tip that an elderly couple had continued taking in children long past the point where they could really care for them. They had five kids in their house, three of them under the age of five. Sam didn't even have a separate bedroom, she was sleeping in the living room in a little nest of filthy blankets. It was a Friday night, and I couldn't find any place to put her for the weekend, so I took her home. She's been there ever since."

"Does she think of you as her parents?"

Edelman was a lawyer, but he wasn't glib. He thought seriously about Jackie's question, taking it apart in his mind and examining each word. "We think of her as our daughter. She calls us Mom and Dad. But she's aware of not being related to us by blood."

"Has she ever asked about me? About her mother, I mean?"

Edelman shook his head. "It's always been assumed her mother was dead. That's why we find ourselves in this delicate situation."

"What situation?"

Again, that same nervous exchange of looks among Edelman and the other two. *You tell. No, you.* Again, Edelman was stuck with the short straw.

"As Ms. Chu said, the state has official custody of Sam, but your parental rights were never terminated. You were thought to be dead and Sam's birth certificate listed no known father. But you're alive."

"I knew that when I came in here," Jackie snapped. "What I don't know is what you're dancing around here."

The general counsel sighed. "Samantha King is your daughter.

You are within your rights to petition the Foster Care Review board to return her to you. Given the circumstances, there is nothing we can do to keep you from taking the girl from the Edelmans."

Tess could see Jackie was at once attracted to this idea—and terrified of it. *She could have her daughter back.*

"What does—" Apparently she wouldn't allow herself to say her daughter's name. "What does *she* want? Does she want to stay with you, or would she want to be with me?"

"I wouldn't presume to speak for Sam. Her biological mother has always been an abstract idea to her, just a name, Susan King, nothing more. We tried to find her death certificate once, but when it didn't show up, we assumed she must have died somewhere outside of Maryland."

"Then you're inept, as is the state," Tess broke in. "I found Susan King in less than three days. A Chicago Title search would have taken you right to her. You would have found the name change. You're a lawyer, you should have known that much."

Jackie put out her arm, as if to hold her back, the same gesture a driver might make when making a sudden stop. "I was at Penn ten years ago. Even if they had found my name change, they probably wouldn't have tracked me there."

"We did file a lien against you, for child support," the general counsel offered, a little abashedly. Tess remembered that stray lien against Susan King that Dorie had picked up, the one she had dismissed as so many unpaid parking tickets. "We're entitled by law to collect support retroactively, given your present circumstances. But we're going to waive that in this case."

"Big of you," Tess muttered. "Awfully big of you."

She had expected Jackie to be even angrier than she was, but Jackie was as dazed as a sleepwalker. She opened her purse, staring into it as if all life's answers might be resting beside her lipstick, checkbook, and Mont Blanc pen, then snapped it shut resolutely.

"Do you have a photo of her?" she asked Edelman.

"What?"

"Do you carry a photo of her, in your wallet?"

"An old one. She wouldn't let me buy this year's school picture. She said it made her look fat." He pulled it out and flipped past photos of two freckled, red-haired boys to a girl with tawny hair, brown eyes, and a dark olive complexion. Jackie stared at it a long time, then handed the wallet back to Edelman.

"I'd like to see her," she said.

"You just did."

"I'd like to see her in person. You don't have to tell her who I am, just yet. But I have to see her before I can decide what I'm going to do."

"We're the only parents she's ever known," Edelman said. He sounded as if he might cry. "She's so happy with us. Our sons worship her. We wouldn't be a family without Sam."

"I believe you," Jackie said. "Now when can I see her?"

TWENTY-FOUR

THEY FINALLY AGREED ON WEDNESDAY, AFTER SCHOOL. JACKIE AND TESS would have tea with Molly Edelman, all very civilized, make polite chit-chat while Jackie observed her daughter. But Wednesday was also the day of the crab feast at her mother's, and Tess also had to make a fruit salad. Not just any fruit salad, either, but Gramma's favorite, with a particular poppy seed dressing and all sorts of conditions and regulations involving the fruit. (No kiwi, green grapes not red, extra strawberries, all melon must be balled.) She was assembling it in the small kitchen in her office when Tull knocked.

"Hi," he said.

"Hi," she said, holding up her hands. "I'd shake, but I'm juicy."

Tull reached into the cookie jar and tossed Esskay a bone. The dog gulped it down gratefully, then returned to the kitchen to keep her vigil near the fruit salad. Esskay liked melon, balled or not.

"The baby—" Tull began.

"Laylah."

"Yeah, Laylah. She's been moved to a group home. The sister-in-law took her for a few days, then decided she couldn't handle it."

"I can't decide if that's good or bad."

"I did some checking on the place where they put her. It's pretty nice. Out in the country, lots of land. Woman usually takes in HIV-positive babies and special needs cases, but she had a vacancy just now."

"Great. I mean, not great, but okay, I guess." Although Tess wondered if Laylah, who had no "special" needs, would get as much attention as the others. Being an eight-month-old orphan wasn't considered all that special, not alongside children with disabilities and the AIDS virus.

Tull continued to stand there, looking strange and uncomfortable.

"About Luther Beale," he said.

"What about him?" She had gone back to her fruit salad.

"Just be careful, okay? The double homicide—it turns out he doesn't have an alibi. Home alone, listening to the radio."

"But you said it was probably drugs. You said you were going to question him just to fuck with his head."

"Yeah, well, Lavon and Keisha weren't involved in drugs, as far as we can tell. Sure, she was ripping off Social Services, claiming the baby's father wasn't around. But Lavon was doing painting work on a cash-only basis. Real reliable, according to his boss. No sign that either of them used drugs, much less sold 'em."

"So what are you saying?"

Tull met her eyes. There was no oneupmanship in his gaze, no sense of triumph or I-told-you-so, just concern, direct and simple. "I'm saying someone killed Destiny Teeter and made it look like a trick gone bad. Someone bashed in Treasure Teeter's head and tried to make it look like he burned himself up. And someone killed Lavon and Keisha in a way that made us suspect a drug hit. I'm saying I want you to keep carrying your gun, and I want you to be careful."

"Even if Beale did any of these things—and I don't think he did—why would he hurt me?"

"Because this killer is crazy, and getting crazier. Because this killer is beginning to strike out at anyone even tangentially related to Donnie Moore. We're keeping watch on the prosecutor from the case, the judge, the Nelsons down in D.C. But you're on your own, Tess. I can't protect you from your own client."

"And Sal?" Tess asked. "You're watching Sal?"

"Sal's the easiest one to protect. He's staying at Penfield for the summer session. They even got him a bodyguard for when he wants to leave the premises."

Tess bet Sal just loved that. A bodyguard. Just another reminder that he wasn't anywhere near as tough as he thought he was.

Tull turned to leave.

"Martin—" Funny how strange his first name felt in her mouth.

"Yeah?"

"Tell me something about yourself, something personal. Anything. Something about your marriage, or why it ended."

He deliberated for a moment. "We had a cat."

"The marriage ended because you had a cat?"

"Give me a second. You asked for a story, then you charge right in, interrupting me. We had a cat. He was named Stanley, because he had this weird meow, it sounded like he was yelling 'Stella.' I kid you not. I loved that cat. The night my wife left me, she took Stan. She also took everything else—our bed, the air conditioning units, the major appliances. I mean, she took the fucking stove, okay? But she left the litter box. I think she was trying to tell me something."

"And that was?"

"I'm still trying to figure it out. You got any ideas?"

"My guess is that she was a greedy head case who wasn't anywhere near good enough for you."

Tull smiled, walked back to the desk, and grabbed another biscuit for Esskay, then gave Tess a comradely thump just above the elbow. "Be careful," he said. "Please be careful."

LESS THAN FOUR HOURS LATER, TESS AND JACKIE SAT IN A GAZEBO behind a gingerbread Victorian in Mount Washington, a neighborhood full of gracious old homes. Molly Edelman was serving them iced tea, homemade cheese straws, and ham sandwiches with the crusts cut off. Her hands shook as she poured the tea. No one was eating.

"Just think," Jackie murmured, almost to herself. "When I came to Fresh Fields, I was practically in her backyard. I might have seen her here. She might have been over at Starbucks. Or walking through the little business district, looking at the clothes and jewelry at Something Else."

The boys came home first, as their grade school was at the foot of the hill. There were two of them, red-headed boys, almost close enough in size to be twins.

"Sandwiches. Excellent," the older one said, grabbing a handful.

"Remember your manners, Henry," Molly said. "Henry, Eli, say hello to my guests, Miss Weir and Miss Monaghan."

"'lo," Henry said around bites. Eli looked up shyly from luminous green eyes, too bashful to speak.

"Can we practice, even though you're having guests?" Henry asked.

"Sure," Molly said. "Just keep control of it. I don't want a lacrosse ball coming at us."

The two boys disappeared into the house, returned with lacrosse sticks scaled to their height, and began throwing the ball against a netted backdrop, passing it to one another. As they played, a Volvo station wagon stopped in the alley and a long-legged girl climbed out. They dropped their sticks and ran to her, falling to the ground and grabbing her by the ankles.

"Thanks, Ms. Reston. See you at school tomorrow, Hannah." The girl looked down, an amused giantess. "Get off me, you spazzes."

She wore the short blue skirt of a local private school—Bryn Mawr, Tess thought, or Roland Park County. Her body was hard and slender, the tea-colored legs criss-crossed with scratches. The honey-colored hair was pulled back into a plait, but small, tight curls had popped out along the forehead and at the nape of the neck. The face was a lighter version of Jackie's—the broad forehead, the expressive mouth, the deep-set eyes.

"Sammy, Sammy," the boys yelled, still holding on to her ankles. "Will you work on our drills with us?"

"I'm tired of practicing," she said, but she was smiling. "Let me get something to eat and I'll be right out."

"Mom's got cheese straws and little sandwiches in the gazebo. She let us have some."

"Cool." Samantha King bounded up the steps of the gazebo, stuffed a cheese straw in her mouth, then gave Molly Edelman a kiss on the cheek, leaving a few crumbs behind. Molly didn't seem to notice. "I finished my science notebook today and turned in my final paper for English. I'm cruising."

Again, Molly made the introductions, but her voice was more strained this time. Sam reached out and shook their hands with a heartiness so familiar that Tess could almost imagine their overlapping DNA meeting at the fingertips. After all, she was related to her, too. There was as much Weinstein as there was King in this striking young girl.

"So what's Mom trying to save this time? A house, a whale, some Guatemalan kid? If she's not careful, she's going to give it all away and we'll have to get athletic scholarships to college, in which case my brothers are really in trouble."

"I'm a fund-raising consultant," Jackie said, her eyes drinking in the girl before her, taking in every detail. "We're going over strategy."

Sam was busy loading up a napkin with sandwiches and cheese straws. *I know that appetite*, Tess said. *I just never knew which side it came from.*

"I'm going to play with the pests, then walk over to Darla's house, okay? She wants to try on her new bathing suit for me, ask if I think it makes her look fat."

"Okay," Molly said, her voice croaking a little. And the girl ran away, long legs carrying across the lawn in a few quick strides.

"She's beautiful," Jackie said.

"She looks like you," Tess said. "I'm surprised she didn't notice."

"Girls that age, they're a little self-centered," Molly offered apologetically. "I don't think they can see anyone's face but their own."

Jackie stood. "Okay, that's enough."

Molly looked up fearfully. "Enough?"

"I've seen what I needed to see. I won't take her from you. She's a good girl, and she's happy. You've given her a life I never could have. Thank you."

Tears fell down Molly's cheeks, but she tried to control herself so the children wouldn't realize anything was amiss. "We could work something out, you know. I'm sure she'd love to know you, to have you be a part of her life. We'd have to talk to a psychologist, of course, but it could work. I know it could."

"I don't think I can do it halfway," Jackie said. "I know I'm being selfish in a way, but I can't settle for just a piece of her. I gave her up thirteen years ago. I have to live with that."

"We could tell her you're alive, at least, that you're not dead as she always assumed."

Jackie shook her head. "Maybe later, when she's a little older. But I'd like to help out, if I could. I could help with her college, or even the private school tuition."

Molly wiped her eyes. "Oh, Sam was kidding about my causes. David makes plenty of money, we're not hurting."

Well, someone is, Tess thought, looking at Jackie's face. *Someone is definitely hurting right now.*

FOR THE FIRST TIME, JACKIE LET TESS TAKE THE WHEEL OF HER BELOVED Lexus. She crawled into the passenger seat and stared ahead, her face unreadable.

"For what it's worth, I think you did the right thing," Tess offered, cautiously. "It's hell for a single woman to bring up a kid."

"I've got money," Jackie said in a dull, flat voice. "Money makes it easier. I could raise her if I wanted to. But what do I have to give her? My life is sterile. I don't have any real friends, any life. All I do is make money."

"I wouldn't say that," Tess said nervously. "You're . . . self-contained, self-sufficient, but not sterile."

"I am what I am, Tess. I adapted and I survived. The question is, what did I give up along the way? I gave up my daughter. I gave up myself."

Tess thought of the *Just-So Stories* in Sal's *Kipling Compendium*, each one the story of someone who had changed in order to survive. The camel had to have a hump, the leopard had to develop spots, the elephant needed a nose, if only to remind him of the perils of satiable curiosity. For several miles, neither woman spoke.

"Are you going to be okay?" Tess asked as they headed east toward Butchers Hill. "I mean, there's this thing at my mom's tonight that's absolutely mandatory, but if you need me, I'll go late, or leave early."

"No, your job is done," Jackie said. "I asked you to find my daughter and you did. How much do I owe you?"

"The retainer more than covers it. You don't even owe me mileage. We always used your car."

At the curb outside Tess's office, Jackie suddenly pressed a hand to her forehead.

"Do you have an aspirin in your office? I don't think I can make the drive back to Columbia feeling like this."

Tess dashed inside and returned with a generic ibuprofen, a glass of water, and a panting Esskay, who also wanted to pay her respects. Jackie drank the water gratefully, patted the dog, then slid over to the driver's seat, handing Tess her backpack along with the empty glass.

"Thank you," she said formally, offering her hand. "I actually came to like you over the past two weeks."

"Hey, me too. How does the song go? You may have been a headache, but you never were a bore. Besides, we're connected, aren't we? We're family, if you think about it."

"You and Sam are connected. There's really nothing between us."

"Oh," said Tess, feeling rebuffed. She thought they had shared quite a bit. Then Jackie smiled.

"What's so funny?"

"Oh, I was just thinking about our adventures together. Meeting Mr. Mole, going to that lesbian bar, that stupid story you made me tell about *Fresh Lake Trout*. Did you ever find that kid, by the way?"

"Yeah." Insular Jackie had to be the one person in Baltimore who didn't know she had found Sal Hawkings. "It didn't quite turn out the way I expected, but I found him."

"And that white trash Willa Mott, the rabbit holes she sent us down. You think there ever was a Mr. and Mrs. Johnson, who planned to name their baby Caitlin?"

"I guess we'll never know."

"I guess not," Jackie said, waved, then drove out of Tess's life.

Tess and Esskay walked into the office. Tess sat down at her computer and looked at her once unblemished desk calendar. It wasn't so unsullied now. Names, leads, and doodles covered its surface, spilling over into days she hadn't even lived yet. There were rings from Coke cans, rogan josh drippings, greasy smears, and, of course, traces of chocolate. It was messy. Life was messy. She would have to remember to tell Jackie that. Life was messy.

Then she remembered she would never see Jackie again.

TWENTY-FIVE

TESS HATED ALL SEAFOOD. CRAB HATED HER BACK. ONE BITE, THE TINEST sliver of its flesh in a casserole or a dip, and she'd go into anaphylactic shock, her trachea swelling until she couldn't breathe. On the plus side, her allergy had made for an unforgettable eighth birthday party for Noam Fischer. Whenever she ran into him, usually browsing the history table at the Smith College book sale, he still spoke of it with great cheer, as if it were a high point of his childhood. "You turned blue! You almost died!"

So one might think that, given the twenty-nine years she had been hanging around, her own parents would be able to remember this salient fact. But as the crab feast got under way at the Monaghans' house, it quickly became apparent that Judith had forgotten to plan an alternative main course. Unless Tess found something in the pantry, she was going to dine on coleslaw, corn on the cob, and her own fruit salad, which she didn't even particularly like.

"Don't you have any peanut butter?" she asked her mother, pushing jars and cans around. Judith never threw anything out, so her well-organized shelves were filled with the exotic but not-quite-edible foods people send as gifts. Chutney, fruit cakes, jellies in strange flavors. "I could at least make myself a sandwich."

"I could run up to Arby's, get her a roast beef," her father said helpfully. He still had on his summer work clothes, a short-sleeved white shirt and clip-on blue tie, a shade lighter than his eyes. He also had his summer sunburn, one shade lighter than his hair.

Tess thought if someone was going to escape on her account, it should be her. "Or maybe I could just go get takeout from Mr. G's, or the Chinese place over on Ingleside, the one with the dancing cow. That's it, I'll get some dumplings, maybe an order of spare ribs."

"No!" Judith screamed, in a voice so shrill and hysterical that it stopped them both in their tracks as they edged toward the kitchen door. But no one looked more surprised than Judith at the strangled sound that had come out of her.

"I mean—don't leave me. I need you both here. If you get me through this, Pat, I'll go down to the ocean with your family in August, stay in that horrid little condo of theirs, and never say a word."

Tess exchanged a look with her father. This was a serious concession indeed. Judith insisted on staying in a separate hotel when the Monaghans staged their August reunion and usually came up with a reason to leave two days into the week-long vacation.

"Okay, hon," he said. "I won't leave, and neither will Tess. She'll just have to dig up something around here she can eat." He opened his arms and Judith allowed herself to be embraced. As they snuggled, Tess was reminded of the chemistry that had sizzled between her parents all these years, the one constant in their marriage. They had thrown in their lot with one another less than two weeks after Donald Weinstein had introduced his kid sister to this up-and-coming Monaghan kid in the West Side Democratic Club. Both families had predicted, hoped, prayed, that the union would founder. But here it was, thirty-plus years later, and there was still a glimmer of whatever had passed between them at that first meeting. Tess would have found her parents' relationship inspiring if she didn't happen to believe it had warped her for life. Hadn't she sent her last boyfriend packing for the simple crime of being too nice, too easygoing?

"I'll go put the newspapers down," Tess said. "Should I tape them or just weigh them down with dishes?"

"Tape the first layer," Judith said, her words muffled by Patrick's shoulder. "Then spread another over the top, so we can gather them up as the tables get full and put them straight into the garbage bags."

Within an hour, the paper-covered picnic tables in the backyard were full and bits of crab shell flew through the air with each swing of a crab mallet. Even crab-aversant Tess couldn't help being impressed by the professional skills her relatives brought to the dismemberment of this non-kosher delicacy. Uncle Jules and Aunt Sylvie had special mallets, of course, wooden heads on sterling silver handles, their monogram engraved along the shaft. They were messy types, sacrificing large pieces of crab meat to greedy haste. Cousin Deborah was neat, but prone to tiny cuts along her manicured nails, painful when the Old Bay seasoning rubbed against them. Little Samuel sat between his grandparents, pounding on the table with his own monogrammed mallet, as if practicing for the day when he could eat more than Saltines and corn sliced from the cob.

Uncle Donald dissected his crab with a knife and was expert at extracting large pieces of back fin, the best part of the crab. But Gramma was the fastest, cleanest picker of all. She had once won a crab-picking contest for local celebrities, thirty years back, when the proprietess of Weinstein's was considered a certain local celebrity. She told the story at every family crab feast. She was telling it now.

"The second-place winner, the woman from the little ice cream store, what's her name, she wasn't even close. Her wrists were strong, from all those years of scooping, but her skin was soft, and she was squeamish." Gramma rotated her wrist, as if scooping something hard from a carton, chocolate chip or Rocky Road. "But that little ice cream business was bought out by Beatrice Foods last year, so I guess she had the last laugh. Her husband knew how to manage a business. She could afford to have soft hands."

Tess, munching unenthusiastically on her butter-and-guava-jelly sandwich, studied her grandmother. She understood Gramma's bitterness now, these repeated jabs about Poppa's failures as a breadwinner. Gramma must have known, or guessed, of his betrayal. Then again, Gramma had always been a sour, unhappy person. There was no Jackie around in the early years, when she was monitoring Tess's time on the flying rabbit. Or was there? Was Jackie a one-time thing, or one in a string? She put down her sandwich, what little appetite she had gone.

She got it back quickly enough when she saw Aunt Sylvie bringing out her homemade German chocolate cake. Whatever her other failings, Aunt Sylvie made good cakes. Gramma was standing at the head of the table, tapping her fork on the side of her glass, while Samuel continued to pound at the table with his mallet. Gramma gave him a look. She didn't like to be upstaged, even by the two-year-old great-grandapple of her eye. Both lost their audience when a police car pulled up in the driveway.

"Someone probably complained about all the cars parked out front," Patrick grumbled, getting up to go to the gate.

But it was a county cop car, not a city one, and the two officers seemed tentative and embarrassed.

"Is there a Miss Tess Monaghan here?"

Everyone in the family turned to look at her, their eyes so accusing, so ready to believe the worst of her, that Tess felt just the tiniest bit affronted.

"That's me," she said, putting down the garbage bag of crab shells she had been tying up, brushing her hands off on her jeans.

"You don't have to say anything to them," her father assured her. "Let me go call our lawyer."

"You want I should call the chief of the state police, or Arnold Weiner even?" Uncle Donald asked. "I don't see how the county cops have jurisdiction here."

Penfield School is in Baltimore County's jurisdiction, Tess thought as she walked toward the gate, her mouth dry and ashy. If something had happened to Sal Hawkings, it would be county cops who would investigate, the county cops who would want to question her, the county cops who would want to know about Luther Beale's unvarying alibi.

"How can I help you, officers?"

"We found someone," said the taller cop, a strapping near-giant, his name plate at Tess's eye level. Officer Buske. With his broad chest and shiny black hair, he reminded Tess of the smiling boy in red-and-white checked overalls, hawking burgers at Shoney's Big Boys.

"Is he dead?" she asked.

The big cop, Buske, looked at her strangely. "Dead? He? No, it's a she and she says she's not going anywhere until she talks to you. We found her walking barefoot along the Hanover Pike, up toward the state line. She said she had been kidnapped, but she didn't want to press charges, that you would take care of it. She had your business card in her pocket. We took her down to your office, and when you weren't there, we went over to your apartment. Your aunt said we'd find you here." Buske suddenly blushed. "She sure is pretty, your aunt."

Tess couldn't help imagining this broad-shouldered lad sitting at the breakfast table, wearing the flannel robe that Kitty kept for all her gentlemen callers. Husky Buske.

"Back up a minute," she said. "You found *who* on the Hanover Pike? Some kidnap victim who wants to speak to me? This doesn't make any sense."

The smaller cop—actually, he was almost six feet, but Buske Big Boy dwarfed him—opened the back door of the patrol car and Willa Mott limped out, her bare feet as red as her perpetually stuffed-up nose, but much more painful looking.

"Willa?"

"I told them you'd take care of me," she said stiffly. "That you worked for my lawyer."

Tess decided to play along, even if she wasn't quite sure just what game was afoot. "Of course. Tyner will be so upset when he hears what happened. Your ex-husband again? Are you finally ready to press charges?"

"I think we should talk about this in private," she said, stumbling forward. Not only where her feet raw and swollen, but her ankles were criss-crossed with tiny scratches and insect bites.

The big cop lowered his voice. "Truthfully, ma'am, we think she ought to go in for psychiatric observation. She was muttering to beat the band the whole time she was riding around in the back seat, using every curse word in the book."

"She has problems, but she's okay as long as she takes her medication," Tess said. "It's the same old story. She starts feeling good, then decides she doesn't need to take the lithium any more. This happens every six months or so."

Willa glowered, but didn't dare contradict her. The officers retreated to the car somewhat reluctantly, called in on their radio, and backed out of the driveway about a minute later. As soon as they were out of sight, Willa turned to Tess.

"That crazy nigger bitch friend of yours did this to me," she screamed. Tess couldn't believe such a loud sound was coming out of mousy Willa Mott. "That crazy nigger bitch kidnapped me, took my shoes, and then put me out on the road in the middle of nowhere."

Tess glanced back at her family. Her mother looked stricken, as if she had always feared exactly this: some white cracker friend of Tess's crashing an otherwise pleasant family gathering, screaming expletives and epithets. Cousin Deborah leaned forward, a hint of delight in her shocked face, while Gramma merely looked impatient. Baby Samuel continued to pound on the table with his crab mallet. "C'azy nigga bit. C'azy nigga bit," he chanted happily.

Tess said the only thing that occurred to her. "Would you like to join us for dessert?"

* * *

WILLA MOTT PASSED ON THE CAKE, ALTHOUGH SHE LET TESS'S FATHER tend to her feet, whimpering as the hydrogen peroxide bubbled and hissed over her open wounds.

"That just means it's working," Patrick assured her.

"Now tell me what happened with Jackie," Tess said.

They were in the upstairs bathroom, away from the rest of the family, although Judith had insisted on being here, too. It was her house, after all. Willa sat on the closed toilet, Patrick at her feet, while Judith blocked the door. Tess was left with the rim of the tub, wedged in tight by Willa Mott's side, so she was facing her profile. Willa seemed to prefer it that way, making eye contact with Patrick instead of Tess.

"About four-thirty today, after the last of the kids had been picked up, that nigger bitch pulled up in her fancy car, said she wanted to talk to me."

"Jackie," Tess corrected. "Her name is Jackie and if you keep calling her that, I'm going to smack you."

Willa shrugged, as if so much had happened to her today that one more smack wouldn't make a difference. "So then she says, she knows. She knows, and she's going to kill me if I don't give her what she wants."

"Knows what?"

Willa's voice was inaudible.

"Speak up, Willa."

"She knows I have the records from Family Alternatives, and she's going to kill me if I don't turn over her file."

Patrick and Judith were completely bewildered, but Tess had an instant image of Willa walking back and forth through her living room, her arms full of juice packs. The whole operation had taken much longer than it should have, but Tess had chalked it up to Willa's general ineptness.

But it was only after she had returned from the garage that she began to remember the details of Jackie's case. A quick peek at the records had probably done more to freshen her memory than all the twenties Tess had dropped in her lap.

"How did Jackie figure it out?"

Willa shrugged, indifferent. "I don't know. Something I said about the baby's father. Besides, I wasn't in a position to argue with her, the way she was yelling and threatening to kill me. So yeah, I had the records. So what? Those creeps I worked for left in the middle of the night, owing me two weeks' salary. I figured the files could be my severance."

"What good are adoption files for some defunct agency?"

"You think you're the first hot-shit investigator who's tracked me down, looking for one of the babies we placed?"

Yes, in fact, Tess had thought she was. "So you sell the information."

"Only after talking to the adoptive parents."

Now Tess was confused, but her father was nodding. He had seen his share of graft in his years as a city liquor board inspector, and he was a quick study when it came to such schemes. "A bidding war," Patrick explained to Tess and Judith. "She gives the adoptive parents a chance to pay more *not* to reveal the information. And the parents have to go on paying, right, because you can hold it over their heads forever."

"I never thought of that." Willa looked dejected, contemplating her lost blackmail opportunities. "I just charged them a flat fee of five thousand dollars. That's how I got the money to put down on my house, start my business. But it had been a long while since anyone had come around. Maybe I should have worked with some of those adoption rights groups, let them know what I had. But they would have shut me down."

Something didn't fit. Tess drummed her fingers on the tub's rim, trying to pinpoint what was wrong.

"Jackie's baby *wasn't* adopted. There were no parents to black-mail in her case. Why didn't you name your price and tell her that the baby had gone back into the system? Why didn't you tell us what we wanted to know when we first came out there?"

Willa lowered her eyes. "The people who took her baby and gave her back, their . . . privacy meant a lot to them. They wouldn't have wanted that crazy ni—that crazy bitch showing up at their house, asking questions, making a fuss."

Tess grabbed Willa's arm and shook it, quite roughly. "What did you tell Jackie?"

"I told her what she wanted to know." At her best, Willa Mott was plain and ordinary. Angry, her features seemed to shrink, until her eyes almost disappeared and her mouth was as small as a bug's. "I told her the name of the people who took her baby, the people who gave it back—when they found out it was half-nigger. You see, they paid for a white baby, and they said it wasn't enough if it *looked* white, it had to be white. The agency offered them a discount to keep it, but they said no way. I can't say as I blame them."

Tess leaned to the side until her right temple touched the cool black-and-white tile. It was a big bathroom, but it wasn't built for four people, and it suddenly seemed stiflingly close.

"You didn't tell Jackie that part, did you?"

"I had to tell her," Willa Mott whined. "I didn't have a choice."

"You could have lied, the way you did before. Why did you pick today to become so honest and aboveboard?"

"Because today is the day your fancy friend held a gun to my head and threatened to kill me if I didn't tell her everything I knew."

"A gun? Where would Jackie get a gun?" Tess ran downstairs to the front door, where she had dropped her knapsack by the hall tree. Sure enough, her Smith and Wesson was gone. Jackie must have faked her headache, so she could sneak the gun out of Tess's bag and into her purse. She had been planning this all along, perhaps from the moment they had left the Edelmans'. *Do you think there ever were any Johnsons who planned to name their baby Caitlin? I guess we'll never know.*

"Where did Jackie go after she put you out of the car?" she asked Willa, a little breathless from taking the stairs so fast. "She went to the adoptive parents' house, didn't she? Where do they live? What are their names?"

Willa suddenly looked coy. "Why, I'm not sure I can remember, just like that. What's it worth to you to find that crazy nigger bitch?"

Tess backhanded her, and Willa's head snapped back, hitting the wall was a dull thud. It felt pretty good, probably better than it should have.

"Tess!" her mother shouted. "This is how you do business?" But her father looked impressed.

"You are through making money off your files, Willa Mott. Do you understand that?" Tess held her by the shoulders, the way someone might grip a sullen child, and shook her hard enough to make her head wobble on her skinny neck. "You are never going to sell another piece of information as long as you live. Now tell me what you told Jackie."

"Dr. and Mrs. Becker, Edgevale Road in Roland Park," Willa whimpered. "And that crazy—that woman already took my files anyway."

"So everything you told us was a fucking lie, wasn't it? The name, the location, what the adoptive father did for a living. You were making sure we never got close, so you could milk them instead."

Gramma picked this moment to come upstairs. "Aren't you done in here yet?" she demanded from the doorway. There hadn't been this many people in the Monaghan bathroom since a memorable high school party, in which Tess and her friends had discovered the mixed pleasures of mixed drinks. "You're holding everything up."

"This is kind of important," Tess said between gritted teeth, but too intimidated by her grandmother to just push past her and make a mad dash for her car. "People's lives may be at stake. There's a woman—Jacqueline Weir, you might remember her as Susan King.

She worked for Poppa in the Fells Point store, and she's about to make the biggest mistake of her life."

She couldn't help it, she was curious to see what her grandmother's face would reveal, curious to see how she would react to the name. But Gramma looked unimpressed.

"That troublemaker? Wouldn't you know she'd pop up again just now, when there's money to be made. She always did have a nose for money. Well you tell her that she's not getting another penny, you tell her that. Nothing's changed."

Pop up again? "What do you mean, Gramma? When did Jackie—Susan—pop up before?"

"Oh, she came around ten or twelve years ago, asking Samuel for money for college, but I put my foot down. So he got her pregnant, the stupid man, and had to give her money for an abortion. You think someone who owned a drugstore might have had the means to prevent such a thing, might have taken the time to sell himself a prophylactic kit. But he didn't and he had to pay. I accepted that. Once. Were we to pay for his stupidity for the rest of our lives? When she asked for help again, I told Samuel it was out of the question. Otherwise, she'd never be out of our lives. Now you tell me she's back. I can't say I'm surprised. I wonder how she heard about the land sale?"

"You knew? You knew all this time?"

"Of course I knew. Your grandfather could never hide anything from me. Believe me, he didn't stray again. As I reminded him, Maryland is a community property state. First he was too rich to leave me, and then he was too poor. What's half of nothing?"

"Knew what?" Judith asked. "Who's Susan King? Will someone please tell me what's going on?"

"I'd tell you, Mom, but I have to go stop a woman from committing her second felony of the day," Tess said. "Let Gramma explain it all to you. Besides, she's known about it much longer than I have."

"There's nothing to explain," Gramma said, with a wave of her hand that suggested the past was an inconvenience—a fly to be swatted, a smear on a window pane that could be erased with a quick shot of Windex.

"There's a lifetime to explain," Judith said. "A lifetime of secrets and lies, and I'm sick of it. You're not going anywhere, Theresa Esther Monaghan, until you tell me everything."

Tess grabbed her mother's hand. "I'll tell you what I know in the car, if you insist. But I should warn you I'm going to be driving just a little bit above the speed limit."

TWENTY-SIX

TESS'S DRIVING PROVED TO BE THE LEAST OF JUDITH'S CONCERNS, EVEN as Tess ran every amber and not a few reds on the way to Roland Park.

"So this woman, this client of yours, she's . . . connected to Poppa?" Judith asked tentatively. "And Mama knew, she knew all this time, and never told any of us?"

The sign at the intersection said no right on red, but Tess thought it surely couldn't apply to her. After a quick glance to make sure no cops were around, she tore around the corner.

"She didn't know Jackie put the baby up for adoption, because Poppa didn't know the baby was ever born. Jackie told him she was going to get an abortion, and kept the money. She told me when she asked for his help with college, he said the business was too shaky for him to help her. But I guess he couldn't squeeze that much cash out without going to Gramma, and she put her foot down."

"So I have a half-sibling."

"Yeah, a sister."

"I always wanted a sister," Judith said, then smiled. "Well, that was inane."

"We saw her today. I knew it had upset Jackie, but I guess I didn't know just how freaked out she was."

Tess was on Northern Parkway now. If she had been in her

office, or her apartment, she could have made Roland Park in fifteen minutes. But her parents' house couldn't have been much farther away. If you thought of the Baltimore Beltway as a clock, it was akin to driving from seven o'clock to midnight.

"Edgevale is on the west side of Roland Park," her mother said. "It runs off Falls Road. But how will we find it without the number?"

"I know Jackie's car."

It was dark now, and fireflies flickered on and off as they drove down Edgevale. Whatever Jackie was doing, she couldn't make much noise, for sound would carry easily across these lush, hushed lawns. Unlike Keisha Moore's embattled neighbors, Roland Park residents would never let a gunshot go unreported, assuming they realized it was a gunshot, instead of a car backfiring. Then again, the houses were set just far enough apart to suggest a certain reticence on the part of the owners, a surface neighborliness that didn't go too far beyond mimed "hellos" at the curb. Such places often had an unspoken agreement not to be too nosy. A woman could be beaten here, or a child, and the crime, if discovered, would only prompt the usual banalities. "He was a quiet man." Yet just let a young black man try walking in the neighborhood and the police would be summoned at once.

Jackie, however, had the right accessories to slip under that radar. Her white Lexus was parked in the driveway of a stucco mansion at the end of the street. It blocked a late-model Toyota Camry with an ACLU bumpersticker, but another car had pulled in behind the Lexus, a black Mercedes with "Save the Bay" plates. Tess pulled in behind the Mercedes. An old car like hers might also excite comment in Roland Park if left on the street.

"Stay in the car, Mom."

"Not on your life."

"There's a woman in that house with a gun, my gun. A hysterical, unpredictable woman who doesn't know you, and might not hestitate to harm you."

"My point, exactly. So why don't you call the police, and let them handle it?"

"Because there's a slender hope I can undo what Jackie has done without getting the police involved. *If* she hasn't hurt anyone yet. I'm counting on Jackie not being as tough as she thinks she is." But she would hurt herself, Tess thought. She might be so hysterical over seeing Samantha that she would kill herself in front of the people who had treated her daughter so cavalierly.

The front door was unlocked. Tess stopped in the front hallway, listened intently. Judith came in right behind her. No time to argue about it now. She motioned her mother to be quiet, her mother gestured back that she knew what she was doing. God, she was exasperating.

Now both the women concentrated on the sounds of the house. It was so big, so quiet. It was hard to imagine any child here, running up the stairs so shiny they looked wet, leaving handprints along the expensive-looking wallpaper. There was a murmuring sound from the rear, perhaps a television left on, or even the leaves of the trees rustling together. Tess and her mother moved toward the sound, through the formal living room, into the dining room and through swinging doors into the kitchen, a bright, cold place, all granite and stainless steel.

"Who are you?" a woman asked, and her voice was too loud, too shaky, even for someone seeing two strangers in her kitchen. Short and fleshy, with the kind of silver-blond curls never found in nature, she was sitting on a severe little metal love seat at one end of the remodeled kitchen, where a family room had been created in what once was an alcove or breakfast nook. A small man in glasses was next to her, frowning.

Jackie was sitting directly across from them in a matching chair, her briefcase open on her lap. Was the gun in there? Would she use it before Tess could cross the room?

"Hey," Jackie said languidly, as cool and composed as the day Tess had first gone to her apartment. "I didn't expect to see you here tonight. That your mom? I see the resemblance. You're lucky, girl, if you got that bone structure. You're going to look *good* twenty, thirty years from now, you ever learn how to dress."

Judith, who had been staring at Jackie, perhaps still trying to grasp their connection, blushed. "Thank you. I always did think Tesser favored me, although there's some of her father there, too."

"Tesser? You have been holding out on me."

The whole scene felt surreal to Tess. Here they were, in this $100,000 kitchen with the couple who had turned away Samantha because her mother was black, chatting as if they had run into each other in the dairy section of the SuperFresh. The couple on the love seat looked nervous and edgy. Was Jackie holding the gun behind her briefcase? Had she warned them not to speak? But she had to know Tess wouldn't leave without her, that Tess would never let her destroy her life this way.

The man, Dr. Becker, spoke as if he were impatient with Tess. "We are having a, uh, confidential discussion. Could you and Miss Weir transact your business later, when we're finished?"

Jackie leaned forward and patted the doctor's hands. They were small hands, knitted tightly together on the table top. Something—his hands, his knees, his wife's legs—were shaking hard enough to make the teacups before them vibrate ever so slightly. *Teacups*, Tess thought. What kind of murder-suicide is this?

"It's okay, Dr. Becker. Tess and I don't really have any secrets at this point. Although Mrs. Monaghan—" She looked back at Judith, who nodded shyly. "Well, it looks like she's cool, too. What do you know?" To Tess: "You told her?"

"I had to, when Willa Mott crashed the crab feast."

Did Tess just imagine it, or did the Beckers shift uncomfortably at the mention of Willa Mott?

"So that's how you found me. Well, we're almost done here, aren't we? There's just the little matter of the check. Not so little, really. I mean, a quarter of a million dollars is a lot of money, but it's all for a good cause, isn't it? Seed money for foster care group homes. You know, the places where kids go when no one wants them. Can you imagine such a thing? Not wanting a child?"

"I told you what happened," the doctor said. "I requested the child's medical records. The hospital goofed and sent them to me directly, instead of to the agency, and I saw the girl was biracial. We had been told we were receiving a white child. We decided if the agency would lie about something so fundamental, it couldn't be trusted to tell the truth about anything. The adoption hadn't been finalized yet, so we were within our legal rights to void it."

"It's not as if we're prejudiced," Mrs. Becker broke in. "We give money to all sorts of black causes."

Jackie nodded, smiling, as if pleased by this recitation. "Yes, I understand. You sent an eleven-month-old baby back like she was some sweater from J. Crew that happened to be the wrong color. *'Uh-huh, I didn't order me no taupe sweater, I wanted something in a peachy white.'* "

"We assumed they would find another home for her," the doctor said.

"What if they didn't? Do you know what happened to her? Do you know where my daughter is today, what kind of life she has?"

The doctor and his wife said nothing. Puzzled, Tess started to interrupt, to remind Jackie of the wonderful life that Sam had with the Edelmans, but then she realized how deliberate this was. The money wasn't enough for Jackie. She wanted to plant dark images in the Beckers' minds, see if she could give them a few sleepless nights as well. *Good luck*, Tess thought. If the Beckers ever thought about what they had done, it would be because of the check Dr. Becker was now filling out with Jackie's Mont Blanc pen.

"They have a name for this," he said, even as he handed the check to Jackie. "Extortion. Blackmail. Don't think I won't report this to the police."

"They have names for you, too," Jackie said, examining the check carefully. "Bigot. Racist. Peckerwood. Don't you see, money has to change hands here. Because this whole thing is about *economics*. If I had kept my baby, the government would have given me, say, about $225 a month and some food stamps to raise her. You paid $10,000 for her, but the agency got that, not me. I do hope you got a refund. And when she went into foster care, that family got twice as much as I would have for keeping her. The Edelmans, who aren't hurting by a long shot, collect maybe $500 a month they don't need to raise the baby I would have gotten $225 to raise. Now could someone explain that to me?"

Mrs. Becker actually began to say something, as if Jackie expected an answer, but she was silenced by one stern look from her husband. Tess couldn't help thinking that the voided adoption was one of the best things that ever happened to Samantha King. Dr. Becker would have managed to snuff out that exuberant girl's soul long ago, while his silly wife just looked on.

"You know, I know people," the doctor said. "Important people. You might find your job a lot harder to do in the future if you cash that check."

For the first time, Jackie looked hesitant, unsure. Her career was the kind built by word of mouth, Tess realized, and it could be destroyed by it as well.

"You people think you run the city now." Dr. Becker had found his advantage and was pressing forward, cruel and heedless. "Well, you don't. It's the people with money who are in control, white or black. That check may be the last anyone ever writes you. Think about that."

As Jackie just sat, studying the check, Tess reached out and grabbed the doctor's hand. "Where are my manners? Tess Monaghan, I should have introduced myself when I came in. I'm a private investigator, but I used to be a reporter in town and I still have a lot of reporter friends. I think they would love to hear about the prominent Doctor Becker—ACLU member, friend of the Chesapeake Bay—who reneged on an adoption because the child wasn't white. Throw in the Willa Mott angle and it's a national story, don't you think?"

"We told you, it was because the agency lied," Becker said, almost sputtering in his rage. "You keep making it sound as if we were racists."

"No, I think it was your use of 'you people' that made you sound like a racist. Anyway, that's how it will end up, unless you leave Jackie alone. Trust me. The top editor of the *Beacon-Light* owes me a favor or two, and I'm willing to call the chit in for this."

"And I work at the NSA," Judith put in suddenly. "You don't even want to contemplate what I can do to you."

Tess doubted that her mother could do much more than instruct the clerk-typists under her supervision to write a really scary letter, but it was the National Security Agency. Who knew what powers her mother really had?

The doctor nodded sullenly, but Tess didn't trust him. There was nothing to keep him from calling the police as soon as they left, or setting in motion his grapevine scheme to undercut Jackie's business.

"Now we're going to leave here and I'm going to make sure any paperwork linking you to Samantha King is destroyed, although Jackie will keep a copy. That will keep you quiet?"

Another tight little nod from Herr Doktor.

"He's not going to let it go," Jackie said. "He's going to find a way to get back at me, if only because he's humiliated."

"No, he's not," Judith said emphatically. "After all, you have an alibi. You were never here."

"Oh yeah? Where was I?"

"Across town, at a crab feast with twenty other people."

Tess looked at her mother. She had always thought her ability to lie, to think on her feet, must come down on Patrick's side, but maybe it was a Weinstein trait as well.

"I don't get it," Jackie said. "Who would do that for me?"

"Your daughter's family," Tess said.

* * *

JUDITH DROVE TESS'S CAR BACK TO THE MONAGHANS', WHILE TESS PI-
loted Jackie in her white Lexus for the second time that day.

"You shouldn't have stolen my gun," she chided, once they were
alone.

"Next time, don't leave it untended," Jackie said, not at all repentant.

"You scared me to death. I thought you were going to kill yourself, or them."

"Why would I destroy my life like that after all the work I put
into recreating it? I wanted to hurt them, and money was the way to
do that. Probably the only way with people like them." Jackie
laughed, pleased with herself. For the next mile or two, they didn't
say anything, but it was a comfortable silence. The kind of silence
that friends can endure.

When Jackie spoke again, her voice was soft and tentative. "I was
hurt and I wanted to hurt someone else. You know, I started off by
wanting to hurt you."

"Hurt *me*?"

"Why do you think I hired you in the first place? I wanted to get
back at you for being the girl on the other side of the soda fountain,
the one who had the real childhood, while I had to work my way
through high school, then college."

"Poppa meant to pay for your tuition. Gramma was the one who
wouldn't let him."

"She knew?"

"So it seems."

"Poor woman."

"Poor woman? She forced Poppa to renege on his promise to
you."

"Well, how would you like to be the woman whose husband
comes home and says, 'Remember that eighteen-year-old girl I
knocked up? I think we should send her to college.'"

Jackie had a point. For all her anger, she could always see the big picture, see things outside herself. Tess should learn to do the same. She smiled. Truth be told, it cracked her up, the image of Jackie sitting across from the Beckers at her little extortion tea party, reeling off her facts and figures about the welfare system. Only Jackie would make a revenge scheme so didactic.

"Hey, that stuff you said about the economics of the system. Was that made up, or was it true?"

"Oh, I may have been off on the actual numbers, and everything's different since welfare reform. But the proportions were right. People pay thousands to adopt babies, welfare mothers get pennies to keep them."

"And the foster parents receive bigger stipends than the mothers?"

"Oh yeah. But they also have to meet higher standards than the welfare mothers—separate bedrooms, stuff like that. Remember, that's why they took Sam away from those folks. Why are you suddenly so interested?"

"Just doing some math in my head."

TWENTY-SEVEN

CHASE PEARSON'S OFFICE IN ANNAPOLIS WAS FAR GRANDER THAN TESS would have expected. His was an insignificant job, after all, an appointed position that would evaporate like the dew once the current governor was gone. The special secretary for children and youth. But how foolish of her, how naive. There were no insignificant jobs in the state capital. No small parts, no small actors.

And no small crimes.

"Miss Monaghan," Pearson said. She didn't even rate a flash of his bad teeth at this point in their relationship. Whatever his future plans, he had apparently decided he could get by without her vote. "I thought I had made it clear that I did not wish to hear from you again."

"You made it clear I'd be arrested if I tried to go to Penfield, so I came to see you here. That's okay. You can answer far more of my questions than Sal ever could."

Pearson leaned back in his chair. "Speak," he said, in a tone suitable for addressing a dog, or a trained seal. Seeing as Tess was neither, she roamed his office, inspecting the plaques that lined the wall, checking out Pearson's view. It wasn't very good, just some Annapolis rooftops, not even a silver of the Chesapeake Bay.

" 'To Chase Pearson,' " she read from one of the largest mounted certificates. " 'In honor of his work for Maryland's children.' Now was this award for your current do-nothing job, or the one before, the do-nothing task force on young men and violence?"

"I don't consider saving the next generation a matter of insignificance."

"Neither do I, neither do I," Tess assured him. "But don't you think you accomplished more as a front-line social worker?"

"Beg pardon?"

"A social worker. That is how you started, isn't it? I had a friend pull your resume this morning from the *Beacon-Light*'s files, and there it was. Eighteen whole months in the trenches. Very noble, in the Pearson tradition of community service, but your generation really couldn't afford to be so civic-minded, I gather. About five years ago, just before the mayor appointed you to that task force. What was it that you did for DSS, exactly?"

"I was in the Social Services Administration."

"Right, the division that oversees foster care." Tess smiled at Pearson's discomfort. "As it happens, I've recently had a crash course in the various divisions at the state Department of Human Resources. I know all the acronyms now. DHR, SSA, DSS, CAP, AFDC. This morning, I even learned the wiggly words you guys use for abuse and neglect investigations. 'Indicated' and 'Unsubstantiated.' I have to say, those are the best CYA words I've ever heard, and I've heard a lot in my time."

"CYA?"

"Cover Your Ass. The worker can't be faulted either way, you see. Indicated or unsubstantiated. If the child turns up dead, the worker isn't held accountable."

Given that Pearson always looked vaguely disdainful, it was hard to say that his expression was responding to anything specific Tess had said. But a corner of his upper lip seemed to lift slightly. "Such half-baked cynicism often tries to pass as sophisticated policy analysis. Did you go to Baltimore City schools, Miss Monaghan?"

"Yes, but I can still do math in my head and pounce on the occasional dangling modifier. Or, in your case, the dangling fact."

"Dangling fact?"

"Donnie Moore's mother, Keisha, she would have been 'indicated' for neglect, right?"

"I wouldn't know."

"That's funny, because you knew exactly what I was talking about the night Keisha Moore was killed. 'She always did keep bad company.' That was never part of the public record, how Keisha lost Donnie. But Donnie's social worker would know all about the company Keisha kept."

Pearson's chin moved. It wasn't even a nod really, just a slight tilt of his chin, a sign that he was still listening.

"You placed Donnie in the Nelsons' home, didn't you? Donnie, Destiny and Treasure, Eldon and Sal. Five kids in a three-bedroom house. Five kids who never had nice clothes and looked as if they didn't get enough to eat. Except Eldon. The Nelsons made at least twenty-five hundred dollars a month on that arrangement, possibly more if any of the children were classified as 'special needs.' Where did the money go, Mr. Pearson?"

"You'd have to ask the Nelsons that question."

"Now see, this is where I get confused. Because I'm pretty sure it was *your* job to ask the Nelsons that question. You were in charge of making sure these children were cared for properly. You were one of those reform-minded young workers recruited by the system after the lawsuit. Why would you ignore the rules to put five kids in a run-down house in a terrible neighborhood? What was in it for you?"

Pearson's desk was devoid of props. His hands crept across its surface, looking for something to occupy them, then retreated to his lap.

"The Nelsons were loving, caring foster parents," he said. "Do you know how hard it is to find young, vigorous foster parents still in their thirties? The Nelsons believed they could provide a setting few foster parents could, even if they didn't have much in the way of material things. I believed in their vision."

"How much did they pay you for that particular belief?"

Pearson was cooler than she thought he would be, much harder to rattle. "You're dreaming up conspiracy scenarios again, Miss Monaghan. It's an interesting theory, I grant you. Social worker places children in home in return for kickbacks. I can see how it might happen. In theory."

"It's not that complicated. A fourteen-year-old could figure it out. A fourteen-year-old did figure it out. Sal Hawkings put the pieces together and shook his old worker down until he arranged for a scholarship to Penfield. Of course, you wouldn't pay for it out of your own pocket. Even now, when you're making good money, you're still kind of tight, aren't you?"

She could hear Pearson's knee knocking at the underside of his desk as he jiggled it. "Go on," he said. "I want to see where you're headed with this little story of yours."

"I'm going back to a night five years ago. A boy is killed in front of his four friends. It's a horrible thing, terrifying even for street-hardened kids. But their social worker and their foster parents aren't worried about the fallout from that trauma. All they care about is splitting the kids up as quickly as possible, getting them in new homes so the reporters won't have time to focus on how weird it is for five foster kids to be living in some tiny little rowhouse in a rotten neighborhood where they receive virtually no supervision."

"The compromises made in order to remove children from truly harmful environments are sometimes difficult for laymen to understand," Pearson said. "You can't imagine the conditions that these children had endured. The Nelsons' home was paradise to them."

"Right."

"The twins had an addict for a mother, you know. They lived in a basement without electricity or plumbing. They were assigned to me when she almost burned the place down with a candle. They were ecstatic to live in a three-bedroom house with a toilet.

"Donnie—well, you know what his mother did, how she left him alone for days while she went off to Atlantic City. Then there was Eldon. His father caught him hitting a dog with a stick and decided to administer the exact same punishment to Eldon with the same stick. At least, that was the story Eldon's father told the Foster Care Review Board when he petitioned to get him back. My guess is he beat Eldon first, and Eldon turned on the dog. You know, that's actually a good indicator of violence in a family, violence against pets. As it happens, child abuse laws in this country were derived from the old anticruelty statutes. Until the late nineteenth century, there was no legal prohibition against harming one's children."

Pearson's voice trailed off. He had veered almost automatically into a bureaucratic set piece, the kind of statement he might make before a Senate committee, then remembered his audience. He stared out the window at his undistinguished view.

"What about Sal?"

"Sal?" He looked genuinely confused, as if he couldn't place the name. "Oh, Sal. He was different, a true orphan, which is rare now. His parents were killed in a car accident when he was eight, and there was no other family, no place for him to go. He was sent to one of our best homes, run by a wonderful woman. A saint, an absolute saint. We could have used a thousand like her. But she suffered a stroke when Sal was eleven, and I had to find a new placement for him. He was the first child I put with the Nelsons." He paused. "I always liked Sal, you know. I would have helped him with Penfield under any circumstances. I even gave him a book once, one of my childhood favorites."

The Kipling, Sal's precious Kipling.

"Did Sal ever tell you?"

"Tell me what?"

"What the children saw on Butchers Hill the night Donnie was killed? Why they had to lie, never mention the car, or the other gunshots?"

Pearson looked at her with something almost like pity, except he didn't like her enough to truly feel sorry for her. "Miss Monaghan, give it a rest. Yes, the Nelsons and I had a mutually advantageous financial arrangement, not that you'll ever be able to prove it. That doesn't mean Luther Beale didn't kill Donnie Moore or the twins. Face facts. A man who fires a gun at a group of children is capable of anything."

"Why don't you call Penfield and tell them we're headed there to talk to Sal? Maybe if I threaten to send his benefactor away to prison, Sal's memory will get a lot better."

"If I do this for you—if I convince Sal to tell the truth, whatever it is, you'll leave us alone?"

"Yes." Tess figured it wasn't a binding promise. Chase Pearson's fate could be decided later. "You can put him on the speakerphone, if you like, right now, and I'll be out of your life sooner rather than later."

Pearson reached for the phone and dialed.

"Chase Pearson. Would you find Sal and ask him to speak to me? I know it's the last day of classes, but it's terribly urgent."

Several minutes passed. Tess thought of Jackie's shoe store analogy—the longer someone had to look for something, the less chance there is they'll find it. Finally, there was a torrent of mumbling on the other end, rushed and high-pitched.

"Are you sure?" Pearson asked. "Are you absolutely sure? Well, how long has it been since anyone has seen him? What happened to the bodyguard? How inept can you possibly be?" The last question must have been rhetorical, for he hung up the phone without waiting for an answer.

"He's missing. Along with one of the groundkeeper's trucks. Apparently he ducked into the lavatory about thirty minutes ago and never came out. They found his school uniform in a stall, so he must have planned this, changing into a worker's clothes. He even left a note, telling them not to worry, that he had to leave in order to be safe, that he would travel faster if he went alone."

"Jesus."

"I bet I know where he's gone." Pearson looked up excitedly. "There's a place, a place he always goes back to when he's troubled or unhappy—"

"Tell me."

He narrowed his eyes. "No. I'll go find him on my own."

"You mean you want to get to him first, get your stories straight, convince him to keep lying, as he has all these years." Tess allowed the flap of her knapsack to fall open, so Pearson could see the gun inside. "Where's Sal?"

"He'll run from you, if you go there alone. He doesn't trust anyone but me."

"Fine. Then we'll go together." Pearson started to object, and Tess flipped her knapsack again, showing her gun one more time. "I'd just follow you anyway, so you might as well take me along."

TWENTY-EIGHT

THEY TOOK PEARSON'S CAR, THE SLEEK LITTLE 911 PORSCHE OF WHICH Sal had spoken so longingly. Tess had planned to take the wheel anyway, but seeing the Porsche cinched the deal. Was it bought with kickbacks from the foster child trade? She could ask Pearson later.

"So you going to tell me where we're going?"

"Not yet. Not until we're a little closer."

She drove on. The Porsche was a dream to drive. Eighty felt like fifty-five, and the usual twenty-five minutes from Annapolis to the Baltimore Beltway sped by in fifteen.

"Now?" she said, turning onto Interstate 95.

"Not yet." She wondered what Pearson was trying to pull, if he still thought he might get to Sal first. If so, he was underestimating her. "It's in the old neighborhood, I'll tell you that much."

"Good." She zipped past the exits for downtown.

"Why are you taking the McHenry Tunnel?" Pearson asked suspiciously.

"I think we can make better time going in Eastern Avenue," she lied, as they dipped into the belly of the tunnel. Suddenly, she took her foot off the accelerator and let the car drift forward of its own momentum, its speed plummeting. Horns sounded behind them, echoing harshly off the tile walls.

"You'll get us killed," Pearson yelled, grabbing for the steering wheel, so the car slithered to the left, and then back into the right lane.

"Possibly. I'm more likely to cause a horrible traffic jam, and we won't get out of here for hours, and by then it will be too late to find Sal. Now tell me where I'm going. Exactly."

"Only if you start driving again."

Tess tapped the accelerator. The car was up to thirty now, still a little slow for the tunnel, but fast enough to avoid being rear-ended.

"The Kipling is the key," Pearson said.

"Kipling?"

"Sal made an allusion to one of his poems in his note. He travels fastest who travels alone. It reminded me of another poem he liked, one he taught the other children."

"So?"

" 'By the old Moulmein Pagoda, lookin' eastward to the sea / There's a Burma girl a-settin', and I know she thinks o' me; / For the wind is in the palm trees, and the temple bells they say: / Come back, you British soldier, come back to Mandalay.' "

"Very nice. But what does it have to do with Sal?"

"The pagoda. He'll be at the Patterson Park pagoda."

There's a Burma girl a-settin'. Hadn't Treasure said Destiny had gone to Burma? The pagoda must be the safe place of which Sal had spoken. Not so safe for Destiny, though, she had died at its feet. The Porsche began the slow gradual climb out of the tunnel. Good, the toll lines weren't too long. Tess picked the one on the far right, and flicked a switch to lower the power window.

What if someone was going to kill Sal? What if he had been summoned to the pagoda just as Destiny was, to meet a murderer?

"Hand me my phone," she said to Pearson. "It's in the side pocket of my knapsack."

"Why do you need a phone?"

"I think Sal's in danger. Destiny died at the pagoda, Treasure wasn't far from it. Maybe the police can get there faster than we can."

Or what if Sal had been the one to summon Destiny? What if Sal was the killer? Then who was he planning to kill this time?

Pearson pulled out her phone, lowered his window, then flung it backward in the path of a car that had just emerged from the tunnel.

"You son of a bitch."

"No police," Pearson said calmly. "That was our deal."

Tess wanted to argue, but it was her turn to roll up to the toll booth. She looked over at the far right lane, where a transit cop was parked, surveying the traffic.

"That'll be one dollar, ma'am," the attendant said.

Tess gave her an ear-splitting scream instead. "He's car-jacking me! Oh my God, call the police, he's carjacking me, he's going to kill me!" She rammed the gate, which was slightly harder to break than she had anticipated. Well, Pearson probably had insurance. Not that you could ever really fix body damage. But it was only fair. An eye for an eye, a Porsche for a portable phone.

"What the hell are you doing?"

"Getting us a police escort. There's a killer in Patterson Park, and it's either Sal or the person he's gone to meet. I'm afraid your political future has to take a back seat to such considerations."

"You're an idiot," Pearson shouted back at her, holding onto the handle above the door. "Sal will never tell you what you want to know, I'll see to that."

Technically, Baltimore police had a policy forbidding high-speed pursuits in the city, so the flashing lights Tess saw in the rearview mirror hung back, slowing at intersections. Luckily for her, the lights on Eastern Avenue, maddening under normal circumstances, proved to be perfectly synched when a driver was going ninety mph. She reached the southeast corner of the park in less than five minutes, but the pagoda was in the northwest corner. She zipped along its southern border, then turned north, running up on the sidewalk and scattering a few dog walkers as the car came to rest fifty yards from the pagoda.

She could still see the police in her rearview mirror. Of course, they thought she was a victim, the terrified hostage of a crazed carjacker. Sal was straight ahead, waiting, a windbreaker pulled close to his body, as if the day were cool. His gaze was fixed on a tall, muscular young man in baggy jeans and a tank top, approaching from the east. The man looked vaguely familiar, but she couldn't place him. She threw the car into park, stripping the gears, grabbed her gun from her knapsack and fell out of the car, screaming all the while.

"He tried to kill me, he tried to kill me," she screamed, running toward the pagoda. "Please someone help me, he's trying to kill me."

As she had hoped, her screams distracted Sal and the approaching man. She ran between them, firing once into the air, just to show them she knew how to use a weapon. But wasn't that how Luther Beale had started, firing one shot up into the sky?

"Whatever you have, drop it," she said. She hoped she sounded more confident than she felt. "Both of you."

Sal looked stunned, while the muscular young man smiled. She finally placed him. It was the monitor from the Nelsons' school, very much out of uniform. The one who had lectured her on survival.

"What makes you think I have a weapon?" he asked, his round face innocent and guileless. "He's the killer, aren't you, Sal? He was probably fixing to kill me when he asked me to come here today. After all, I'm the only one left who knows what he did. Once I'm dead, he's home free."

Sal cried, a child's wail. "That's not fair, Eldon. We promised to never tell, not ever. All for one, and one for all. Besides, you're the one who asked me here."

"All for one and one for all. Right. I didn't see you helping the rest of us get fancy scholarships. From the day they split us up, it was every man for himself."

"But I didn't know where to find you. Ask her, she'll tell you. I even broke into her office just to get your address."

So this was little chubby Eldon, all grown up. He wasn't really listening. He was reaching behind himself, Tess saw. To scratch his back, or to pull out a weapon? It was a hell of a split-minute decision to have to make.

The cops made it for her.

"Freeze," one yelled, as six police officers came running across the lawn. "And throw your weapons down, now. *Everybody*. That includes you, miss."

Tess threw down her .38 happily. Eldon dropped a semi-automatic, a cruel-looking gun. Sal pulled a serrated butcher knife from his jacket, and let it fall to the grass. What a flimsy little thing it was, next to Eldon's gun, how inadequate. It would be hard, of course, trying to find a weapon at Penfield on such short notice.

"Eldon said he needed me," Sal said, almost sobbing now. "He said some shit was coming down, and he needed my help. You probably told Destiny and Treasure the same thing, you son of a bitch. Why'd you kill them? What'd they ever do to you?"

"Fuck you, man," Eldon said, his hands on his head as the cops patted him down. "You started it all. If it weren't for you, none of this shit would have happened."

Tess, who was also being patted down, looked at the two of them. She might as well get her questions in now. "There was a car, wasn't there, the night Donnie died. A car, and two more shots fired, just as Luther Beale maintained."

"I don't remember a car—" Sal began.

Eldon shrugged, a small, cramped gesture given that his hands were on his head. "A car? There may have been. It doesn't matter."

"It matters to Luther Beale."

"You really don't get it, do you?" Eldon looked disgusted. "Stupid bitch, stirring everything up, and never really getting it. None of that shit matters because Sal killed Donnie Moore. Didn't you, Sal?

Oh, you were such a big man, carrying your gun around, trying to protect us all. Well, you protected Donnie right into the grave."

AT THE POLICE STATION, AS THE COPS TRIED TO UNTANGLE THE VARIOUS felonies of the day, Tess almost felt sorry for the *Beacon-Light* police reporter, a young man she knew only by reputation. Herman Peters, aka the Hermanator, a man who was rumored to never, ever, be without his beeper. Rosy-cheeked, with dark curly hair, he looked like the kind of smiling boy who should grace a box of instant cocoa. But he was a tenacious, tough reporter, intent on fact and nuance, not as easily satisfied with the little scraps spoon-fed to the television reporters.

"I still don't understand," she heard him saying insistently to Tull, who was handling media while his fellow homicide detectives interviewed Eldon, Sal, and Pearson. Because of the public nature of the crime, the reporters had descended on the police station within minutes of the showdown in Patterson Park. "You say Donnie Moore was killed by his friend Sal Hawkings, but you're going to charge Eldon Kane with the murder of Keisha Moore and her boyfriend, and he's also a suspect in the deaths of the Teeter twins?"

"It's our supposition that Eldon was a hit man, working for the Nelsons. He killed anyone who threatened to expose their operation in D.C. Cops down there just executed a search warrant at the Benjamin Banneker Academy, found a basement full of stolen goods and an attic full of guns. They had expanded the scope of their operation since they moved to Washington."

"Back up a minute," the Hermanator pleaded. "I'm not getting all of this."

"Okay," Tull said with a grin. "It all begins with a couple who figure they can get cheap labor through the city's foster care system. The original mom-and-pop operation, if you will."

Sal should have been reading Dickens instead of Kipling, Tess thought as she half-listened to Tull unspool the dark yarn. The Nelsons had taken in foster children as workers in their fencing operation, at first a small-time operation. The original mom-and-pop burglary ring. The children had stolen car radios and anything else that wasn't nailed down, but the real money was in weapons. Sal had even helped himself to a gun from the Nelsons' cache. So when Luther Beale had opened fire that night, Sal had shot back. Problem was, he wasn't a very good shot, and he had ended up hitting Donnie instead. Or so he thought.

The children had sworn an oath never to tell what had really happened, not to mention guns, or stolen goods. They had assumed lies would keep their little family intact, but Donnie's death had started the inexorable process by which they would be torn apart.

Two years later, Sal had tracked down Pearson and wrangled his scholarship, threatening to expose him. "I was smarter than the others," he had bragged to Tess. "They were dumb motherfuckers." Yet Eldon had done the same thing, convincing the Nelsons to hide him after he jumped bail. They had been glad to do it for a few small favors here and there. And Destiny had been smart enough to try and shake the Nelsons down for money. Or dumb enough, given the outcome.

The Nelsons had strung her along until Eldon could kill her, but they had needed Tess to find Treasure. And when Keisha Moore had started asking questions, Eldon killed her, too. In his own way, Eldon was as much an overachiever as Sal. He just focused his energy differently.

Tyner finally arrived, Luther Beale in tow. There were some charges pending against Tess—reckless endangerment, destruction of property—although Tull was reasonably sure the criminal charges would be dropped. Eventually.

"Pearson's insurance company isn't going to let you off the hook so easily," Tyler said gloomily. "Insurance companies don't make exceptions, even when you're trying to save someone's life."

"Hey, I did, didn't I?" Tess, who had been contemplating her own role in all the deaths on Butchers Hill, felt momentarily cheered. "I wish that made up for Treasure. Or Keisha. I feel as if I led Eldon straight to them."

"He would have found them one way or another," Tull assured her. Another olive branch. Why not? She had been right, after all.

Beale just stood there silently, holding his Panama hat. He was wearing his brown suit, this time with a blue shirt with a white collar. Tess couldn't help wondering if he had a single shirt that matched his one suit.

"So I didn't do it?" he asked. "I really didn't kill that boy?"

Tull shrugged, not so anxious to mend fences with Beale. "We'll never know, will we? You fired, he fired, Donnie died. It could have been either one of you."

"But a jury wouldn't have convicted Beale if they had known," Tyner pointed out. "We'll get a governor's pardon out of this, maybe even some money. I see a big lawsuit here."

Tull rolled his eyes. "You can't sue the state for pursuing its mandated duties, Tyner. But go for it. Maybe you'll shake a little settlement out of them."

Two officers brought Sal out just then. He was still just a boy, Tess reminded herself. Seventeen wasn't as old as he thought it was. And he hadn't covered up his crime because he feared taking responsibility for what he had done, but because he wanted to keep his "family" together. Perhaps, like everyone else in Baltimore at the time, he had assumed Luther Beale would never serve time for his crime. How could a little boy know the intricacies of handgun laws in the city limits?

"The skinny one," Luther Beale said. "You're the skinny one."

Sal glanced up. He looked angry and guilty at the same time, and not a little frightened.

"Yeah, I remember you, too."

"Well, I have something to say to you," Beale announced. "I have something I want everyone here to hear."

Tull looked at Tess, as if to say: I told you he was a son of a bitch.

Even Tess couldn't quite believe that Beale would insist on making a scene. It wasn't enough for him to be proven right. He had to proclaim it.

"The way I see it, a lot of folks failed you," Beale said, the Hermanator scribbling down his words furiously. "Those people you lived with, the man who put you in their home. They didn't teach you right from wrong. But they were grownups and you were a little boy. You couldn't help not knowing any better.

"I was a grownup, too. If I hadn't come out in the street with my gun that night, you wouldn't have fired your gun and Donnie Moore wouldn't have died. Not that night at least. We failed you, all the grownups in your life, we let you down. So all I can say is—" He stopped, playing with the brim of his hat, a gesture Tess remembered from their first meeting. "All I can say is, I'm sorry."

EPILOGUE

August

THE UNSEASONABLY BEAUTIFUL SUMMER HAD FINALLY YIELDED TO SOME-
thing more familiar—hot, humid days, with afternoon thunder-
storms that lasted just long enough to ruin picnics and barbecues,
but didn't deliver enough rain for the city's now parched gardens
and lawns. At Camden Yards, the ground crew was getting more
exercise than the Orioles: at least they got to put out the tarp each
evening and then roll it back, while the Orioles seldom circled the
bases. The Orioles being in something of a slump, their bats were
the only reliably cold place in all of Baltimore.

In other words, everything was back to normal. The bill had
come due for June and July. Nothing to do but pay up, and move on.
Already, fresher scandals were crowding out the twisted saga of
what had happened on Butchers Hill so many years ago. "Butchers
Hill?" Tess had heard a man say at the lunch counter at Jimmy's just
the other morning. "Oh yeah, that place where that kid tried to kill
that old man that time."

"No," his companion had insisted. "The old man tried to kill the
kid, for breaking his window."

In Kitty's bookstore, Tess pushed aside a stack of the latest
Louisa May Alcott discovery—"How many manuscripts did that
woman have squirreled away?" she grumbled—to make room on
the old soda fountain for yet another tray of hors d'oeuvres. Her

mother had been cooking for days, it seemed, bringing by tray after tray of delicacies until Kitty had finally run out of room in her freezer.

"I thought Judith hated to cook," Kitty said, trying to squeeze a plate of miniature quiches between the pasta salad and artichoke dip.

"She used to," Tess said. "I think she's entering some strange new phase. Wait until you see all the outfits she's bought."

"Not all matching?"

"Shockingly, no."

But this party had been Judith's idea, after all. She was entitled to go hog-wild if she wanted. "To celebrate . . . whatever," she had said. "Well, not celebrate, but acknowledge. You know—"

"I know," Tess had said, feeling charitable enough toward her mother to want to bail her out. It wasn't easy, being St. Judith. It wasn't easy being Gramma. It wasn't easy *being*.

Kitty had just tapped the keg, a sweet little microbrew from Sissons, the one that tasted like a blueberry muffin in a beer glass, when the guests began to arrive. Most of the Weinsteins were there, showing their support for Judith even if her meshugah daughter had thrown a monkey wrench into everything. The Monaghans had come, too, if only to gloat at the strange circumstances bedeviling their snobbish in-laws. A black teenage mistress! A discovered heir! Who did Samuel Weinstein think he was, Thomas Jefferson? Still, the Monaghans had to admit the Weinsteins were handling the situation with surprising grace. Even Gramma had behaved reasonably well, which is to say that she had decided not to try and block the sale of the property when she heard of Tess's plan to cut Samantha King in for an equal share.

"All for one and one for all—your exact words," Tess had reminded her grandmother. "You said your grandchildren and children had to learn to get along."

"*My* children and grandchildren," Gramma had countered. But she had added, a sly smile on her face: "I hear she's a smart girl, very athletic and pretty. I know whose genes those are. Blood tells, doesn't it?"

Tess didn't bother to contradict her. Sure, blood tells, but it didn't always tell you what you wished to hear. More than Jackie herself, the long-limbed, auburn-haired Samantha King was a reminder of the secrets that even those closest to you can harbor. Tess wasn't really sorry that Sam was away at lacrosse camp, unable to attend this party today. Everyone was still working on the feelings that she stirred up in them.

Especially Jackie. After the confrontation at the Beckers', she had decided to take up the Edelmans' offer of a limited relationship with Sam. As she had prophesied, it wasn't particularly easy for either of them. While Sam could accept the decisions made by a determined eighteen-year-old, she was perturbed to find out her biological father had been in his sixties. And while she didn't want to leave the only family she had known for Jackie's household, she was more than a little jealous that Jackie had decided to start her own family. She wanted it both ways. What teenager didn't?

Tull came through the door, carrying an insulated freezer sack. "Coffee ice cream," he said.

"Well, I knew whatever you brought, it would be caffeinated. How's life on the killing streets?"

"I'm pleased to announce Baltimore has gone forty-eight hours without a single stiff showing up. Maybe I'll be out of a job soon. Where's the guest of honor?"

"Running late. Jackie's punctuality has taken a severe hit as of late. She's found there are some things in life she can't make run on her own timetable."

But there was Jackie now, coming through the door, in a yellow-checked sundress, the guest of honor balanced on her hip, also in a matching yellow outfit.

"How's my girl?" Tess asked, reaching for Laylah. But Judith had gotten there first.

"May I?" she asked tentatively, bouncing the girl in her arms. "Oh Jackie, you put her in the outfit I sent. She looks adorable."

"*One* of the outfits you sent," Jackie said. "Thank you for having this party to celebrate the adoption. But you know, she won't be officially mine for several months yet."

"A formality," Judith said. "Laylah's your daughter now as far I'm concerned."

Laylah, who had been staring, mesmerized, into Judith's face, made a quick grab for one of her earrings. Judith laughed, slipped them into her apron pocket, and began touring the room with the baby, allowing everyone to make a fuss over the guest of honor.

"I owe you one, Jackie," Tess said. "I think I'm off the hook for producing grandchildren, at least for a few years."

"I helped," Tull said. "Don't forget, I helped."

So he had, tracking Laylah down in the foster care system, while Uncle Donald had called in every chit he had to grease the works at DHR. The agency officials had balked at first. It was highly irregular, he had been told, to allow a single woman to take a child into her home before the adoption process was further along.

"As irregular as losing a woman's kid in the system and then trying to file a lien against her for back support?" Donald had asked innocently. From then on, everything had been simple.

If only everything could be so simple in the future. For Jackie and Sam, for Jackie and Laylah. Would Laylah be better off with Jackie than she had been with Keisha? It wasn't a judgment Tess could make so easily any more. Laylah's material life would be better, and she would be loved. But one day, she would start asking questions and the answers she received would be far more disturbing than the ones Samantha King had confronted. Blood tells. It tells and tells and tells. Sometimes, blood just wouldn't shut up.

Eldon had finally told, too. Stoic at first, he had decided that his loyalty to the Nelsons did not extend to taking the fall for the four murders. So the Nelsons were to stand trial in two jurisdictions now. Double-dipping again, tying up the resources of two criminal systems, two prosecutor's offices, and two juries. Chase Pearson was expected to testify at their Baltimore trial, although he was really a small player. It seemed almost pathetic, how little he had reaped from the literal mom-and-pop operation that had grown into a million-dollar fencing ring. He was a figure of ridicule now, his name synonymous with ignorance and missed opportunities. Recently, when the housing commissioner had done something particularly bone-headed, a *Blight* columnist had referred to it as "pulling a Pearson." It was possible to come back from being indicted in Maryland politics; even convicted felons had enjoyed second chances here. But stealing a cherry when you could have had the whole pie—unforgivable.

Jackie appraised Tess. "You look good, girl. Prosperous." She did. Her hair was up, she wore a black linen sheath that Jackie had picked out for her at Ruth Shaw, with black-eyed Susan earrings—onyx set in real gold. She had balked at the black-and-yellow spectator pumps, however. Someone needed to draw the line at all this matchy-matchy stuff. She wasn't turning into her mother. Not just yet.

"Work is going well. I'm turning down business these days. Everybody wants to hire the private investigator who cleared Luther Beale. No offense, Martin."

"None taken, Tess."

Tess looked at her two friends. She had started the summer feeling so lonely. What had Kitty said? She was a Don Quixote, in search of a Sancho. But Jackie was no Sancho, nor was Tull. They were all Don Quixotes in their own ways, each one dealing with their lost illusions.

In last year's nests, there are no birds this year. But there would be new nests, right? You could lose one set of illusions, but gain another. At least, she hoped it worked that way. She still didn't know what happened to the real Don Quixote.

Sal Hawkings dashed through the door, a small package in hand. He wore jeans and a T-shirt, both splattered with paint. He was spending the end of the summer helping Beale renovate houses along Fairmount. The community service wasn't court-ordered; it had been decided that no criminal action should be brought against Sal for the death of Donnie Moore. It had been an accident, after all, and he had been only twelve. These days, it seemed as if he was seventeen going on ten, trying to recapture the childhood he had never had.

"Mr. Beale is out in the car, but he wanted me to drop this by. Will you open it while I'm here?"

"Sure," Jackie said. She undid the ribbon and lifted a heart-shaped locket from a nest of cotton, a locket that Tess remembered well. She was surprised that Beale would part with it. But then, Beale never stopped surprising her. He had refused to sue the state, settling for a pardon. If she tried to speak to him now of what had happened that night, he said it wasn't important, the past was the past, he was too busy thinking about the future. Where should Sal go to college, for example? He had heard Princeton was nice, but he worried he should be closer to home. St. John's in Annapolis? Johns Hopkins?

"Open it," Sal urged. "It's got a little catch on the side. I'll show you how."

The photo inside was of a boy, his mouth slightly open, his eyes large and bright. The tiny heart shape had been cut from a color photo, grainy and overexposed, but it was still possible to see the joy in his eyes. Perhaps it had been Christmas, or his birthday. Perhaps it had been nothing more than a trip to McDonald's. It took so little to make a child happy. It took so much.

"It's her brother, Donnie," Sal said. "Well, half-brother, I guess. His aunt had some photos, and she let us have one. So one day, when Laylah's older, you can tell her how she had a brother and he was a pretty good kid."

Jackie thanked Sal, tears in her eyes, passing the locket to Tess, who couldn't help wondering how anyone could tell the story of what had happened on Butchers Hill. Where to begin? The night Luther Beale had gone into the street with his gun, the day he had come into her office? Did it begin the day Chase Pearson became a social worker, or on the day Donnie Moore was born? Or the day Luther Beale was born, ornery and resolute, his destiny hurtling him toward a tragic confrontation and a nickname he still couldn't shake? The Butcher of Butchers Hill. Where did anything begin?

Once upon a time, you had a brother, his name was Donnie Moore and he was a pretty good kid.

There were worse ways to be remembered.